THE RIVER HAUNT

EAST TIMOR CRIME SERIES Nº 5

Chris McGillion

Kenmore, WA

Coffeetown Press books published by Epicenter Press

Epicenter Press
6524 NE 181st St. Suite 2
Kenmore, WA 98028.
www.Epicenterpress.com
www.Coffeetownpress.com
www.Camelpress.com

For more information go to: www.Epicenterpress.com

All rights reserved. No part of this book may be reproduced or transmitted in any form or by any means, electronic or mechanical, including photocopying, recording, or any information storage and retrieval system, without permission in writing from the publisher.

No generative AI was used in the conceptualization, planning, drafting, or creative writing of this work. No permission is given for the use of this material for AI training purposes.

This is a work of fiction. All characters and events, along with the hamlet of Lolitu, are creations of the author's imagination.

The River Haunt
Copyright © 2026 by Chris McGillion

ISBN: 9781684922857 (trade paper)
ISBN: : 9781684922864 (ebook)

LOC: 2025942372

Printed in the United States of America

Dedication

For Phil Maguire and Andrew Hordern.
My shout next.

The East Timor Crime Series

The Crocodile's Kill
The Sand Digger's Skull
The Coffin Maker's Apprentice
The Island's Vengeful Dead

Acknowledgments

The Balibo Fort Hotel and Cultural and Heritage Centre was inaugurated in 2015. I've taken some 'poetic' license to depict the fort as still in ruins when this story is set in 2014 but actually the renovation was well underway by then. The hotel is now a beautiful complex with commanding views over the surrounding countryside, splendid accommodation, and very friendly staff. I am thankful to the staff members who made my stay there so pleasant while I researched Balibo and its surrounds for this book. I definitely intend to stay there again. I'd also like to thank Raymond Harding, muse and mentor. And my good friends at Epicenter Press—Jennifer, Phil and Murray.

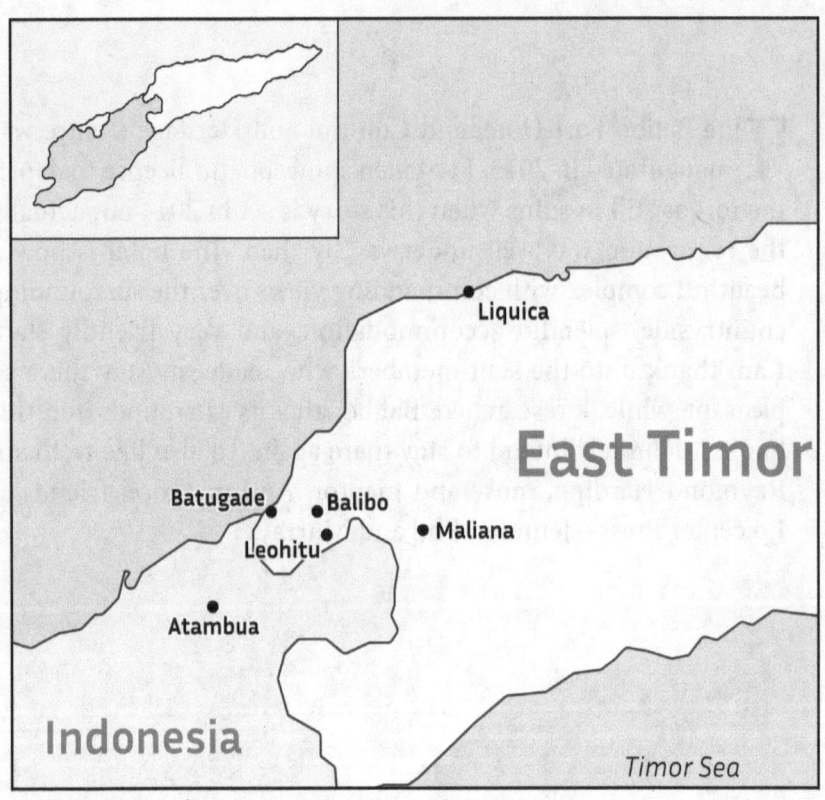

Map by Dominic Andrews

1

When she heard his soul howling from the graveyard near their hut on the East Timorese side of the border with Indonesia, Isa Tavares knew her husband would soon be dead.

As he left the hut the morning before, Kosme was in good spirits and there'd been nothing to suggest he was coming down with any kind of ailment. There were no signs of any injury on his body now. Nevertheless, the voice had wailed on the wind throughout the night and the sound, as much as the agony gripping Kosme's face in the pale pre-dawn light, told her it would not be long before he would leave her and journey to the other side.

She dipped a rag in a bowl of water on the floor beside Kosme and wrung it until the last drips had fallen. She wiped the rag across her husband's forehead as he lay panting on a mat. That done she stood, went to a woven betel bag in the corner of the hut, and rummaged through it. It was where she kept a small number of bills in US dollars—Timor having adopted US currency as its own on independence—including the bill she'd found crumpled up in Kosme's pocket last night. The bag also held valuables such as the picture card of a crucified Christ she was searching for now. She took the card and tucked it, along with a sharp knife, into the cord that secured her sarong. Their children had grown and left to start their own families, so there were no prying eyes to distract her or sceptics to question her actions. She trudged out into the early morning, a smell of rain in the air, knowing full well what she had to do.

In the yard the chickens were already busy pecking and scratching for food scraps on the ground under the green, spindly ferns. She grabbed one of the older hens by the tail feathers, clenched it firmly under an arm, and wrung its neck. When the twitching stopped, she took the knife and slit its throat.

Isa Tavares circled the hut sprinkling the chicken's blood onto the soil as she went. Back at the entrance to the hut she placed the carcass and the knife on the ground and took out the picture card. She held it to her breast and recited what she could remember of a prayer she'd once learned in church to add Jesus-power to the customary protection she'd just invoked. When that was done, she grabbed the dead chicken and the knife and went inside to sit with her husband and watch him die.

She didn't know why he was being taken from her. It must be a black, demonic force that caused his affliction but to dwell on that would only invite the evil to be turned on her. She'd already thought too much about it and wondered if she'd done enough to keep from following her husband into the dark world of the dead.

• • •

Vincintino Cordero had just returned home from a midweek visit to his widowed sister Ana and prepared himself a cup of rich, dark Timorese coffee on his prized Italian-style stove-top percolator. The gurgling of the coffee pot finished, and the aroma of the fresh brew engulfing the room, he poured a cup and sat down to sugar the result. On the armrest of his chair he'd opened the first page of a book on the Cuban revolution that he'd been intending to read for several months. The Timorese, essentially abandoned by the West, had taken inspiration from Cuba as they struggled against the Indonesian occupation after it invaded in 1975 and walls could still be seen painted with defiant images of Che Guevara in some villages. Cordero was musing over this when his cell buzzed. He wasn't expecting a call and so he stared at the cell for a few seconds before reacting.

He placed the book on the floor next to his easy chair and checked the caller ID. It was Sara Carter. She was an FBI Agent assigned to INTERPOL in East Timor and by now a very good friend. He immediately answered when he recognized it was her calling.

"Hi," he said. "I thought you were on a mission to train the local police in Balibo."

"I'm not training anyone," Cater said. "I told you I'm collecting information on how INTERPOL can help with border management. Or at least I'm supposed to be. That's why I'm calling."

He sipped his coffee as she paused and he felt a little apprehension rising.

"Go on," he said.

"I need you to come get us and take us there."

He relaxed. It was nothing more serious like a run-in with dangerous criminals—not that there were many of those in Timor—or an argument with a senior government officals—the type of thing he'd come to expect with Carter. And by 'us' it was safe to assume she was with the young Timorese police officer Estefana dos Carvalho who had been assigned to her as a translator.

"Take you? Where? Why? I've just—"

"It's those silly bloody rickshaws that jam the road around Liquica," she said cutting him off.

He put down his coffee cup and rubbed his brow.

"They're called *ojeks*," he corrected her. "*Ojeks*. It's a Bahasa word although some say it's derived from an African language. It means a motorcycle taxi. They're popular around Liquica because it's close to the border and has a large Chinese population which—"

"Enough with the lecture," she said. "African, Indonesian, Chinese—those things are a damn nuisance. They're forcing everyone else to drive at a snail's pace behind them which means they're causing traffic jams all around here." She took a breath. "Then there's your stupid potholed roads," she added.

"I don't—"

"We were half way to Batugade when we were held up by a dozen of the damn rickshaws clogging up the road. Why do people bother to ride those silly things?"

She was agitated—which was not unusual. He blew out a breath before answering.

"Well usually they're going to or from markets and carrying—"

"Anyhow," she cut in again, "Estefana left the road to get around the things and 'clunk!' We did an axle in a pothole as deep as a mine shaft."

"She what?"

"She broke an axle."

"How on earth—"

"It wasn't her fault!" Carter said. "It's your goddamn potholes. She couldn't judge how deep it was because it was filled with water, alright? It happens. It's raining here. Listen!"

He imagined her holding the cell at arm's length so he might hear the rain even though he couldn't.

"We've got to get to Balibo," she continued, "and you're our only hope."

He glanced at his coffee cup.

"Can't you get someone from Balibo to come get you?" he asked.

"We've tried," she said. "The local police commander took their only SUV to Maliana and hasn't returned yet. The other cops only use motorcycles and are out on jobs."

"What about the police in Liquica or Batugade?"

He thought he heard a sigh at her end.

"The police in Batugade said they have a huge traffic accident to sort out," she said. "I don't wonder given your roads."

"They're not *my*—"

"And Liquica isn't answering the phone. We've tried five times."

Someone passed by on Carter's end of the call: "*Manu no etu, manu no etu!*" It was a woman's voice and she was hawking chicken and rice lunches even though it was now close to 4 o'clock in the afternoon. Another, younger, voice broke in "*Pulsa, pulsa!*"—a teenager trying to find a buyer for the cell phone recharge card Timorese used.

"Can't you hire something else until your axle's fixed?" Cordero complained.

"Do I need to remind you we're in Timor?" Carter said. "Where are we supposed to find a car rental place this far out of Dili? And the repair could take days. Estefana spoke to a local guy who calls himself a mechanic and he's arranging a tow. Or at least we hope he is."

"*Pulsa, pulsa!*" came the cry again in the background.

Cordero regarded the cover of the book he wanted to read and picked up his coffee cup. He took another sip to keep from expressing annoyance at this disruption to the relaxing afternoon he'd planned.

"Well?" she persisted. "You've nothing better to do. You've been suspended, right?"

"Because I disobeyed my superior and involved you in the investigation of that murder on Atauro," he said, referring to the island off the coast from Dili. "And now you want to involve me in your affairs in Balibo! What's that expression you use? Once bitten, twice—"

"Listen," she interrupted him again. "You were told not to involve me in that Atauro investigation because the Timorese police wanted all the credit. Well, they got it, didn't they? And all you got was a temporary suspension on half pay. So stop complaining."

"It's still a suspension!" he insisted.

"That's right. A suspension. Which means you've got nothing to do. So why not come up to Balibo? Your cousin lives there as I recall."

He turned to the window and considered the drizzle running down the pane.

"Yeah, Moises," he said. "And Cipriana, his wife." He'd dropped a television set off to them when he, having grown up in Australia and so with a perfect command of English, was given the job of chaperoning Carter on her first INTERPOL assignment. "Remember how she thought you were my girlfriend?"

He allowed himself a chuckle at that.

"Yeah, very funny," she said. "But if I don't get to Balibo I'll be back in Dili drowning in paperwork."

"You can't drown in paperwork," he said and she sensed he was weakening.

"Well come anyhow. Please!" she said, now adopting her best pleading tone.

"Listen, it'd take me over an hour to get to Liquica, longer to get to wherever you are and by then it'd be getting dark. The road from the coast up to Balibo is treacherous at the best of times. In the dark it's close to suicidal."

"Well you'd better get started," she said, becoming more insistent. "And hurry!"

They were both quiet a moment while he finished his coffee. He'd known her long enough to accept there was little point in arguing when she'd set her mind to something. He also knew she was right—he had nothing better to do. A visit to his cousin Moises was overdue and, the more he thought about it, actually preferable to yet more idle hours sitting at home on his own.

"I don't know," he said to suggest it was a big ask on her part.

"What's there to know?" she said. "Can I count on you or not?"

He stood and placed the empty cup on the table. He was silent a moment.

"Where will you be?" he asked finally.

"On the side of the road, where do you think?" she said. "Hold on a minute."

He could hear her talking to Estefana although he couldn't make out what was being said.

"Estefana says we're about 12 miles east of Batugade," Carter told him. "We just crossed a culvert about a hundred yards back and the stream flows out onto what would be a lovely stretch of beach if it wasn't raining, we weren't stranded, and we hadn't been instructed to come here in the first place."

He scratched his neck.

"Okay," he said, adding an audible huff for effect. "I'm on my way."

• • •

Dario Freitas slid out of the driver's seat of the Hilux he'd bought at a sale of used United Nations vehicles, took off his bill cap, and ran a hand through his hair. It was late afternoon. He'd pulled up on a vacant block of land under a large strangler fig, the branches of which hung dripping following the break in the rain.

Goats were tethered beneath the branches, their coats damp and their attention focused on the weeds they were munching.

On the far corner of a muddy road that ran down one side of the block stood a store with wet, weathered posters along its side. Old tyres from trucks and cars had been thrown on the tin roof to keep it in place during storms. A truck loaded with packaged foods, fuel, used clothing tied in huge bunches, pipes, and building materials had taken up what parking space there was out front.

Dario replaced the cap on his head and made his way around the truck. As he approached the door of the store an aging Chinese man shuffled out from inside. He was lanky but his body had not yet begun to curve with age even though he was quite old. He wore the dull, loose-fitting pyjama-like clothing favored by a certain type of rural Chinese. He had a high brow below thinning hair and skin stretched across his face giving him chiseled features. His eyes were fixed on a slip of paper he held in his hand.

"*Botarde Senyor* Feng," said Dario, wishing the old man a good afternoon. "So the goods I ordered have arrived?"

Feng looked up from the paper as a heavy-set Timorese man, the truck driver, came out of the store and stood beside him rubbing his hands on a soiled singlet as though he had just finished eating something.

"No," said Feng. "This is a shipment of rice I ordered. I was told your things will come tomorrow."

He handed the piece of paper to the truck driver who pocketed it before clambering onto the tray of the truck.

"You told me that yesterday," Dario said, irritated. "I've been waiting almost a week."

Feng ignored the complaint.

"All I can do is order the goods," he said. "When they come is not up to me."

The truck driver began to pass down bags of rice to the old man whose agility in stacking the large, hefty items belied his advanced years.

Dario grunted, lifted his cap, and scratched.

"I'll return tomorrow," he said to no one in particular.

The driver handed Feng another bag of rice.

"I lot of people are coming, you know," Dario continued. "I don't want anything to go wrong."

The driver tossed the last bag of rice to Feng, jumped down off his truck, and climbed into the cabin. He waved a hand at the store owner and started the engine with a belch of black smoke from the exhaust. Dario waved the fumes from his face.

"Things are quiet now in Balibo," Feng said as he picked up one of the bags of rice and swivelled to carry it inside the store. He stopped and gazed directly at Dario. "Nothing will go wrong. Your things will come tomorrow, I think."

Dario approached the stack, took a deep breath and heaved a bag up onto his chest.

"Gaspar was a *dato*, you know," he said. "That means—"

"You've told me what that means many times," Feng said, adjusting the bag in his arms for a better grip. "An important village elder."

"A village *nobleman*," Dario said, emphasising the term. "That means he had authority here and commanded respect."

"You also told me he's been dead for many years," Feng said. "Another day or two until your father is put in the ground won't cause him any harm now."

2

Small houses of cement blocks covered in tin roofing were scattered like grains of rice across the ridges and folds around Balibo. A thickening knot of electrical wiring signalled the outskirts of town where the centre, such as it was, spilled along a main road past a new church, a collection of drab government buildings, several colonial-era houses, and the occasional junkyard before forking. One arm of sealed road went south to the district capital of Maliana. The other—*Rua de Frontera*—formed by gravel, rock, and mud, snaked west down to the border.

They arrived on nightfall. In the dim light a damp sheen covered what could be seen. Cloud hung low, suppressing the smoke from cooking fires to create an eerie fog hovering just above ground. No one was about in the soggy outdoors, but dogs scrounged in the watery gutters along the sides of the road and bats fluttered leathery wings as they flew from trees on their nightly hunt.

Cordero pulled to a stop next to an SUV flecked with mud in front of a cinder block building sporting a drooping Timorese flag and a weathered sign that read *Eskuadra-Polisia*—Tetun for 'Police Station'.

"Welcome to Balibo," he said, cutting the engine. A yellow light glowed dimly in the window of a front room of the building. "Someone's here anyhow. Probably the commander by the looks of that," he added jerking a thumb toward the SUV.

Carter blew out a breath and unclipped her seatbelt.

"Phew. That was some road," she said. "If you could even call it a road."

"Told you," said Cordero glancing across.

"Don't gloat," she replied.

They stepped out into the night to stretch bodies aching from the crammed confines of the vehicle. Carter was in excellent shape at thirty years of age—athletic without compromising on shapely and attractive. Cordero was well preserved for forty even if his body was stiff from the driving and he had to shake the circulation back into his arms and legs. Estefana, younger than Carter by eight years and a much slighter build, was the least affected by the drive as she'd had the whole of the rear seat to herself. She slipped out and took a deep breath of air that was warm and muggy even though they'd ascended 2,000 feet from the coast.

"You okay Estefana?" Cordero asked.

"Yes, *maun*," she said, feeling relaxed enough in his company these days to refer to him by the informal title of 'brother'.

"In that case, let's go and announce our arrival," Cordero said, and he strode off to the front door of the station. Carter walked around to join Estefana on the driver's side of the vehicle and rubbed her shoulder in a friendly way. The two followed Cordero into the building.

A man with gorget patches on the collar of his shirt was hunched over a stack of papers under a small lamp, a pen twirling in his left hand. It was the local police commander, Mateus Salsinha. He appeared to be the only one in the building as all the other rooms were in darkness. Mateus lifted his eyes when Carter knocked on the door frame to his office.

"Commander Salsinha?" she said. "I'm Agent Carter. From INTERPOL."

"Enter, enter," Mateus said, placing his pen gently on the desk and rising from his chair. "Please, call me Mateus, please. And welcome. So you're the American one. I've been expecting you for hours."

He came around the desk, switched on the single bulb meant to light the entire room, and shook her hand gently in the Timorese fashion.

"Our vehicle broke an axle east of Batugade. My colleague—" Carter gestured to Estefana —"Officer dos Carvalho has arranged for it to be repaired which could take a few days. Our friend here had to come to the rescue. This is—"

"Investigator Vincintino Cordero," Mateus said, completing the hand shakes. "I heard you speak at a police conference some months ago. Very good, you were. I thought you were suspended."

Cordero couldn't hide a degree of embarrassment. He raised a hand in a palm-up shrug of indifference.

"I am, *senyor*," he admitted. "A trifling matter and only temporary I assure you."

Mateus chuckled. "A disagreement with Jada, I understand," he said, referring to Cordero's superior, Chief Inspector Francisco Jada.

"News travels fast," Cordero said.

"Few secrets are safe among police," said Mateus. "You should know that by now. I was in the police academy with Jada many years ago. He is easily offended and, how you say…*ulun-toos*?"

"Headstrong," offered Cordero.

"Yes, headstrong," echoed Matues. He waved at some plastic seats along one wall of his office and returned to his own wooden chair. "Sit, please," he said.

"You speak good English," Carter said taking a seat. She noticed that the face of the clock hanging on the wall was cracked and the hands were showing 2 o'clock when it was well passed 8 o'clock.

A smirk broke out on Mateus' face as he switched off his desk lamp and eased the paperwork to the one side.

"Before I became a police officer I study for the priesthood," he said. "We have a confessor who loved English literature very much. Don't ask why; he was from Portugal. But he teach English to some seminarians so he can discuss the books he read. I was one of the lucky ones and I love reading your Graham Greene. There's one in my drawer here: *The Quiet American*. You have read it, *senyora*?"

Cordero coughed slightly.

"Graham Greene was English not American," he said. "And *The Quiet American* is set in Vietnam."

Mateus allowed a smile to fade.

"Yes. You right then," he said showing no embarrassment. "But doesn't matter. A writer's true country is the page. Our confessor say that often."

"That's quite a career move from the priesthood to the police," Carter commented.

"No, not really," said Mateus. "It's on same line: a police officer catches sinners and a priest forgives them. Human frailty is what both work with."

The commander was in his early fifties. He had a soft, round face, a generous smile, and a head of lush dark hair. His uniform jacket on a hanger to the side of his desk was weighed down by an impressive row of medals affixed above the left pocket. Clearly he'd been judged good at the vocation he'd chosen to pursue.

"I only receive the notification two days ago," he said.

He leaned forward, reached for a folder on the far side of his desk, and opened it. He took a document out of the folder. It comprised several sheets of paper stapled together and he read aloud the cover page in English pronouncing each word carefully as he translated from the Tetun: "*'INTERPOL scoping study for capacity building initiative in migration and border management'.*"

He looked up at Carter, pressed his lips together and flicked through the rest of the document in silence. A few minutes later he re-ordered the pages.

"Your organization takes many words to say simple things." He replaced the document in the folder and pushed it away. "Like mine," he added, lifting a finger toward the pile of papers on the near side of the desk.

Carter smiled at that.

"Basically they sent me here to find out what you need to strengthen your ability to police the border," she said.

"We don't police the border," Mateus said. "The regular police I mean. We have specialized border police who do that."

Carter drew in a breath.

"I am aware of that," she said. "I think some people in Dili believe improvements could be made in inter-agency coordination."

"Inter-agency coordination?" Mateus repeated slowly and deliberately. He snorted. "You know any agencies that coordinate well when competing for resources, for influence?"

Carter didn't. On the Navajo, Hopi, and Apache reservations where she often worked out of the FBI office in Flagstaff, Arizona, she would usually have to juggle the arcane jurisdictions of tribal police, county police, state police, and Bureau of Indian Affairs police when investigating crimes. At times Drug Enforcement Agency personnel, Bureau of Land Management agents, and Bureau of Alcohol, Tobacco, Firearms and Explosives officers would be involved and sometimes even Homeland Security. All had their own ways of operating and their own self-serving agendas that typically tied investigations in knots.

"And these people in Dili who want improvements," he continued. "Who are they?"

He pushed away from the desk and stood. His face sagged a little.

"I don't expect an answer," he said. "You've been sent to gather information, not provide it." He thrust his hands in his pockets. "But why here? Why not Batugade, Maliana, or Suai? They are the main towns people enter from West Timor."

Carter pinched the bridge of her nose.

"They'll all be subject to other investigations," she said and immediately regretted the term. It was unusual for her to choose her words in an ill-advised manner unless she was tired--and she was tired. Too tired for detailed explanations, rationales or justifications. "Or I should say fact-finding missions. On this particular trip I've been tasked with examining more remote border areas."

"Remote," Mateus repeated without further comment.

"Any information or insights you can offer will be most appreciated and we'll be on our way as soon as our vehicle has been repaired," Carter said.

Carter's tone was flat. Mateus studied her a moment.

"You don't like this assignment, I think," Mateus said.

Carter met his gaze.

"Let's just say I prefer to work active cases," she replied, trying to brighten her expression.

Mateus smiled at what he perceived as an understatement.

"I went to Maliana today," he said, as he began to pace behind his desk. "I manage to persuade the Border Patrol Unit to send someone here tomorrow to talk to you."

He stopped pacing and leaned over his desk.

"But I can tell you what we need. Money for officers' salaries. The budget is locked up in Parliament for the past two months while everyone argues over how much they can give to their own supporters. Fine for them, not for us. My men not paid in all that time. What reason they have to do their job? If I push, they not show up. This happens all the time. How can my men and their families live? How can I do my job?"

He took a loose cigarette from his top pocket and a plastic lighter from his trousers. He popped the cigarette in his mouth, lit it, and casually tossed the lighter onto the desk. He took a long drag and stood upright, smoke drifting from his nostrils.

"You Officer dos Carvalho," he said in Tetun. "When were you last paid?"

Estefana raised her eyes, glanced at Carter and back to the commander.

"I'm paid through INTERPOL," she said in English.

"INTERPOL," Mateus huffed. "Then you are lucky." He'd reverted to English now. "I'm sorry to be angry," he said. "It is not up to any of you here. But if people in Dili did their job, we could do ours. Pass the budget. Get things done."

He slumped into his chair and took another drag on his cigarette. Carter found herself warming to him as a man whose cynicism about politicians she shared.

"I'll take note of that," she said, "in compiling a full report on your resource needs as well."

"Resource needs, huh?" Mateus said. "I'll tell you about resources. There are not many televisions in Balibo but I show American movies here, at the police station, on the computer," he said and pointed to an old desk top computer atop a side table.

"DVDs, you know? Tourists leave them. I watch to practice my English. My men come, sometimes their wives too, not to learn English but because they like the action. Guns, shooting. Lots of shooting. But a gun won't tell you if someone shot on purpose or not. And if it's on purpose, a gun won't help you to understand why."

He tapped a finger against his temple.

"You need to think for that," he continued. "Ask *Maun* Cordero. He talked about that at the conference I mentioned. Using a gun is easy. Using your brains is hard. You need to know how. So my officers need education. Not training"—he held up a finger to emphasise his point—"but education. Education about how to think."

"I'll note that as well," said Carter. With a wave of her hand she indicated Cordero. "I don't think our friend here has ever carried a gun," she said to lighten the mood.

"Do you?" Mateus asked.

Carter was taken slightly aback by the directness of the question.

"Back home?" she said. "Kids in elementary schools carry guns where I come from. So yeah, I carry a weapon there. It's a matter of survival. Here, in Timor, I have no enforcement powers with INTERPOL so I'm unarmed."

They fell silent for a moment.

"Where are you staying?" asked Mateus.

"We've booked a night in a guesthouse just down from the center of town," Estefana said.

Mateus shifted to face Estefana. He straightened and stubbed out his cigarette.

"You speak good English too, *mana*," he said, using the standard vocative of 'sister'. "But I don't think you went to the seminary like me."

"No *senyor*," she said. "I was taught by Filipina nuns in school."

"Ah, Filipina nuns!" said Mateus, smiling. "That explains it. Timor's most recent colonizers. They don't use swords and guns; they use rosary beads and blackboards. They don't try to *overpower* people. They try to *win* them over. Brains you see."

Estefana smiled a little uncertainly at that.

"I have a cousin who lives just out of town," Cordero said to change the subject. Mateus shifted his gaze to him. "I'm staying with him and his wife. I'll return tomorrow to help these two women in any way I can."

"You're suspended," Mateus said.

"I can drive them around and explain things to them," Cordero said. "I'm familiar with the area."

"You say your vehicle might take a few days to repair?" Mateus asked Estefana.

"It could be a few days, *senyor*," she replied. "I'm sure we can extend our stay if we need to. The guesthouse said they have no tourists booked in all this week."

Mateus grunted his satisfaction at that reply.

"Have you eaten?" he asked. "My wife, Graziela, said to invite you for dinner if you haven't. I may be the commander of police but she commands me."

"Thank you, maybe another time," said Cordero. "We grabbed something before we left the coast and everyone is feeling quite tired."

"As you wish," said Mateus. "Mind you, my wife makes a good goat curry. What guesthouse are you staying in?"

"It's called *Uma Konvidadu Bandeira*," Estefana answered.

"Which one?" asked Mateus.

"*Senyor*?" said Estefana.

"There are several Flag Guesthouses in Balibo," said Mateus.

"It's the one on *Rua Ermera*. Off *Estrada Balibo-Liquica*," said Estefana.

Mateus nodded.

"Why is the name so popular?" Carter asked.

"Why?" Mateus repeated, surprised at the question. "They're named after the house where the Australians were staying when the Indonesians invaded. They were reporters. They'd painted an Australian flag on the house to identify themselves, you see. It's in the center of town. You'll see it tomorrow."

"And?" asked Carter still no wiser.

"And the Indonesians took them out and shot them!"

said Mateus. "All five of them. Locals were reporting that the Indonesian military were coming across the border for weeks and nobody took any notice. But when a foreigner is reporting it, it's harder to ignore."

He grabbed the keys to lock up and leave.

"I think that's why they sent you here," he said to Carter. "Because you are a foreigner. People may listen to you. So be careful. The border can still be a dangerous place for foreigners."

• • •

Cordero drove Carter and Estefana to their guesthouse. He helped them with their bags to the door, said good night and drove back through town to his cousin's house.

The guesthouse was a drab cement block building of four bedrooms, a small common area with a table, six plastic chairs, a fraying couch, and a shared bathroom addition outside. An old dour woman caretaker had materialized when she heard Cordero's vehicle pull up and she led Carter and Estefana inside to one of the rooms that had twin beds. She handed Estefana a key to the main door, wheeled around, and left. The woman's severe manner suggested to both Carter and Estefana that they should abide by her direction to share the same room even though other rooms were empty and they could have had one each.

A dusty icon of Jesus, his flaming heart emitting rays of light from his chest, adorned one wall of the common room opposite a much smaller picture of the independence hero and first president of East Timor—Xanana Gusmao. The two stared down on the table as though expecting company. Carter and Estefana circled the table and entered their designated room, where they chose their beds, both mattresses sagging in the middle, and laid out their things under the mosquito nets.

"*Mana?*" said Estefana, the bed creaking as she sat on it.

"Yes Estefana," Carter said, leaning against the doorframe and yawning.

"It was good of *maun* to come all the way from Dili and drive us here to Balibo," Estefana said.

"He didn't have anything else to do," Carter said knuckling her eyes. "Besides, he has a cousin here."

"He didn't have to come, *mana*. He wasn't planning to visit his cousin. And now he'll have to stay here until our vehicle is fixed. We should do something to thank him."

Carter pushed herself off the doorframe, blinked to more fully open weary eyes, and frowned.

"Like what?" she asked.

"I don't know, *mana*. What I do know is that if Josinto came all that way for me, I'd do something nice for him as well. To show him I appreciated him."

"Josinto's your husband," Carter said.

"Yes *mana*. And so I would expect him to come but I'd be grateful when he did. *Maun* Cordero isn't your husband or mine and so he didn't have to come. He did. Why did he do that?"

Carter shrugged and yawned a second time.

"Like I said, he's nothing else to do," she answered.

"Why do *that*? If he had nothing else to do, he could have done anything. He could have stayed at home."

Neither spoke for a moment.

"Let's sleep on it, okay?" Carter said. "Maybe we can cook him dinner or something. How's that sound? Let's talk about it tomorrow."

3

"How did you sleep?" Cordero asked, as he waited for Carter and Estefana to finish a breakfast of stale bread rolls, cold fried eggs, and delicious strong coffee in the small common room under the gaze of Jesus and Xanana. Outside a cloudless blue sky was leaching colour in the heat and the day was steamy from the rain the night before. The sound of a nearby rooster cock-a-doodling reverberated down the hallway.

"Good, *maun*," Estefana said, pulling apart a bread roll. "We were tired. How are you this morning?"

"Yeah I'm good too," he said. "I'm running a little late though because of all the traffic coming into Balibo. Beep, beep, beep—that's all I've heard all morning."

A second rooster joined in the crowing and the two began to compete for attention.

"Every time I hear a rooster from now on, I'll think of Timor," said Carter as she pushed her empty plate away.

"Do you not have roosters in Arizona, *mana*?" asked Estefana.

"Only ones locked up in chicken farms," Carter said. "Which is another reason I'll think of Timor when I hear them. Roosters and chickens roam freely all over the place here."

"The fighting roosters are usually tied by the leg to a peg in the ground, *mana*," said Estefana. "It's so they don't lose strength roaming as you say." She popped part of the roll into her mouth and covered the lower part of her face with a hand. "But most roosters are not fighting roosters."

"Mateus was quite engaging," said Carter, changing the subject. She poured Cordero a coffee into the same cup she'd just drained as there were no other clean cups to choose from. "And he certainly has a high opinion of you."

Cordero's grin broke through despite his best efforts to feign humility.

"Did you see those medals on his jacket?" he asked.

"Yeah," Carter responded. "A good cop by those accounts. Doesn't make him a good judge of character."

She winked at Estefana as Cordero considered what to make of that.

"How was your night?" Carter asked, throwing an arm across the back of her chair. She was dressed in dark blue cotton slacks and a plain white blouse, and her hair was tied in a short ponytail. As usual, Estefana was neatly dressed in a clean and somehow pressed light blue police uniform.

"Moises and Cipriana were glad to see me," Cordero said, brightening. "The kids too, of course." He laughed. "Cipriana refuses to accept that you're not my girlfriend. Said why else would I be still hanging around with you after we came through here a few months ago."

"What did you say?" Carter asked, amused.

"Say?" Cordero repeated, a trace of surprise in his tone.

"Yes, say."

"I told her we occasionally work together," said Cordero, searching the table for sugar.

"Did she buy that?" Carter persisted.

"What? Um, no," Cordero replied.

Estefana handed him a small wooden container with a little raw sugar encrusted on the bottom.

"I'd already told Moises I'd been suspended so Cipriana asked how I could be working with you if I didn't have a job."

Carter leaned forward and folded her arms on the table.

"And you said?"

Cordero fidgeted with the sugar container.

"Didn't know what to say," he admitted. He wiped the blade of a knife clean and used it to scrape a little sugar from the container into his coffee. "Just let it go."

"So much for working with your brain," Carter said and rose from the table.

Cordero shook off the taunt and sat moodily over his coffee.

Estefana collected the breakfast plates and cutlery, excused herself, and went outside to find the woman who'd brought them breakfast and hand the tableware over for cleaning.

"I have to go to the store on the way to the police station," Cordero told Carter. "Cipriana asked me to get her some cooking oil."

"Cooking your goose is she?" quipped Carter.

"Goose?"

"It's an expression," she said.

"Oh. No, she needs it for a children's party she's hosting on the weekend." He downed the contents of his cup, grabbed his keys, and stood. "Come on. Let's go."

• • •

They drove to the edge of town where the road forked. On the far corner outside the store a man was pacing up and down along a row of headless mannequins adorned with second-hand clothes. Cordero pulled up in front of the store, exited the vehicle, and leaned in through the window of the driver's door.

"This'll only take a minute," he said and pushed off for the entrance to the store. "Wait here," he called back.

"*Mana*," Estefana said, twisting around to gaze out of the rear window.

"Yeah?" Carter replied.

"That must be the house the commander was talking about last night," she said, pointing. "The one our guesthouse is named after. Where the Australian reporters were staying. You can see the flag painted on the side."

They both stepped out of the vehicle for a closer inspection. Carter noticed a tortoiseshell cat under the wheels of a motorcycle on its stand in the near distance. Another cat—bigger and black—was grooming itself next to the front wheel.

"Lots of cats here," she said to Estefana who was admiring the surrounding buildings not the cats.

Their presence had caught the eye of the man pacing up and down. He stopped and tried to make out what had caught their interest.

He was middle aged, neatly dressed in trousers and a checked shirt, and was clean shaven. A large silver wristwatch sparkled when the sunlight struck his right forearm.

Across the road was a hillock rising up from the road they'd taken up from Batugade the night before. A crumbling stone perimeter enclosed the ruins of a burnt-out garrison, its roof a jumble of skeletal beams and the odd blackened tile. Tufts of grass grew out of a cobblestone drive that led from the twisted entrance gates to the main building. It was all that remained of a fort built 400 years earlier to defend Portuguese Timor from the Dutch colonisers to the west. The man guessed it was that which had taken their interest.

"*Ami iha planu atu halo otel husi ida-nee forte tebes*," he said. "*Ba turista*," he added.

Estefana merely smiled in acknowledgement.

"The man thinks we are looking at the old fort over there, *mana*," she said to Carter. "He says they have plans to develop it into a hotel for tourists."

The man edged closer.

"I don't see too many tourists around here, do you?" said Carter.

"They may come if there is a hotel, *mana*," Estefana replied.

Carter let it go and returned to the vehicle.

"Where are you from, *mana*?" the man, now alongside Estefana, asked.

"Dili, *senyor*," she answered.

"Ah. Welcome to Balibo," he said. "And your friend there? She is a foreigner. Interested in the house with the flag painted on its side. She's Australian perhaps?"

"American," said Estefana, keeping her answers short so as not to encourage the man in conversation.

"Ah, American," he said. "That's interesting."

• • •

Inside the store items for sale were stacked, dumped and spilt with scant regard for order. Cans of fruit, vegetables, and prepared meals with Indonesian, Chinese, and Arabic writing on the labels occupied shelves alongside loose screws and nails, plastic bottles filled with gasoline and other liquids of various colours, and a collection of herbs most of which had dried to dust. Along one wall were the dismembered arms, legs, and torsos of broken mannequins opposite cartons of two-minute noodles piled high on burlap sacks of cement that had hardened solid with age. Water bottles stood upright along a bench like votive candles. The store reeked of stale air, and motes drifted in slithers of light angling through the slits in the wall that passed for windows.

It took a while but eventually Cordero found what he was searching for—a small can of cooking oil—and he called out for someone to come so that he could purchase it.

Silence.

He called a second time.

A thin curtain with a faded floral design was thrown open at the back of the store, there was a soft tinkling of coloured beads attached to it, and an old Chinese man emerged.

"*Bondia, senyor*," said Cordero.

"*Dia*," the man replied in what amounted to little more than a whisper.

The man was carrying incense sticks. He made his way across the room to a small Buddhist altar that had been assembled in one corner. He replaced three charred incense sticks with the new ones, lit a candle sitting on the floor in its own wax, bowed with his hands together, and used the candle to light the incense. Soon the sweet, aromatic smell of incense was wafting through the store.

The man turned, put one hand on a chair to steady himself, and faced Cordero.

"My name is Feng Lee Hung," he said in Tetun. "Feng will do. This is my store. You are a visitor here. Perhaps passing through. How can I help you?"

"Do you have any sugar, *senyor*?" Cordero asked.

The man nodded, shifted stiffly toward the curtain and reached into a large polyester fiber bag. He pulled out a plastic container half full of sugar and shuffled over to a set of scales sitting on a bench off to the side.

"Just a little," said Cordero. "Enough for coffee for a few days."

The storekeeper unscrewed the top of the container and began pouring the sugar into a paper bag.

"That'll do," said Cordero, holding up a hand.

The man weighed the contents of the paper bag on a set of ancient scales.

"Twenty centavos," he said—the equivalent of twenty cents.

Cordero nodded.

"A lot of stuff you have here, *senyor*," he said.

"I am the only merchant between Batugade and Maliana," Feng said with a note of pride. "Only a few people in Balibo have money to spend. Others more fortunate pass through and they buy from me. I have to stock whatever they may need and it's not always easy to know what that might be. People's wants and needs vary. You need sugar. Others need salt."

Cordero held up the cooking oil.

"And this," he said.

The old man squinted.

"Sixty centavos," Feng said.

Cordero reached inside his pocket and brought out two fifty centavo coins. He handed them over, took the sugar, and pocketed his twenty centavos in change. He thanked the storekeeper and went outside into the glare of the sun shielding his eyes with the hand that held the bag of sugar.

He noticed a stranger standing beside Estefana who looked less than comfortable in the man's presence. He walked over.

"*Bondia, senyor*," Cordero said to the stranger. "Can I help you?"

The man turned and smiled at Cordero. Estefana saw her chance and retreated to the vehicle.

"*Bondia*," he said. "My name is Dario Freitas. And you are?"

"Why do you ask?"

"I am curious," Dario said. "A lot of people are arriving today for the burial of my father, Gaspa. You could be one that I don't know."

Again the stranger smiled.

"I noticed a lot of traffic coming into Balibo this morning," said Cordero. "Now I know why. Do you often come to the store to look for people you don't know?"

The man laughed at that.

"I am waiting for my goods to arrive, *senyor*," he said. "I am hosting the burial and must provide for the kinfolk of my late father. The ritual will go on for days. Gaspa was a *dato*, you see."

"I'm sorry to hear that he is dead," said Cordero as he reached for the door of his vehicle.

"Oh he died many years ago, *senyor*," said Dario. "But you know how a man must be laid to rest in the presence of all of his kinfolk. And the troubles Timor has faced since he died have prevented them coming." Dario smiled. "Until now," he added.

At that moment the police SUV swung in off the main road, Commander Mateus Salsinha at the wheel. He pulled up abruptly, splashing a pool of muddy water in Dario's direction. An officer jumped out of the passenger's seat and strode, head down, toward the store.

"*Bondia, Senyor* Dario," Mateus said to Dario who was checking that the legs of his pants had not been smeared with mud. "I didn't mean to splash you and apologize if I did. My officer there is chasing up a complaint from the Chinaman about a break-in a few days ago," he said, as though that somehow explained his driving. His attention shifted to Cordero. "We'll have to postpone our meeting, *maun*," he said. "You can tell the American I'll be back in an hour or so."

"Where are you going?" Cordero asked.

"Down to the border," Mateus said. "A body's been found."

He threw the vehicle into reverse. Two officers in back, one a young female, lurched forward with the motion. "I must go," he said.

"Wait," said Cordero. "The American's here, with me, in my vehicle. Why don't we follow you? It's a good chance for her to see the border for herself."

Mateus pursed his lips.

"That's what she's here to report on isn't it?" Cordero added.

"Okay," Mateus said. "Follow me." He spun his SUV back onto the road. "Try to keep up!" he shouted to Cordero through the passenger's window and roared off.

4

"Any idea what this is about?" Carter asked, clutching the grab handle for support as Cordero drove at speed over the ruts and rocks in an effort to keep up with the police commander.

"None at all," he said. "Mateus just said something about a body."

They continued on for several miles down *Rua de Frontera* and through barren country. On their left were heavy patches of acacia and palm: on their right, unfarmed stretches of tall grass, flowering thistles, and bird's-nest ferns. Houses had given way to huts of bamboo and thatch spread out sparsely across the terrain. They passed a group of women in grubby sarongs and shabby headscarves washing clothes under a pipe spouting water from the embankment into a culvert. Further along small children, naked and streaked with mud, splashed through the slush in which they played. For a short time, their progress was slowed by a man bouncing along on a pony, his toes inches off the ground, hogging the centre of the road to avoid pools of cloudy water sloshing onto his feet.

Mateus pulled up behind a mud-slicked jeep which itself was parked behind a police motorcycle. Three men standing around the jeep glanced up, nothing more. One, the oldest, was dressed in heavily soiled work clothes and a scruffy ranch hat and was hand rolling a cigarette. Another, middle-aged, was dressed in shorts, a blue checked shirt and flip-flops. The third wore the black cassock and white collar of a priest.

Cordero steered onto the edge of the road behind the commander's SUV and cut the engine. The young female officer, thin limbed with frizzy hair, bolted out of the SUV and up to the three men holding out her arms as if to corral them. The other officer, a solid middle-aged man, grunted as he dragged a tarpaulin from the SUV and threw it over his shoulder. He grabbed a camera with his free hand and slammed the door shut with his foot. Mateus was the last to slip out from behind the steering wheel. He waved to the three men up ahead, walked back to Cordero's vehicle, and stood over Carter's door. She opened it and shifted sideways to face him.

Mateus squatted down to be eye-level with her.

"A farmer found a body this morning," he said and gestured toward the men. "He's in the hat. He called the man next to him. That's Juno Cabral. He's up for re-election as village head so he makes a point of getting to know everyone around here and involving himself in everything that's going on. He called me and brought the priest, Father Francedez." He stood and placed one hand on the roof of the vehicle above Carter. "This is a good opportunity for you to see the border area." He pushed himself off the SUV. "Oh, and you told me you like active cases," he said. "Consider the body a bonus. It may tell you something about how people live here and what the police have to deal with."

He signalled to Juno Cabral, the priest and the local farmer that he'd be back soon and led Carter, Cordero, and Estefana through the scrub for thirty yards. The police officer with the tarpaulin and camera trudged on behind them in silence.

In a small clearing grew a wild pomegranate tree in fruit. A little further on was a police officer in his early thirties, a slight growth on his chin, his shirt wrinkled. He stood over a body curled into a foetal position on the ground.

"*Dia*," Mateus said to the officer before facing the others. "This is Officer Eduardo Sobado," he said in English. "Edi for short." He swung back around and spoke to Edi in Tetun. "What can you tell me, *maun*?"

"Not much commander," Officer Edi said, as Mateus stepped carefully around to the far side of the body. "I haven't moved him or let anyone touch him. The priest wanted to bless him or something. I told him to leave the body alone until you arrived."

"Good," said Mateus. He surveyed the area near the body. "All three of them tramped around the body and disturbed any tracks by the looks of it."

"Before I came, yes."

"You know this man?" Mateus asked.

"No sir," said Edi. "Never seen him."

"Any identification?"

"None I could find, commander."

"You searched his pockets?"

"Yes, commander," said Edi. "Carefully."

"No identification? No papers?"

"Papers?" Edi scoffed. "What good would they do? People down here can't read." Mateus crouched and leaned over the body.

"And you found nothing?"

"Nothing."

Mateus ran his eyes over the body. The dead man wore a long-sleeve blue shirt, flecked with mud and opened at the front to reveal a grimy singlet underneath. Baggy shorts and a pair of old army boots without laces completed his wardrobe. The man's hair was dark, his stubble grey, and his face furrowed in a way that suggested he was well advanced in his years.

Mateus took the cell from his pocket and took two quick photographs of the dead man's face. He pocketed the cell and told the officer who brought the camera and tarpaulin to take detailed images of the body and the area where it lay. When that was done, the commander squatted down and examined the man more closely.

"No sign of wounds," he said in English. He ran his fingers around the head and neck. "No sign of any kind of blow and no indication of broken neck or strangulation." He stood. "See for yourself," he said, gesturing to Carter and Cordero. "I can't find anything that might have killed him. Heart attack maybe."

Cordero crouched down on one knee and ran his eyes over the body, Carter watching over his shoulder.

"Rigor mortis has set in and livor mortis is well developed and unaltered," he said. "Blood's pooled on the side nearest the ground where he's lying so the body hasn't been moved."

"Yes, I noticed that," said Mateus. "I'd say he's been dead at least twelve hours."

Cordero didn't argue with that estimate and continued to examine the body.

"So, no identification?" Mateus asked Edi a second time.

"Nothing."

"And you've never seen him?" Cordero asked this time and the officer merely shook his head.

Mateus scanned the surrounding countryside.

"Any sign of where he was coming from or going to?" he asked.

"There are some prints over there on the other side of the *romã*," Edi said, using the Portuguese word for pomegranate. "They match his boots. They're all over the place. I think he was coming this way." The officer raised his arms and slapped them against his side. "It's hard to tell."

Estefana had been translating the officer's answers for Carter.

"Was he curled up like this when he was found?" Carter asked and Mateus put the question to Edi. The officer was uncertain at first as though the question might be accusing him of disturbing the body.

"Yes," he said, finally.

"And you say the footprints are all over the place? Could he have been stumbling?" Carter asked and Mateus translated for the officer.

Edi nodded uncertainly.

"What do you have in mind?" asked Cordero.

"Ask him if he saw any sign of vomit," Carter said to Mateus, ignoring Cordero's question.

Edi said he hadn't.

"It rained last night, remember?" said Cordero. "It would've washed anything into the soil."

"Maybe," she said.

"What are you thinking?" he asked.

"It's like he's holding his stomach. Like he had a severe gut ache or something." She edged Cordero out of the way and began to inspect the body. She lifted each of the eyelids and examined the eyeballs closely. "I think he's jaundiced," she said. "You can just make it out on the whites of the eyes. I wouldn't swear to it. It could be his ethnicity." She opened the dead man's mouth, leaned in carefully and put her nose to the lips. She pulled back and did it a second time, and a third. "I detect a slight fruity smell in his mouth."

Cordero looked from Mateus to Carter who rested on her haunches.

"Maybe he was eating a pomegranate before he died," suggested Cordero.

"You ever eaten a pomegranate?" Carter asked. "There's no sign of juice on his fingers or his clothes and I can't see any evidence of husks or seeds." She glanced along the length of the man's body.

"So you're thinking what? That he ate something and it poisoned him?" Cordero asked.

"Ate or drank. That'd be my guess," she said and stood, wiping her hands on the sides of her slacks. "We really need a toxicology report to know for sure. And if it is a case of poisoning, we need to know what type of poison it was."

"*We*?" said Cordero but instead of elaborating she turned to Mateus.

"Can toxicology be done here? In Balibo, I mean," she asked.

"Well…," Mateus said, scratching his chin. "We only have one doctor. Cuban trained. Good with infections and broken bones. Not sure if he could do a toxicology examination. Not one you could put much trust in. Anyhow he went to Viqueque until the end of the week."

"There's no one else?" Carter asked. "Not in Maliana or Batugade?"

Mateus clamped his jaw by way of a negative to that.

"Can you get Brooks up here?" Carter put to Cordero.

He looked doubtful.

"If this guy was poisoned we need to know what it was and where it came from because other people could be at risk from the same thing," Carter said.

"I've been suspended remember," Cordero said. He thought for a moment. "Can you request it, Mateus? Dr Howard Brooks is an English pathologist currently working at the morgue in Dili. He's very good. I've worked with him on several cases."

"I'll get in touch with headquarters when I return to the office and see what I can do," Mateus said. "I'll need to know what he'd be looking for if he agrees to come and what he needs to bring. I don't think there's much in Balibo that would help." He eyed the police officer who'd taken the photographs. "Cover him and take him to the health clinic," he said in Tetun. "Stay with the body and make sure nobody touches him until we know what caused his death. Use my vehicle. I'll go with Investigator Cordero."

"I'm *suspended*, Mateus," Cordero reminded him.

The commander waved that away.

"I'll call Jada," he said in English. "I may need you in an official capacity."

Carter thrust her hands in her pockets and gazed down at the body.

"If we're right to suspect poison, it was most likely accidental," she said. "Most poisonings are. Maybe he consumed something that he shouldn't have or made a mistake when mixing things together." She hesitated a moment. "But it could be rat poison mixed in with rice or flour that he got his hands on or something in his cooking oil. We need to be sure it was an isolated thing and nothing more."

Mateus didn't comment. He looked at Estefana.

"Anything you notice or want to say, *mana*?" he asked.

Estefana hesitated a moment.

"No, *senyor*," she said.

The commander turned to the officer he called Edi.

"When you've helped get the body into my vehicle I want you to go over those tracks you spotted. Follow them as far as you can, searching the area on one side. Do the same on the other side. You follow? Keep an eye out for anything dropped, thrown or brought up if he'd been sick. If you find anything—anything at all—I want you to bring it to me at the station."

"Even vomit? What do I do if I find vomit?" Edi asked doubtfully.

"Scrape it up. We'll need to test it." Mateus checked his watch. "I'll be back at the station by ten o'clock."

• • •

While the two police officers attended to the body, the others followed Mateus to the road. He approached the three men being corralled by the female officer.

"*Bondia maun*," Mateus said to the one he'd called Juno Cabral. "And you *amu*," he added to the priest, using the colloquial Tetun term for 'Father'. He gazed at the man in the ranch hat. "And you are?"

The man took a drag on his cigarette and cleared his throat. "Nario," he said. "Nario Gansoso."

"You live around here Nario?" Mateus asked.

The man waved a hand off vaguely west through the trees, his cigarette dropping ash.

"What were you doing out here this morning?"

"Picking pomegranates, what else? Fruit's ripe now," Nario said and pointed with his cigarette toward a hessian sack by his feet. Mateus guessed he'd find pomegranates in it if he cared to look. "I come over here every few days," Nario added.

"You know who that man is? You seen him before?"

"I don't know who he is—or was," Nario said, tossing away his cigarette. "I've never seen him."

"What time did you find the body?"

The man lifted his hat, cast his eyes down, and ran a hand through his hair.

"He rang me about eight o'clock," Juno said. "He doesn't have a watch and can't read time on his cell."

Mateus nodded.

"Did you see anyone else out here this morning?" he asked.

Nario shook his head and took the makings of another cigarette from his trouser pocket.

"Did you touch the body?"

"No! He was dead," Nario said with alarm. "I don't touch the dead. Spirits, you know."

"And you don't know who he is or where he's from?"

Nario raised a hand to indicate that he didn't.

"Who else lives around here?" Mateus asked.

Nario licked along the edge of the cigarette paper before answering.

"Around here? No one."

"Except you," Mateus said.

"Me. My family," he said. "Letencio Tiago and his family. But we're all closer to the village."

"Leohitu?"

"Yes."

"No other huts near here?"

"One or two. Not close. No. More near Lolitu."

"What about strangers? Do you get a lot come through this way?" Mateus asked.

The man lit his cigarette and rubbed the loose tobacco off his hands. "Sometimes," he said, drawing smoke into his lungs. "It's easy to cross the border here without being seen. The road's rough and the one to Lolitu is even rougher." Smoke came out of his mouth with his words. "Border police don't come often."

Nario dropped his eyes and regarded the cigarette in his hand. He clearly had nothing more to say on the subject of the unknown dead man.

Estefana quietly translated the gist of the exchange for Carter's benefit. Mateus next approached Juno. The man was in his late forties or early fifties. He had a full head of dark, curly hair above probing eyes, and a firmly set jaw.

"Thanks for calling," Mateus began. "You didn't touch the body?"

Juno shook his head.

"Or see anything or anyone other than this man?" he asked and flicked his thumb toward Nario.

"No."

"And you don't know the dead man?"

"Never seen him," Juno said. "I just called you and brought Father Francedez down here. I don't know anything more."

Mateus stepped sideways to speak to the priest who pushed his glasses higher on the bridge of his nose and tried to smile. He was a short man with the beginnings of a paunch and he blinked purposefully and often.

"You *amu*?"

"I wanted to give the poor man a blessing. The police officer said I couldn't touch him until you came," the priest said. "So I haven't touched him, no." The priest fidgeted with the small parcel in his hands. "And I have never seen him before either," he added.

"You have a stole there?" Mateus said, referring to the band of cloth that signified priestly authority.

"And holy oils," the priest said. "Yes."

"Okay *amu*," Mateus said. "When my officers bring the man out, you can bless him here." He turned back to Nario Gansoso. "I may want to talk to you again. You called Juno so you have a cell. Give the number to my officer here," he said and nodded toward the policewoman.

With that the commander started off toward Cordero's vehicle, his hand placed lightly around Carter's back.

"So none of them claims to know anything," he said to her. "Probably true. But since we're down here we might as well go a little further. I'll show the photos on my cell to some locals. Someone may recognize our dead friend. And you'll get to see the border and why it's difficult to patrol."

5

"They call people down here *Kaladi*," Mateus was saying over his shoulder to Carter. "It means yam-eater. It's not a nice word. It suggests people here are ignorant, primitive. Some of them were settled here from West Timor when the Indonesians occupied the country. That adds anger about the land they were given to the prejudice long time residents feel."

He had to raise his voice to be heard above the rattle of the SUV on the bumpy road.

"But they're not stupid. It's just that this area hasn't seen much development. No schools beyond the first years of primary, few roads. Without a motorcycle, it's a long walk to Balibo and most people here live off what their gardens produce. They don't buy and sell in the Balibo market. All of that adds to a strong sense of local identity and a traditional outlook where people are suspicious of outsiders and very defensive." He turned to face forwards again in his seat. "That makes policing here a challenge."

The road twisted along a narrow gorge through forests of spindly casuarina trees on the southern side and open savannah to the north. Soon it veered to the left through a small copse of beech before opening onto Leohitu. The village consisted of run-down cinder block houses and thatch huts together with a collection of official buildings with faded signs out front that had once indicated their purpose.

Dogs lazed in what shade they could find and chickens pecked along the side of the road. Mateus searched for someone he could question. The only sound was of someone hammering well out of sight. He could see no one.

"If this place is as undeveloped as you were saying," Cordero said, "people could be working plots a long way from their huts or even foraging in the forest."

"That. Or simply staying indoors out of the sun," Mateus suggested.

They drove down the deserted road.

"There!" said Estefana pointing to a woman hanging washing on a frangipani tree on the side of a hut.

Cordero pulled the SUV to a stop.

"Wait here," said Mateus. He climbed out and took off zigzagging his way around puddles.

They could hear the police commander introduce himself as he trudged toward the woman explaining his purpose. She made no reply, a blank expression on her face as she spat a blob of red spittle from the betel she was chewing onto the ground. Mateus drew closer to her, out of earshot of the others. They watched him produce his cell and show the woman the images of the dead man. She shook her head, indicating she didn't know anything about the man.

There were a few more questions and more headshaking. A child ran out from the hut and wrapped arms around the woman's legs. It was a small boy, wearing only a ripped singlet. The boy gawked at the stranger in silence. Finally, Mateus pocketed his cell, nodded his thanks to the woman, and made his way back.

"Never seen him and doesn't know anything about where he was found," he said as he climbed into the passenger's seat. "Let's go on a little further."

They came to the last huts on the edge of the hamlet where a man was approaching on the other side of the road where it petered out completely. He looked like he'd been working in a garden plot, his T-shirt rolled up to reveal a chest slick with sweat, the legs below his cut-off jeans spotted with soil. He carried a bunch of spring onions in one hand and with the other rested a machete on his shoulder.

Cordero drew alongside.

"*Bondia, senyor,*" he said.

"*Dia*," the man replied in a coarse voice without breaking his stride or turning toward Cordero.

"A moment please!" Mateus called.

The police commander jumped from the vehicle and caught up with the man. Cordero cut the engine and waited.

The man slapped the machete repeatedly against his thigh as though annoyed by this interruption to his day as Mateus introduced himself and explained why he was in Leohitu. The man said nothing. Mateus took his cell from his pocket and showed the images he had taken. The man put the machete down on the ground and took the cell. He glanced at the images before showing more interest in the device itself which he turned this way and that in his hands.

"Well?" asked Mateus.

The man handed over the cell.

"I've never seen him," he said, gathered his machete, and started off down the road.

"Any good?" Cordero asked.

"Said he'd never seen him," said Mateus taking his seat.

"You want to stop here and see if anyone else comes along?"

"No. Let's go," said Mateus. "We'll try Lolitu. It's back a little off a side road. If no one can help us there we'll go on to Balibo."

Cordero engaged the ignition and made a three-point turn. Mateus threw his arm across the back of his seat and twisted side-on to Carter.

"Less than a mile beyond this village is the Talu river," he said. "The border runs down the middle of it here. For most of the year you can cross it without much difficulty. In the wet season, it's more of a challenge but a little easier near this next place we're going to where a tributary has pushed rocks into the main channel. All through this area"—he waved a hand around the cabin—"you can see few people live here. You can cross the border without anyone noticing."

"What about the Border Patrol?" Carter asked.

"What about them?" replied Mateus. "There's a lot of ground to cover and no roads beyond here. That means you have to patrol on foot. So they don't come this way often. Besides, nothing much of value can be carried across the Talu. What comes in here are mainly small items for local consumption or sale in Balibo."

"What about drugs? People? Weapons?" Carter asked.

Mateus faced forward.

"Whatever demand there is for drugs and illegals is in Dili, not out here," he said. "And there are easier ways to get both to Dili than to bring them across country like this and then arrange transport to the city. As for weapons, that's what the Indonesians were most generous with in Timor. When they agreed to hold a referendum on independence in 1999, they handed them out to their militia friends to intimidate Timorese into voting No." Carter caught him in the rearview mirror smiling to himself. "It didn't work."

• • •

The 'side road' Mateus had mentioned proved to be little more than a bush track. It ran along a low dry ridge below which was a waterway with the occasional large pool glistening in the sun. Cordero had to stay sharply focused to keep control of the SUV as it jerked from one rocky outcrop or sunken crater to another and he pulled the vehicle this way and that to avoid stretches where the edge of the track had collapsed entirely. Mateus steadied himself with one hand on the dashboard, one on the center console. Carter and Estefana jostled in the back like string puppets.

The heat building in the vehicle added to the discomfort. Even though the windows were down to encourage airflow, Carter's blouse was damp with sweat and was sticking to the back of the seat. Cordero kept wiping his forearm across his face when the driving allowed. Even Mateus took a kerchief and passed it around his neck several times. Only Estefana showed no sign of being affected by the conditions.

Another half mile on and a small hut came into sight nestled between two palm trees off through the scrub. Its walls were made of slit bamboo and the roof of thatched palm fronds. There was a crude door for an entrance and no windows. A chestnut brown Timorese pony stood motionless, tethered to a log off in the shade of a tree. A heavy blanket had been tied across its back to serve as a saddle.

As Cordero drew near, a boy emerged from the hut and made for the pony. He watched the SUV approach and, when it pulled up, he came to a stop as if sensing a threat. Mateus shouted for the boy to stay where he was, climbed out, and trudged off to speak to him. Cordero decided to stretch his legs and so he slipped out of the driver's seat and followed Mateus. Carter sat in the vehicle, fanning her face. Estefana sat calmly, her eyes on Mateus.

"The commander is not having much luck, *mana*," Estefana commented.

Carter watched the two men mount the rise to where the boy was standing.

"Not yet," she said. "Few adults around and none of them all that sociable. Maybe he'll have better luck with this kid."

Mateus reached the boy.

"*Dia, alin*," he said, using the Tetun title for a younger person.

The boy wore a grubby singlet which exposed his too-thin arms. On his feet he wore sneakers with the toes exposed on one, and a length of twine around his waist tied shorts that were too big for his hips. Close up, he looked to be in his early teens. He offered no reply.

Mateus quickly introduced himself and asked if there were any adults at home. The boy looked toward the hut before answering.

"No," he said finally.

Mateus sighed his disappointment.

"What's your name?"

"Amando," the boy replied.

"You live around here, right Amando?" Mateus asked.

The boy said nothing.

"I need to know something," Mateus said. He reached for his cell and pulled up the images of the dead man. "We're trying to identify this man." He handed the cell to the boy. "You ever seen him?"

The boy held one hand over the cell to block the glare of the sun and narrowed his eyes, studying the image for a moment. His frown suggested uncertainty about something.

"Is he asleep?" the boy asked.

"No. He's not asleep. He's dead," replied Mateus. "Have you ever seen him?" he repeated. "He was found not far from here down toward Leohitu. Do you know who he is?"

The boy examined the image again although he didn't bother to shade the screen.

"Is there a reward for information?" he asked.

Mateus lowered the cell to his side.

"A reward!" he said. "Why ask me that?"

"My father says the *bapa* offered rewards when they wanted to know about people," the boy said. *Bapa* was the colloquial expression Timorese used for Indonesians.

Mateus straightened and sucked in air through his nostrils.

"Your father is talking about the time the *bapa* invaded this country," he said in an exasperated tone. "They offered rewards when they were chasing people to kill! People who fought for your freedom! You're a citizen now, not a slave. You have responsibilities. So I'm asking you again: have you ever seen this man?"

The tone and volume of Mateus' reprimand had made the boy slink back a little toward the pony.

"I've never seen him," he said.

Mateus put his cell in his pocket and calmed himself.

"Okay," he said to Cordero. "Let's go."

Cordero was patting the pony's forehead.

"Would you have seen him if there was a reward, Amando?" he asked the boy with a grin.

The boy considered Cordero for a moment, face blank of expression.

"Well?" Cordero asked again.

"No," said Amando. "I guess not."

"Good-looking horse you have," said Cordero.

"It's not a horse, it's a pony," the boy corrected him. "Be careful. If he doesn't know you and you touch him he'll kick."

"Oh, okay," said Cordero and he took a step back from the animal. "Yes, it is a pony. I get so many things wrong. Like I got things wrong about you. I told the commander here I was sure a boy like you, who gets around on a fine horse—I mean pony—like this one would know about the man in the photo. Wrong again."

Cordero shook his head feigning disappointment with himself.

The boy considered him as Cordero reached out and ruffled the pony's forelock, turned, and made to walk away.

"Bobu may know," the boy said.

"Bobu?" repeated Cordero. The word means 'clown' in Tetun.

"You'll find him further on," the boy said pointing vaguely down the track. "I heard him there earlier. He knows lots of people here."

"Heard him?" repeated Cordero.

"He plays the guitar," the boy said. "And sings."

Cordero nodded.

"Does he now? Thank you, *alin*."

• • •

They found the character known as Bobu sitting under a candle nut tree in a clearing amid a small cluster of traditional huts. He looked to be in his mid-twenties, tall and lean from the way his legs were extended and he wore old jeans and a faded plaid shirt. His long, frizzy hair was arranged into cornrows and tied with bright red beads in a bun. A wispy goatee sprouted from his chin. The folds on either cheek were prominent as though he'd known periods of hunger and an incisor was missing on the left of his upper jaw.

The gap where the tooth had been was easy to see because the man was singing a melancholy song about a lost love as he strummed an old box guitar. A little girl danced at his feet but to a different tune that was all her own. The approach of the SUV distracted neither from their performance. It was only when Cordero and the others got out, slamming the doors of the vehicle like a drum roll that the man strummed the last chords of his lament with a theatrical flourish and the girl twirled herself to the climax of her dance.

Mateus approached.

"Are you the one they call Bobu?" he asked.

The man looked up and smiled.

"At your service," he replied. "What can I do for you?"

"Answer some questions," replied Mateus.

"Do you have a cigarette?" Bobu asked, placing the guitar beside him on the ground.

"I don't smoke," said Mateus.

"That's good for you, *maun*, not for me," he laughed.

"I'm police commander Salsinha," Mateus said. "Bobu's your name?"

"That's what people call me. It's not my Portuguese church name if that's one of your questions."

"What is that?" asked Mateus.

Carter and Estefana had followed Mateus and Cordero over to the candle nut tree. It was cool in the shade and a slight breeze blew eucalypt leaves across the clearing from the forest behind the few scattered huts. Carter positioned herself to take full advantage of the shade. She looked around the clearing before her attention was drawn to the girl, her cheeky smile and sparkling eyes disturbing Carter for reasons she couldn't quite arrange into some kind of comprehensible order.

"Josefa!" someone called from a hut on the fringe of the clearing. "Josefa *mai, mai!*" and in a flash Carter felt the sensation pass.

The girl wheeled around toward an old woman in a tattered sarong who was standing side-on outside the nearest hut. The girl's flip-flops slapped loudly as she ran off. When she reached the woman the girl took her gently by the arm and led her back into the hut.

"Umbelina," said Bobu, tugging at a blade of grass and raising his chin toward the woman. "Her grandmother." He looked up at Mateus. "What did you ask?"

"I asked for your name," said Mateus. "Your real name."

"Fábio," he said. "Fábio Aparcio."

"You live here, Fabio?" Mateus asked.

"Bobu, please," the man said. "It's what they call me and I like it."

"If you insist," said Mateus. "Now answer the question—Bobu."

"At the moment I'm staying here, yes," Bobu said.

"At the moment? Where are you from?"

Bobu stood and brushed the dirt and grass from the backside of his jeans.

"You might say I'm from all over the place," he said.

"Let's start with where you were born," said Mateus.

"Viqueque."

"And from Viqueque?"

"Los Palos, Ermera, Dili," said Bobu. "I get around."

"What are you doing here?"

"I'm here visiting Josefa," Bobu said. "My daughter." He raised his hand in the direction of the hut into which the girl and the woman had gone. "I'm staying with her there. Helping out."

"Helping out?"

"Umbelina doesn't see well anymore," Bobu said. "Things block her sight. In the past two weeks she's only come out of the hut to call for Josefa," he said. "Then she goes back inside. The darkness in there means nothing to her. She sleeps a lot too. So I help out." He shrugged. "I cook and clean, you know, that sort of thing."

Mateus produced the image of the dead man on his cell.

"You know this man, or seen him around here?"

Bobu studied the image and shook his head.

"You sure? Take another look," said Mateus.

Bobu took another look.

"I'm sure. Never seen him," he said.

"Did you know someone was found dead near Leohitu this morning?"

"I haven't left here all morning," said Bobu. "And no one's come. Except you. How would I know about a dead man being found?"

Mateus pocketed his cell, cast an inquisitive eye over the man, and nodded.

"Why do they call you Bobu?" Cordero asked as the police commander went off to their vehicle.

Bobu smiled broadly.

"I'm an entertainer, *maun*. It's what I do. I play the guitar, I sing, I tell jokes. Sometimes I paint my face, you know, to brighten up these dull surroundings." He picked up his guitar. "Around here that's enough to be called a clown."

• • •

Osorio Lima died a day after Kosme Tavares.

Like Kosme there had been nothing to suggest Osorio was unwell before he took to his bedroll, no physical injuries that he'd suffered, no bites or infections afflicting him to indicate anything that might kill him had damaged or entered his body.

His wife had urged his mother to come to their hut between Lolitu and Leohitu and help care for him when Osorio started vomiting until there was nothing more in his stomach to bring up. The two women had sat up with Osorio all night by the light of a kerosene lamp, the glow too dim for them to notice the pallor of his skin until the sun had risen high enough to throw a shadowy light across the room. By that time they knew what was to come and needed no further signs to convince them.

Osorio's mother took the children to her own hut nearby and informed her husband when he, and his other son João, returned from the river. The two ran to Osorio's hut immediately they received news he had died. João was solidly built although timid and child-like in his movements. His father Helio, heavy-set with an imposing presence, was a traditional leader. He wore a string of beads around his neck under a grimy T-shirt and an old wrap atop his head. His face was brown and hard like the hide of a buffalo, his nose flat at the centre of his cheeks, the beard and moustache white. A small leather pouch dangled from his belt.

The brother stood at a distance from where Osorio's body lay. He was trembling, whether in fear or grief it was hard to tell. The father examined the body, asked his daughter-in-law a few brief questions, and cut off a thin strand of Osorio's hair. He went outside, inserted the hair into his pouch, and shook it while mumbling something under his breath. He emptied the contents onto a patch of ground under a small, nearby stand of Timor pine.

Chicken bones, feathers and pebbles spilled out. It was a crude attempt at divination that he had devised for himself on the basis of scattered memories from a time long ago. The old man bent over the debris and searched to see how the hair lay within it. He remained tight-lipped, his eyes narrowed, and studied the hair from several angles.

When he was satisfied with what he was seeing, he stood and hurried into the hut. He took down the skull and jaws of the eel that had been hung on the wall over Osorio's bedroll and placed both on his dead son's chest.

"We must bury him quickly and without ceremony over in the trees," he instructed João. He spoke next to his daughter-in-law. "In time you can conduct the *halo ema mate*," he told her, meaning 'the making of the dead'—a ritual to despatch Osorio's soul to the place where it would reside in peace with the ancestral spirits. "His body is too hot now, too dangerous to any who come near it. We must quickly seal it in the ground where nobody will find it."

Helio regarded his dead son, his lips tightening. He wrapped the body loosely in the blanket that had covered it and João helped him carry it outside.

Once they had buried Osorio in a hastily dug grave, Helio and João went to the hut of Rodrigo Duarte to escape Osorio's widow's constant wailing. Rodrigo was heavyset for a Timorese with large brown eyes like a cow, bushy eyebrows, and a wispy growth on his chin. He welcomed them gruffly and the three men sat under an arbor staring into the smoldering embers of a fire Rodrigo had tried to light with the damp wood.

"First Kosme Tavares and now Osorio," Rodrigo said.

Helio grunted and nodded.

"I saw Kosme only two days ago," Rodrigo continued in a gravely voice. "There was nothing wrong with him."

"There was nothing wrong with Osorio," said João.

The three sat in silence a moment, watching the smoke curl up thinly from the embers.

"I think there's a witch at work," said Rodrigo, gritting his teeth. "How else do you explain why two healthy men—your brother, João, a young man too—both died for no good reason?"

Helio poked at the fire with a stick.

"It wasn't a witch," he said.

"What's that you say?" grunted Rodrigo.

"I said it wasn't a witch that killed them," Helio replied. "You're getting hysterical."

"How can you be so sure?" Rodrigo challenged him.

"My son's fingers and fingernails did not change colour," Helio said. "I checked. When a witch kills, the colour of the dead one's nails changes. Osorio's nails didn't change. Kosme's nails hadn't changed either when I saw his body. I checked, you didn't. You were too angry to think clearly." He shifted his weight. "They died in the same way too. Witches kill in different ways to disguise what they do. You know that. This was the same way."

Helio threw the stick into the fire, stood, and wiped his hands on his trousers.

"We need to have a proper meeting," he said. "With Fidalgo."

Rodrigo regarded him doubtfully.

"Fidalgo?" he repeated.

"He was at the river that day too," Helio said. "He needs to come."

6

"Your Dr Brooks said he'd be here by three o'clock this afternoon," Mateus was saying. "I said you had asked for him specifically and that it was urgent. Not sure which of those two comments worked best."

He had settled Carter, Cordero and Estefana in a quiet room in the rear of the police station following their visit to the border region and left them there to make coffee while he attended to his calls. He'd now returned to fill them in on the result. "And I finally reached Jada," he said, speaking to Cordero as Estefana handed him a coffee. "Still the same man I remember from the police academy," he snickered. "Even so, I talked him around. You're reinstated."

"As an investigator?" Cordero asked.

"What else?" answered Mateus. He took a sip of his coffee. "Ah, that's good, Estefana. Thank you."

"When we were examining the body, you said you thought you might need to use Cordero in an official capacity," said Carter. "What were you thinking?"

"The jaundice in his eyes, the sweet smell in his mouth? Poison's a distinct possibility." He took another sip of coffee. "Since no one appears to know him, I'd say he came from across the border. I want to know what he was doing here. Cordero can help us find out."

"I thought you said it was Border Patrol who policed the border," said Carter.

"The border, yes," said Mateus. "But once someone is on this side, they're my responsibility."

"He could've been known to people in Leohitu or Lolitu and they're lying when they say they don't know him," suggested Cordero. "You did say they protect their own."

"Possible," Mateus said. "But a woman drying her washing, a farmer, a boy with a pony, and that minstrel—I don't see why any of them would have a reason to lie."

"You said anyone crossing the river now would likely need help—especially if they are carrying supplies of some kind," Carter said.

"Usually, yes."

"So someone must've known him," she added.

"He could have got help from the other side. Or he might have crossed near Lolitu and didn't need help," Mateus said. "We just don't know."

"Without any obvious sign of vomit, my guess is it was something he drank that killed him—something that soaked into the ground with the rain, as Cordero suggested," said Carter.

"I noticed Edi's just come back. Let's see if he found anything out there," Mateus replied. "And let's see what your Dr Brooks discovers."

An officer knocked on the door frame and leaned in.

"The Border Patrol officers are here, commander," he said.

Mateus finished his coffee and made to leave the room.

"Right. The real reason for your visit, *mana*," he said to Carter. "Don't tell them too much. I don't want rumors about poison circulating or people could get scared and start throwing out food. God knows we've little enough of that here already."

• • •

Just inside the front door of the police station two men in camouflaged shirts and pants and tactical army boots stood laughing over Officer Eduardo Sobado—Edi—who was sitting at a desk, a broad grin on his face. The older of the two Border Patrol officers, whose uniform suggested he outranked the other, saw Mateus approaching.

"*Dia maun,*" he said, warmly. "It's always good to come here and get the latest gossip from Edi."

"Gossip? Gossip about what?" said Mateus.

"You'll have to ask him," said the Border Patrol officer, nodding toward Edi.

Mateus directed the two visitors to the room where Carter was waiting. As they sauntered down the corridor laughing at a shared joke, Mateus leaned over the desk. "Find anything more out there, *maun*?" he asked.

"No commander," Edi replied. "Nothing."

"Did you have a good look? No sign the man vomited anything before he died?"

"I looked very closely, commander. I saw no evidence of that."

"Okay," said Mateus. "You didn't tell them anything, did you? The Border Patrol I mean."

"Not about the dead man, no. I was telling them how the mechanic was cheating on his wife."

Mateus straightened.

"Everybody knows that—except the wife," he said.

"Everybody but them," beamed Edi.

Mateus caught up with the visitors just as they entered the room where Carter, Cordero and Estefana were sitting. Introductions were made and pleasantries exchanged. The purpose of Carter's visit was explained as was Estefana's presence as a translator. Cordero excused himself as did Mateus once assured by Carter that she didn't need him there.

Estefana offered to make coffee for the two Border Patrol officers. Both accepted and neither expressed gratitude. Carter gestured to two chairs and she and the men sat in silence while Estefana prepared the drinks. Carter detected smugness in the senior officer's expression and a look of indifference on the face of the other which suggested to her that the meeting would produce little by way of useful information. Nonetheless, she affected a smile and, when Estefana brought the coffee, asked the men to explain the challenges they faced in their work.

"Well," the senior officer said and he ventured into what sounded like a well-rehearsed spiel about the virtues of the Border Patrol force designed to dull the senses of even the most ardent listener.

Meanwhile Mateus directed Cordero out to the front of the police station. He found a half-smoked cigarette in his pants pocket, lit up, and checked his watch.

"Three or four hours before your pathologist Dr Brooks arrives," he said. "We should get something to eat."

Cordero nodded and checked back to the building they had just exited.

"We can bring something for them," said Mateus. "I'm sure the American can handle herself in the meantime."

Cordero looked doubtful still.

"It's not her I'm worried about," he said.

• • •

It was late afternoon when Fidalgo de Queiroz, a tall and boney man who dragged one foot behind the other, Rodrigo Duarte, Helio Lima and his son João met in the *uma lulik*—the sacred house. The structure was in an isolated grove between Lolitu and Leohitu so clan deliberations wouldn't be disturbed by any of the women or by the prying eyes of men who weren't members of the same lineage. Without windows the sacred house offered only a dim light inside even though outside the sun blazed down from a cloudless sky. It was cooler inside as well and the smoky smell of charcoal from a caldron lit occasionally for ritual purposes permeated the air. The skulls and shedded skins of eels adorned one wall of the room.

The four men sat in a circle. They'd come straight from their garden plots in tattered pants and ragged shirts. Rodrigo was airing his doubts.

"How do you know they were police?" he asked.

"I told you," insisted Fidalgo, waving a finger. "I recognized that one from Balibo—the one who's in charge. And the young female wore a police uniform."

"You were close enough to recognize the one from Balibo?" Rodrigo said, unconvinced.

"Yes. I was behind one of the huts," Fidalgo said. He sounded jittery. "I saw him!" he insisted. "They were talking to that clown. Why would they be talking to him?"

They all considered that without speaking.

João scraped his foot across the floor raising a small pall of dust.

"Do you think the clown knew it was Osorio who found the woman naked in the stream?" he asked, breaking the silence.

Fidalgo studied the outline of João's face in the shadowy room and grew more uneasy considering the question.

"He knows everything else about people in Lolitu and Leohitu," scoffed Rodrigo.

"Or maybe the girl does," muttered Helio. Nobody caught what he'd said.

"He's always known things ever since he came here," said João. "How do you explain that? It's like he's lived among us before in another life."

They fell silent again.

"We'd only just buried Kosme when his wife started demanding a grave marker," Fidalgo said. "She went on and on about it."

"Isa Taveres believes all that shit the priests told her when she was young," said Rodrigo. "But what's she going to do about a marker, eh? She's got no money. You think a priest will give her one of those church statues to put on Kosme's grave? It's what those priests sleep with at night when they don't have a woman in their bed."

João giggled at that but the mood was too somber for the rest to appreciate any humour in the comment.

"Why would the clown get others involved?" grumbled Rodrigo, returning to the main topic of discussion. "And a foreigner you said one was. Why would he be dealing with a foreigner?"

Fidalgo stood, rested his weight on his good leg, and slapped his hands on his sides.

"I don't know who the other two were," he said. "The man and the woman with the police officers. It doesn't matter."

"They must be with the police too," Rodrigo said. "So why bring them now? If that bastard killed Osorio and Kosme without the police, why would he need them now?"

"He could have brought them here to finish what he started because he thinks we'll suspect him now but we won't suspect them," Fidalgo argued.

Rodrigo leaned forward and ran his hands roughly through his hair.

"Or now he wants to kill us and he needs help," said Rodrigo, wringing his hands together. "Kosme and Osorio were easy to kill. They were both reckless and foolish."

"My brother was not foolish," João objected. "Don't say that. Don't!"

João began to stamp his feet on the floor causing more dust to fall from the thatch covering the house. Helio put a hand on his thigh to calm him.

"Your brother was easily led," Rodrigo stated. "That's why the clown was able to kill him. He tricked him somehow. Kosme was up for anything too. That's why it was even easier for him to finish Kosme off."

"You keep talking as if the killer was a man," Helio said.

They all glanced at him.

"Well Bobu is a man," insisted Fidalgo.

"What if she's taken that form to confuse us," said Helio.

"The woman?" Rodrigo said, his voice rising in pitch.

"She wasn't given a proper burial," said Helio. "Her spirit could be wandering. Or…."

They waited for Helio to finish. He only sat there leaning on his hands over his thighs.

"Or what?" demanded Rodrigo.

Helio stayed silent.

"Or what?" Rodrigo snapped, rising and standing over Helio now.

"Or the girl called her spirit forth in the form of a man," said Helio.

"The girl?" said Rodrigo, bewildered by the comment.

João stared at his father, not knowing what to make of the statement either.

"What are you thinking?" asked Fidalgo, twisting awkwardly on his good leg.

"That the girl has summonsed her mother's spirit to avenge her loss," said Helio, staring off into the gloom.

Fidalgo was rubbing his hands down the sides of his legs.

"And the mother's spirit has taken the form of Bobu? That's crazy," scoffed Rodrigo.

"Kosme and Osorio dying without warning was crazy too," said Helio. "As João said, the clown knows everything and everyone in this place. It's like he's lived here before in another life. Whose life do you think that could be if not the girl's mother?"

Their thoughts were broken by the excited shrill of children passing outside by the sacred house. Fidalgo was shaken from his fears.

"If what you say is true," he began, "we need to warn them off. Bobu and the girl who commands him."

"Warn them off how?" Rodrigo demanded to know.

Fidalgo stared down into the blackened bowl of the cauldron.

"A fire," he said. "A fire will make them run. I'll set their hut alight."

7

Dr Howard Brooks pulled up outside the police station ten minutes before 3 o'clock. He swiveled around and grabbed a bag from the rear seat of the vehicle he was driving and stepped out into a puddle splashing water onto his trouser cuffs. He heard a giggle: two small children—a girl and a boy with a runny nose—were balancing on what there was of a fence off to the side of the building and were greatly amused by his misfortune. Brooks ignored them, shook the water from his shoes, cursed under his breath, and took off to find the commander.

He found him at his desk in the front room and introduced himself. They shook hands and Brooks followed Mateus to the room where Carter had finished talking to the Border Patrol officers who had now left the building. She and Cordero were discussing how the briefing had gone.

"I'd say they think they don't need anyone telling them how to do their job," she had said, "or interfering with the way they do it."

"Well they're a specialized force and highly trained," Cordero replied. "That can breed contempt for outside advice."

Estefana had just excused herself and gone to the guesthouse complaining of a headache.

"Ah Tino, dear boy," Brooks said, entering the room and using Cordero's nickname. "I heard you were suspended. Did I hear wrong?"

"No, I *was* suspended," Cordero replied. "Now I'm back on duty."

"What a marvelous country this is," said Brooks, smirking. "Enemies one day are friends the next and reprimands become rewards." He glanced over Cordero's shoulder. "And Agent Sara Carter," he said, easing Cordero out of his way with the bag. "How nice to see you in"— he looked down at his shoes —"muddy old Balibo."

"Hello Howard," she said. "Damp but undaunted, I see."

Brooks smiled and fixed his eyes on Carter for a moment before shifting his bag from one hand to the other and addressing Mateus.

"I would have been here earlier except there was a lot of traffic coming up from Batugade," Brooks said. "What's going on?"

"There's a big burial ceremony planned for Saturday," explained Mateus.

Brooks nodded.

"So, as I understand it, you want me to do a toxicology examination on some poor soul found near the border," he said.

"A body not a soul," said Mateus.

"As you say," Brooks accepted, bowing slightly.

"I'm sorry we couldn't send the body to you in Dili," said Mateus, "but that would have taken a day or two to arrange and we need to know what killed him as soon as possible."

"You mentioned it was urgent, not why," Brooks said. "What's the rush?"

"We suspect he died as a result of ingesting some kind of poison," said Carter. Brooks faced her. "And there could be more of it about to put the locals at risk. As the commander said, a lot of people are coming into Balibo for the burial of a former village notable. We can't be too careful."

"Plus there's a market and a cockfight planned for Saturday," added Mateus.

"Quite a big day then," said Brooks.

"Did you bring what we suggested?" Carter asked.

Brooks laughed.

"We're in Timor, Agent Carter, not Texas," he said. "This is a land of improvisation. Technology is limited here—where it exists at all."

"I keep getting reminded that we're in Timor," Carter said, lightly brushing hair from her cheek. "It strikes me as the standard excuse for a lot of...shall we say unsatisfactory situations. But I know you'll do your best."

"I never do less," said Brooks. He shifted the bag between his hands again. "Well if time is of the essence, I suggest you take me to your deceased," he said. "You can tell me the circumstances of how you found him as we go."

• • •

On their way to the clinic Carter explained to Brooks that the dead man had been found apparently clutching his stomach as if experiencing abdominal pain, the whites of his eyes suggested jaundice, there was a faint, sweet odor in his mouth, and he appeared to have been stumbling about erratically just before he died. He nodded at each point she made.

"All consistent with poisoning," Brooks said. "Also with a multitude of other things."

"That's why you're here, Howard," Cordero commented.

"Quite," Brooks responded.

The police officer ordered to stay with the body showed them into a small back room where it had been laid on the floor. Cordero cleared a table of a stack of clean sheets and towels, removed the tarpaulin from the body and helped Brooks lift up the dead weight for examination. Brooks opened the bag he'd been carrying, took out a pair of gloves, and unceremoniously waved them away.

"I don't need the kind of chatter I know you two engage in to distract me when I'm working," he said.

Carter and Cordero looked at each other, accepted his point, and left. They seated themselves under the shade of a banyan tree outside the clinic while Brooks examined the body. Mateus had gone to his office after driving them to the health clinic and there was nothing Cordero could do now unless whatever Brooks found warranted a police investigation that might involve him. As for Carter, she could think of nothing more to add to the information she'd already gathered for her report on border management.

So they sat, killing time as children skipped by happily enough, women with bags of rice balanced on their heads and bunches of green vegetables in their hands smiled as they went passed, and two nuns giggled to each other as they nodded a greeting to the strangers and continued on sharing some risqué gossip.

"People look happy here, don't they?" Carter said. "And that's good to see."

"You don't see that back home?" Cordero asked.

"Back home people come and go in cars and pickup trucks," she said. "You don't actually *see* much of them at all. Not like here. The streets here are sociable. In Arizona, actually throughout most of the US, they're more functional—you know, a way to get from A to B and nothing more."

The fragrance of the banyan tree caught his attention. He raised his eyes, examined the branches above them, and took a deep breath.

She watched what he was doing.

"You enjoying the fresh air?" she asked.

"What's not to enjoy? It beats diesel fumes in Dili," he said.

She closed her eyes and breathed in. She held it in.

"You're right," she said. She breathed again. "Ever smelled a desert after rain?"

"This is the tropics we're in," he said.

"I've heard it called an orchestra of fragrances," she said ignoring his geography lesson. "All the aromatic plants coming to life."

"You miss it?"

"Of course," she said. "It's beautiful."

He looked straight ahead and nodded.

"A banyan tree is a strangler fig," he said. "Birds drop seeds on top of other trees and the banyan sprouts and sends down roots that use the host tree for support while they strangle it." He smiled to himself. "I've read about a banyan tree in India whose canopy covers nearly five acres."

"You know a lot about banyan trees," she said.

"How can you not admire them?" he said. "They're beautiful too."

"Even though they throttle their hosts?" she asked.

"It's the way of things," he said. "It's nature."

He stifled a laugh.

"What?" she asked.

"We enjoy the same things, you and me," he said. "Just in different parts of the globe."

She stared at him. Neither spoke for a short, uneasy time.

"So the Border Patrol officers weren't much help?" he asked to break the silence.

"No," she said. "Although that in itself is useful to know. I'll find a way to make something of it in my report."

"Something?"

"Yeah. Something about communication channels or rather the absence of them."

He reached up and tugged a low-lying leaf off the tree and played with it in his hands.

"I didn't thank you for coming to our rescue," Carter said. "And driving us here. So thank you."

He glanced across at her.

"I was happy to help," he replied and sniffed.

"That's my point," she said. "You always are. From my experience that's a rare quality."

He felt himself blushing and was unsure what to say. When he looked up, a little boy, shirtless, sucking on a corn cob was staring at the foreign woman next to him.

"You have an admirer," he said to Carter.

Carter waved to the boy and he quickly ran away.

"Estefana helps you all the time," Cordero tried.

"She's female," Carter said. "It's part of a woman's makeup. It's not the same with men."

He scraped a shoe across the dirt.

"What about Mateus?" he protested.

"The commander?"

"Yeah," he said. "The commander."

"What about him?"

"You said he's engaging or something."

She leaned forward, elbows resting on her thighs.

"Yeah, he is. And he's considerate." She joined her hands together. "You notice how he involves Estefana in everything?"

"So?"

"So she's twenty-two years old, Cordero! She's relatively new to policing. And she's a woman. How many other Timorese men in senior positions do you know would acknowledge her presence let alone ask her opinion about something, anything?"

She sat upright.

"You don't."

"Well I—" he began.

"Why are you trying to argue with a simple thank you? And don't push your luck with excuses for why you're not a well-rounded human being," she said, suppressing a smile. She bent down. "We're cooking dinner for you tonight to thank you for coming to our rescue."

"You're what?"

"Estefana doesn't have a headache. That was an excuse to avoid any arguments. She's collecting ingredients and when we're finished here she and I will cook dinner. Brooks'll be invited too, of course. After all, he'll have to stay at our guesthouse. Even so, you're the honored guest."

"What about Mateus?"

"He wants to have dinner with his wife."

Cordero tossed the leaf away and for a moment he was quiet.

"I feel a little embarrassed by this, you know," he said.

"What? You're not used to gratitude?" she teased him.

"Well, not so much from you," he said. "And Estefana," he quickly added.

She glared at him for just a moment.

"You'll get over it," she said and leapt to her feet. "I'd better get back to the guesthouse and see what I can do to help Estefana." She wavered a moment. "This'll be interesting. I can't remember the last time I actually cooked for a man. It's usually home delivery or something shoved in the microwave."

8

It was early evening when Cordero and Brooks arrived at the guesthouse after they'd finished at the health clinic and reported to Mateus at the police station. The day had cooled slightly and there was a purple and rose-coloured tinge to the sky as the sun dropped below the horizon. The light inside the guesthouse was weak and flickering. Three kerosene lamps could have brightened the room but only one had any fuel.

Carter told Brooks to take any of the empty bedrooms he liked. He gave the three available rooms a cursory glance, chose one across the hall from Carter and Estefana and tossed an overnight bag on the bed. He extracted a bottle of gin and one of tonic and re-entered the dining area holding them up like trophies.

"The sun is well and truly over the yardarm so who's up for a drink?" he asked.

By way of reply Carter retrieved the two coffee cups and placed them on the table, avoiding the plates and cutlery she had laid out and a large bowl of salad in the centre.

"These are the only cups we have," she said.

"Not to worry, my dear," Brooks said. "In this country it pays to be prepared."

He put the gin and the tonic on the table, slipped into his room, and came out with two paper cups.

"Voila!" he declared.

"So, what did you find?" Carter asked Brooks as she sat and he stood preparing the drinks.

"I told the commander my findings, of course," he said, "but I'll give you the gist of what I concluded."

He handed Carter and Cordero their drinks, scrutinized the room, and checked through the door of Carter and Estefana's bedroom.

"Where's that lovely young police officer from Suai by the way?" he asked.

"The cooking facilities, which amount to an open fire, are outside near where the caretaker lives," Carter explained. "Estefana insisted on cooking the rice and chicken"— she glared at Cordero —"the chicken I prepared, I might add, and will be in shortly."

"Right," said Brooks.

He sat down at the table and took a generous sip from his paper cup.

"Ah," he uttered.

He smiled, about to enjoy himself by impressing them with his medical expertise.

"From the look of him, and what you told me, I assumed it would be poisoning by ingestion of ethylene glycol or methanol and most probably the latter," he began before taking another sip of gin.

"What led to that assumption? Cordero asked.

"Those two toxins are, first, consistent with the suspected gut ache and the jaundice, and, second, fairly common ways for people to be poisoned in this part of the world."

"Illicit liquor?" Carter said.

"Most likely," said Brooks. "Good guess."

He drained his cup and refilled it.

"Only a trained pathologist, however, could confirm that," he said with a hint of professional arrogance. "It could also have been the case that the deceased merely suffered from severe hypoglycemia. Diabetes is not well understood in this country. The most common treatment, if you could call it that, is for the diabetic to eat avocado leaves on a regular basis. What does that tell you? If he'd been an untreated diabetic and hadn't eaten for a day or two, hypoglycemia would have been a distinct possibility. And of course it would have left few visible traces."

"So you found nothing in his stomach that would indicate what killed him?" Cordero asked.

"There was nothing or virtually nothing in his stomach," Brooks answered. "He may have preferred drinking to eating in his last hours. That would essentially leave only liquid in his stomach. Had he vomited up that, you wouldn't have necessarily found it because I'm told it rained during the time between death and the discovery of his body."

"I'd thought of that," said Cordero.

"You are always excellent after the fact, dear boy," said Brooks, patting Cordero's forearm.

He sipped his gin, uttered another satisfied 'Ah'.

"Now to positively test for an ingested toxic substance one would normally use gas chromatography, but nothing is normal in Timor and I doubt they've even heard of it here. My second go-to would be to ascertain the osmol gap. Except I doubt there're more than two osmometers in the country and they'd be under lock and key in Dili." He snickered. "Probably under lock and key somewhere to avoid the risk that they'd actually be used and so worn out and not replaced! It happens."

He regarded them, satisfied his command of technical detail had made the right impression.

"So what did you do?" asked Cordero.

"I took a sample of blood, added acid to unlock the carbon dioxide from the bicarbonate in the blood fluid and measured the level of bicar—"

Estefana entered the room carrying a plate of chicken pieces fried in a wok. The aroma was mouthwatering. All eyes followed the wok to the table.

"Hello, my dear," Brooks said to Estefana. "So very nice to see you."

She smiled a greeting, put the chicken down, and went back for the rice.

Brooks' eyes followed Estefana out the door and he sighed in admiration of her youth and elegance. When she was gone he refocused his attention on the others.

"Do you really want the details, Tino?" he asked. "My educated guess is methanol."

"Methanol?" asked Cordero.

"Methanol," Brooks confirmed.

Brooks was staring at the chicken pieces, salivating.

"So toxic liquor?" Cordero asked to confirm.

"Most likely," said Brooks.

"Commander Mateus thinks the dead man might have made his way over from West Timor," said Carter.

"I think that's right," said Brooks. "Being such a good Muslim country, illicit alcohol is rife in Indonesia and the amount of methanol that killed our friend suggests it was obtained in the worst of all worse ways."

"Which is?" asked Cordero.

"Antifreeze," said Brooks. He eyed Carter. "Not much use for it in a tropical country," he said, leaning toward her, "and so easily taken from the radiators of new imported or locally-made vehicles and substituted with plain old water."

Estefana returned with a pot of steaming rice. She placed it next to the chicken pieces and sat down.

"Dr Brooks prepared a gin and tonic for you, Estefana," Cordero said and handed her the cup. "He was just telling us that the dead man was likely poisoned by methanol used to produce some very strong liquor."

She nodded. He reached into his pocket and pulled out the sugar he'd bought that morning at Feng's store.

"And I haven't had a chance to give you this," he said and handed her the package. "I thought you could use it."

Carter was impressed enough to raise an eyebrow.

"Thank you, *maun*," Estefana said. She waved a hand across the table. "Eat before it gets cold."

At Brooks' insistence, Carter and Estefana helped themselves first.

"On a lighter note, how are they treating you at the hospital?" Cordero asked. Brooks had been brought to Dili's Guido Valaderes National Hospital from his usual job in Suai to fill in for the sole pathologist who had gone to New Zealand on a training course.

"The nurses are treating me fine," Brooks said. "Just fine. Especially the young ones. Management however is another story." He raised his hands in exasperation. "They ask a lot and provide little. Like managers everywhere. Managerialism is a disease, dear boy. Like cholera only even more pernicious. It knows no boundaries and no cures."

Cordero laughed at that and Carter smiled.

"So, Estefana," Brooks said. "I haven't seen you since your wedding. How is married life treating you?"

Her eyes lit up.

"I am very happy, *senyor*. Thank you," she said.

"Well as someone who has been married twice, I am something of an expert on the subject and I can say you should be happy because it is a wonderful institution," said Brooks. "But as with management, some of the people who fill the roles can be a problem."

Brooks and Cordero served themselves.

"This chicken is really delicious, Estefana," Cordero said taking his third eager mouthful.

"Thank you, *maun*, but *mana* mixed the spices for the chicken," she said indicating Carter with her fork.

Cordero noticed the satisfied grin on Carter's face.

"And you, Agent Carter," Brooks said. "You've signed up for a three-month extension I understand. You must be growing to like Timor." He started to eat. "Be careful. I came for a short visit and I'm still here years on."

She bunched her lips to one side of her mouth and made no comment at that.

"As for the case in hand," Cordero began.

"The case?" said Brooks.

"Our corpse," said Cordero. "Do you think we could have a smuggling operation on our hands?"

"I'd say that's a distinct possibility," Brooks replied. "Probably a localized thing. You can't bring too much across the border around here."

"What makes you confident to say smuggling?" Carter asked.

Brooks placed his fork on the table and picked up his gin.

"You put two and two together," he said. "He came from West Timor, and he died from drinking the kind of liquor people make illegally there. His clothes and the general state of his body suggest he was impoverished and so likely in need of money. Few people along the border here have money. So what else could he have been doing except smuggling a small quantity of liquor for sale in Balibo and making the fatal decision to celebrate the fact that he'd crossed without being seen?"

"If he came from West Timor," said Cordero.

Brooks smiled.

"Did either of you check his upper arms?"

"It wasn't our role to examine the body too closely," Cordero said.

"Quite," agreed Brooks. "But had you done so, you may have noticed that the skin had been burned. I'd say a red-hot metal, like an iron or something, had been pressed against it. That's usually how it's done. Why, you might ask. He was trying to erase a rather large tattoo. A little of it escaped the iron." Brooks sipped his gin. "It's against the rules to tattoo oneself in an Indonesian prison. Often you'd be beaten if caught doing it. But it's one way to pass the time and signal your membership in one group or another. In the 80s and 90s, however, it became a deadly thing to do. Sections of the security forces waged war on suspected criminals and the suspects were often identified by their tattoos. So there was a rush to get rid of them and a hot iron scarring the skin was the usual way to do it. He was old enough to have been part of that era."

"What makes you think his tattoo was done in prison?" asked Carter.

"I analyzed the ink in the remnant that was left," Brooks said. "A difficult job, especially with such a small sample and an old one at that. All the same, there are ways if you know how. And I know how. The result was Norit, which is a medication for diarrhea, and blackened cooking oil mixed with ink from a ballpoint pen. Standard Indonesian prison tattoo ink."

"How can you be sure?" Cordero said, still a little doubtful.

"Must you question my expertise, dear boy? I lived in Brazil for some years. Married to the lovely Yara, remember? The actress. What do you think I did for a living while she was impressing audiences with her charms? I worked in prisons in Sao Paulo. Few people are prepared to do that and so the job was mine for the asking. Tattoos are a veritable art form in Brazilian prisons. They took my interest. I've been studying them ever since."

• • •

Brooks woke at seven to the buzz of his cell phone. As he reached for it, he could hear Carter and Estefana preparing the table in the common room for breakfast. He took the call standing on the side of the bed. Once the call had ended, he hastily dressed and threw his things into his overnight bag.

As he made to join the others for breakfast, he heard an angry quarrel erupt in the corridor and so he paused to let it conclude before he left his room. Feeling the effects of several generous gin and tonics the night before Cordero had decided he was too groggy to drive to his cousin's house and didn't need to do so since there were two empty rooms in the guesthouse.

Estefana had made arrangements for Brooks to stay. By contrast, Cordero's decision was a spur-of-the-moment thing, and the old woman caretaker was not taking kindly to having discovered him there. She was arguing: Cordero was explaining, apologising, and trying to offer her a payment. Eventually she accepted ten dollars from him and grumbled that she'd fetch more bread rolls, eggs and coffee.

"Well, now that you have that sorted, dear boy, good morning all," said Brooks striding into the common room.

"How did you sleep, Howard?" Carter asked.

"Like a lamb, dear lady, like a lamb."

They sat to have coffee, the two paper cups Brooks had produced from his bag the night before having to double now as coffee cups. Cordero was a little ruffled by his run-in with the caretaker. Estefana placed the sugar he had given her next to his coffee cup and his spirits began to lift.

"I'm afraid I've been recalled to Dili," Brooks said, loading his plate from the fried eggs and bread rolls provided.

"What? Why?" asked Cordero.

The old woman returned with two fried eggs and a bread roll which she plonked down unceremoniously in front of Cordero. She moved around the table without speaking, picked up their coffee pot and shook it, and left satisfied that there was enough for all of them, and she could take up whatever other duties the day held for her.

They were all quiet until she'd gone.

"You'll remember the Cuban who operated on your sister when she had appendicitis—Dr. Carlos Montoya," Brooks began finally. "He just rang. Overnight two patients came in with meningitis. One is a girl of ten, the other a man in his fifties." He quickly accounted for the eggs on his plate and picked up the bread roll to break in his hands. "He fears an outbreak. What he's not certain of is whether it's the result of a virus, bacteria, fungi or parasites."

He took a bite of bread and spoke out of the side of his mouth.

"All can cause meningitis, you see, but knowing which it is will be critical if there's a need to deal with any outbreak." He washed the bread down with a slurp of coffee. "So I have to retrace my steps to Dili as soon as possible. And that means I leave now."

"If what you were saying last night is correct," Carter began, "and I have no reason to doubt it," she quickly added, "we could be looking at the poisoning of dozens of people. There'll be a lot of people in town on Saturday. That means a lot of potential victims. You're probably the only person this side of Dili who could help manage any mass poisoning, Howard."

"Dili has a population of around two hundred thousand people, dear lady," said Brooks. "An outbreak of meningitis there could be a catastrophe. The village of Balibo has, what, three, four thousand and about the same in surrounding areas? And how many of them are likely to want to drink strong liquor? Not the women. Not the children. Besides," he said, wiping his hands on his trousers and standing, "Montoya has actual cases. Conjecture has it that someone died here after smuggling toxic liquor across the border. Sound conjecture, perhaps, but conjecture nonetheless. And if it is correct, how much liquor are we talking about? Again, it's a matter of conjecture at this stage. You've more work to do to establish a threat beyond any doubt. And if you do, it's the job of the police, not me, to do something about it."

He took the last draught of his coffee.

"I'll leave you all another bottle of gin. Consider it payment for last night's excellent meal. It's in my room beside the bed. Unopened, before anyone asks," he said, holding up a finger for emphasis. "Thank you for your hospitality. I bid you all adieu."

With a theatrical wave of one hand and his overnight bag in the other, Brooks strode out of the guesthouse. For a moment no one spoke. Soon they could hear Brooks' vehicle revving up the hill to the main road to Batugade and on to Dili.

Carter rose and began collecting the plates from their breakfast.

"What now?" Cordero asked.

"You heard Brooks," said Carter. "We've work to do."

9

A bank of heavy black cloud was building on the western horizon and the wind was picking up. They could smell moisture in the air as they arrived at the police station.

"More rain," said Carter, dipping her head to get a better view of the sky through the windshield. "Bit early in the day, isn't it?"

Cordero snatched his key from the ignition and dropped his head to follow her gaze.

"Hot day yesterday and warm night," he said. "It is the wet season after all."

He straightened and opened the driver's door.

"Rain or not, as you put it, we've work to do," he said.

They left the vehicle and entered the building. One officer, bent over a desk, was absorbed in a sheaf of papers in a room off to the side and ignored them. The commander's office door was open. Mateus caught sight of them and called them in.

"*Bondia, bondia,*" Mateus said rising from his chair. Across the desk from him sat a bedraggled woman.

She wore a work sarong that was drab and flecked with dirt and grass stains, a faded orange scarf to keep a tangle of greying hair in place, and a pair of old sneakers the sole of one held on with twine. Her lips and teeth were red from chewing betel. She could have been in her late forties or early fifties although the harsh conditions of subsistence farming tended to age people before their time.

"This is *Senyora* Tavares," Mateus was saying, "and Officer Natalia," he added gesturing to the side of the room where stood, expressionless and silent, the young police officer who'd gone with him to investigate the dead body the day before.

"*Senyora* these are my colleagues," Mateus said to the woman. "From Dili. If you'll permit, I'll speak to them in English."

Mateus resumed his seat.

"*Senyora* Tavares came into Balibo this morning," Mateus began, "to arrange a headstone for her late husband's grave. Her husband—Kosme—was not a Catholic but the *senyora* wanted a cross as well as the traditional animal skulls to adorn his grave." He eyed Carter. "Hedging her bets, you see."

A faint roll of thunder could be heard outside.

"The Chinaman in the store can arrange such things through his connections," Mateus continued. "And so the *senyora* went to see him." He nodded at a bank note laid out on the desk between them. Carter glanced at the note which looked to be American and, leaning across the desk, thought she could make out the image of President Grover Cleveland. On closer inspection she saw it was an American bill to the value of $1000—a note which went out of circulation before Carter was born.

"The *senyora* has no idea about the value of the note," Mateus said. "Nor can she read. Even if she could read," he said and pointed to the note with his index finger, "I doubt she could read in English what it says in the green bar across the top of each side." What he was pointing to read: 'Hell's Bank Note'.

Mateus clasped his hands together over his stomach.

"When she gave the note to Feng, he saw immediately that it was his joss paper—what Chinese burn as an offering to their ancestors." He rubbed his chin and regarded Cordero. "Remember yesterday I dropped off an officer at the store to investigate a break-in? Feng thought nothing had been taken until *Senyora* Tavares showed up with this note. That's when he realised his bundle of joss paper was gone. That's when he called Officer Natalia." He faced *Senyora* Tavares but continued to address Cordero. "She brought the *senyora* and the note over to me just now."

There was a second roll of thunder, louder and longer this time. Clouds were blanketing Balibo, and the daylight was fading.

"Where did you get this note, *senyora*?" Mateus asked the woman in Tetun.

Senyora Tavares looked up at the police commander. She showed bewilderment rather than guilt in her eyes.

"It was in my husband's pocket," she said. "What is the problem? Why have I been brought here to sit in front of you like this?"

"There is no problem, *senyora*," Mateus reassured her. "Just a few questions, that's all. Where did your husband get this note?"

The woman shrugged.

"When did your husband die, *senyora*?"

"Two days ago," she said in a soft voice.

"What caused his death?"

The woman shifted uneasily in her chair.

"His soul was calling him," she said. "From where the dead are buried."

Mateus rubbed a hand across his face.

"Was he sick or injured?" he asked.

"No. He just died when his soul called."

"What was your husband doing in the days before he died?"

The woman raised a shoulder.

"Working his garden plot," she said. "Like every day."

"He didn't go anywhere, see anyone?"

"Not that I would know," she said. "He worked in his plot every day. I stay in the hut. I never kept an eye on him or what he was doing."

Mateus shifted in his chair and tugged at his belt.

"How old was Kosme?" he asked.

The woman frowned and lowered her eyes as though the answer to such a question was beyond her. She rubbed her hands together lightly.

"Two of my sons were born before my daughter but when she was born, I wanted a priest to make all my children *sarani*," she said, meaning baptised Christians. "So, I took them to the church. My husband wouldn't come. He just finished the time he had to do in the *bapa* army and wanted to celebrate his freedom. When I reached the church, I remember there was a lot of crying and praying because *amu-bispo* Teodoro had died. Soon after we came to where we live now, a lot of us did, because floods destroyed our land over there."

"So you're from the West originally and you're talking about Bishop Theodorus?" asked Mateus.

"*Amu-bispo* Teodoro," the woman repeated. "Yes."

Mateus cupped his chin in his hand and creased his face in thought.

"Bishop Theodorus died in 1991," he explained to the others in English. "He'd been the bishop of Atambua in West Timor. I remember news of his death because I was in the seminary. At that time Indonesian men had to do two years military service from the age of 18. So Kosme would have been born about 1971. It's now 2014 so that would have made him mid 40s when he died."

The woman showed no reaction.

"You came from Atambua?" he put to the woman.

"No," she said. "We lived a day's walk from Laran. There was a flood there that washed the crops away and they moved us here."

Mateus looked up at Carter and Cordero.

"So, she and others were brought here from West Timor as part of an Indonesian resettlement program. I mentioned that to you yesterday," he said.

He lent over the desk toward the woman.

"This may be hard for you, *senyora*, but can you describe how your husband died? I mean, did he collapse, was there any sign of him bleeding, did he clutch his chest?"

The woman tucked a strand of hair under her scarf. Her lips quivered.

"The soul took his legs away first and he couldn't use them," she said. "Next, his hands. He couldn't hold a cup. His voice was taken too and when he made a sound, I didn't know what he was saying."

She wiped a tear from her cheek.

"Last to go before he died were his eyes," she said. "It was like he was blind. His soul took him, a piece at a time, and he was gone."

Mateus shot a glance at Carter and Cordero.

"Consistent with what your Dr Brooks told me about the effects of methanol poisoning," he said in English.

He smiled weakly at *Senyora* Tavares.

"If you've come here to organise a headstone, has your husband been buried already?" he asked.

"Yes."

"Why so soon after his death?"

The woman fidgeted with her hands.

"They said he had to be put in the ground before more souls called other people," she said.

"They? Who's 'they'?" asked Mateus.

"Helio and the elders."

"Helio?"

"Helio Lima. He's an important man in our village."

"Ah, yes. I know him. And so he buried your husband?"

"He and the others buried Kosme. They live near us. They knew my husband."

Suddenly rain began to pelt down outside, pinging off the metal roof of the police station and causing people outside to run past the window, bags held over their heads for cover. Mateus craned his neck to check how heavy the rain was.

"Where are your children now, *senyora*?" he asked, facing her again.

"Three of my sons are in Dili," the woman said. "My daughter, too. Young people move these days. They say life is better there. My other son married in Maliana."

"How did you get here?" Mateus asked. "To Balibo this morning, I mean."

"I walked," the woman said.

"All the way from Leohitu?"

"We live this side of Leohitu," she said. "Near Lolitu. I left early."

The phone on Mateus' desk rang. He excused himself and picked it up.

"Commander Salsinha," he said.

Whoever was on the other end was speaking excitedly enough to be heard, if not understood, by everyone in the room.

A woman's voice. Shrill. Mateus stood. He faced away from the others and thrust his free hand into his trouser pocket.

"When?" he said.

More chatter from the other end.

"And you're sure?"

He nodded as he was given the confirmation.

"I'll be right there," he said and replaced the handpiece in its cradle.

For a moment he stared out the window, silent and expressionless.

"*Mana*," he said addressing Estefana. "Could you drive *Senyora* Tavares home, please? In *maun*'s SUV. It's a long way and…." He waved a hand at the rain falling beyond the window.

Estefana stood, came forward and took *Senyora* Tavares gently by the arm.

"What about my husband's grave marker?" the woman asked.

Mateus managed a smile.

"I'll talk to the Chinaman," he said. "To *Senyor* Feng. Leave things with me."

He picked up the keys to his own SUV and watched as Estefana led *Senyora* Tavares out of the room.

"What's going on?" Cordero asked.

"Juno Cabral's son has been taken to the clinic. He drank something and it's nearly killed him."

• • •

Mateus drove Carter and Cordero to the health clinic where the three of them ran out of the rain to the portico and scrapped mud from their shoes. A nurse noticed the commander and came from her desk to open the front door and usher them inside.

"What can you tell me?" Mateus asked the nurse.

"Arturo was found on the far side of the old fort," the nurse said. She scurried over to the desk, picked up a clipboard, and consulted it. "He'd been vomiting, complained of a headache and dizziness, was confused, unable to coordinate his legs. Some girls found him on their way to school and hailed down a microlet to bring him in. When they carried him in, his breathing was rapid and shallow and he couldn't see clearly. He was yelling out something. He made no sense."

She replaced the clipboard on the desk.

"We've put him in a room down the corridor. There's no doctor here to diagnose what's wrong with him and I fear he's getting worse," she added.

Cordero had been translating for Carter.

"Ask her if she knows how to treat methanol poisoning," Carter said.

Cordero did and the nurse stared at him as though she didn't know what he was talking about.

"Ring Brooks," Carter said. "Now! He's probably caught up in that traffic jam with all those rickshaws around Liquica."

Cordero angled off to the side and made the call.

"Has Juno been informed?" Mateus asked the nurse.

"A message has been left at his home," the nurse said.

"What about his wife?"

"She took the message but I didn't go into details."

"The girls who found Arturo," Mateus began, "have they gone on to school?"

"As far as I know, yes," said the nurse. "They didn't hang around here."

"Did they say exactly where they found him?"

"I'd have to ask Manuela," the nurse said. "She spoke to them not me."

The nurse hurried off to find her colleague just as Cordero returned, lowering the cell from his ear.

"You're right," he said to Carter. "He's caught in traffic in Liquica."

Carter gave him a knowing glance and reached out for the cell.

"I'll put you on to Carter," Cordero said and handed the cell over.

Carter pressed the speaker icon and held the cell flat so the others could listen.

"Methanol metabolizes into formaldehyde and formic acid," Brooks was saying. "Both are extremely damaging to the central nervous system and, wait—there's another bloody rickshaw in my way, 'Clear out!'—and the gastrointestinal tract and impact quite soon following ingestion."

"Slow down, Howard," Carter said.

After an audible sigh, Brooks continued.

"As you had noticed, the dead man I examined was probably clutching his stomach as he died. Nausea and headaches occur quickly after ingestion and clinical symptoms present within hours. Sooner if a large quantity has been consumed."

"How would you treat a patient?" Carter asked.

"I'm getting to that," said Brooks. "First you need to stop the metabolism. For that we recommend injecting fomepizole into a vein."

"Wait," said Carter. "Was that fomepizole?" She said the word slowly for Cordero's benefit.

"That's right, fomepizole. I noticed that by chance there is some in the clinic. Only two or three doses, mind. A nurse should be able to locate it. It's in the top drawer of a cabinet in the dispensary. Get it into the patient as quickly as possible."

"Okay. I take it there's a second step?" asked Cater.

"Yes. The second step is to eliminate the toxin from the body which usually requires the ingestion of vitamin B9."

"Vitamin B9," she repeated, facing Cordero.

"I couldn't find any in the clinic and I doubt you could buy it in Balibo. If the patient can be stabilized, I'd be pumping folates into him. That's raw peanuts, sunflower seeds, lentils—all of which are fairly common around there."

"Raw peanuts, sunflower seeds. Okay, got it. Thanks Howard," said Carter.

"If this spreads into an outbreak of poisonings, you're in for trouble," Brooks added before ending the call. "Balibo won't cope and I doubt that either Batugade or Maliana would do much better. So prevention will be critical. You need to find the source and quickly. Good luck."

The first nurse scurried down the corridor with her colleague.

"This is *Mana* Manuela," she told Mateus.

Carter suggested Cordero take the first nurse aside and brief her about what Brooks had said while she made her way to the dispensary to find the fomepizole. Mateus remained in the foyer to question Manuela.

"Did the girls who brought Arturo in say where they had found him?" the police commander asked.

"Yes *senyor*. They were very excited and they talked over each other but they agreed they found him on the far side of the fort where the land drops off below the remains of the swimming pool."

Mateus phoned the police station. He instructed two officers to go immediately to the location Manuela had mentioned and search it thoroughly for any bottles or containers. They were to bring whatever they found to the station without tipping out any residual liquids. As he ended the call, Juno Cabral stormed through the door of the clinic, the rain swirling in behind him.

"Where is he?" Juno shouted. "Where's Arturo? Where's my son?"

"He's being cared for," said Mateus, arms outstretched to block Juno's progress.

"I want to see him!" Juno insisted and he tried to push past the commander.

"Soon," said Mateus, holding him back. "The nurse is with him now and you'd only get in the way."

"He's my son!" Juno shouted.

"I know that," said Mateus. "And that's why I need to talk to you first. Sit down over here," he said and tried to direct Juno to the chairs along one wall of the foyer.

Juno continued to glare down the hallway, his nostrils flared. Mateus took his arm more forcefully. Juno glanced at the commander's hand on his arm and then into Mateus' eyes. He allowed himself to be led to a chair.

The two sat, side by side, Juno on the edge of his seat and his attention focused down the hall.

"Tell me what's going on," Juno demanded. "I've been told nothing. Only that Arturo was brought in and is very ill."

"Your son looks to have ingested something that didn't agree with him," Mateus began. "Possibly illicit liquor. Tell me what he's been up to the last few days."

Juno wheeled around to face Mateus.

"What are you talking about? Liquor? The boy's only fourteen!"

"We're not sure yet what he ingested," said Mateus. "Liquor's a possibility, that's all."

Juno's breathing slowly calmed. He rested his elbows on his thighs and stared at the floor.

"What's Arturo been doing the last couple of days?" Mateus repeated. "And who with?"

Juno grunted.

"What do you think fourteen-year-old boys get up to?" he said. "He's been hanging around with his friends. That's all I know."

"I'll need a list of their names," Mateus said.

Juno sniffed in a demonstrable fashion.

"He's a popular boy," he said. "A list could be made of half of Balibo and still not include everybody Arturo knows."

"They say he was found on the other side of the fort this morning. Do you know why he'd be there? Who he might've been with?"

"No idea. He gets around."

Juno sat up and faced Mateus.

"Is he going to be all right?" he asked.

"I'm sure he is," said Mateus.

"When does the doctor get back?"

"A day or two," said Mateus. "My colleagues rang a doctor in Dili, a specialist, who gave instructions over the phone on how to treat him. The nurse is doing that now."

"Liquor?" Juno said. "Illicit liquor you say?"

"We haven't confirmed that yet," Mateus said. "I've told you that."

"I thought I knew what goes on in Balibo," Juno continued, "but I never knew about this."

"At the moment it's only a suspicion," Mateus said.

"Based on what?" Juno asked.

Mateus exhaled a long, deep breath.

"The body we found yesterday, for a start," he said. "We had someone examine it and he concluded that methanol poisoning had caused the man's death. He also found evidence that he'd spent time in an Indonesian prison. I circulated his photo to my Indonesian contacts this morning and they're investigating. He could have been smuggling supplies of liquor across the border. We don't yet know for sure. However your son's symptoms are also consistent with methanol poisoning."

"Shit!" was all Juno could manage in response.

"The severity of the harm depends on how much has been consumed. I wouldn't expect a fourteen-year-old to drink much—if that's what he did."

Juno was nodding while ignoring all attempts to suggest how tentative the suspicion remained.

"I know who's behind this," he said, suddenly rising to his feet. "It's Dario Freitas."

"Dario? Why?" asked Mateus.

"It's his way of getting people to like him."

"You don't know that," said Mateus tugging Juno's sleeve to make him sit down.

Juno shook him off.

"He's brought it in for that burial. To hand it out like a big man to all those people gathered here." He sneered at that. "Gaspa's been dead for years and his body's been rotting outside Dario's house all this time. You can almost smell it from here."

He started pacing.

Mateus stood as Carter returned. She handed something quickly to the first nurse Cordero had briefed and the nurse put it in the pocket of her tunic and took off down the corridor.

"We'll need to speak another time, Juno," Mateus said. "For the moment we'll leave you with the nurses here and pray your son makes a full recovery."

"I don't know how my son's involved in this," Juno said, "but I know that bastard Dario is to blame!"

10

Unlike the panic that had gripped people trying to escape the rain in the centre of Balibo, indifference was the order of day among people caught in the downpour in the rural outskirts; their attitude proved appropriate when the rain stopped as abruptly as it had started. In only a short time a sliver of golden sunlight broke through as clouds dispersed east towards Dili.

Isa Tavares was huddled in the passenger's seat holding firmly to the door handle with both hands as though she had not experienced riding in a vehicle before. Estefana was driving down *Rua de Frontera* and shot her a glance, noticing how the woman's lips were also sealed tight. She tried to engage *Senyora* Tavares in conversation to distract her from any anxiety she may have felt.

"So you live down near Lolitu," Estefana said. "We drove down there yesterday. It's a pretty little hamlet. It's a long way from Balibo. I wouldn't like having to go all that way on foot."

The woman offered no reply.

They passed a lone grave that had been dug and marked with a simple cross by the side of the road and *Senyora* Taveres watched it go by. Estefana chanced to check on her a second time.

"I was sorry to hear about your husband, *senyora*," she said.

No response.

"My father died unexpectedly some years ago," Estefana continued. "My mother was very upset." As soon as she'd said it, Estefana was cross with herself for being so insensitive to *Senyora* Tavares' feelings. "She soon felt better," she added in an attempt to recover herself. "And now she has lots of interests and takes great joy in her grandchildren."

Another glance across and Estefana noticed the woman's knuckles whiten as she tightened her grip on the door handle.

"Do you feel okay, *senyora*? Are you ill from the drive? Do you want me to stop or slow down?"

The woman gazed out the passenger's window at nothing in particular and started to chew on a betel quid she'd managed to pull from beneath her sarong.

Estefana kept shooting glances at her even though the woman was reluctant to engage.

"I imagine life down on the border—" Estefana tried when the woman cut her off.

"I worry about the stone for my husband's grave," *Senyora* Tavares said in a voice so hushed Estefana had to lean in toward her to hear clearly. "And whether that policeman will do anything about it." She paused and scratched the side of her face. "I don't want my husband shut out of heaven when Jesus closes the door because he can't see where Kosme is buried."

Estefana straightened as the road became more treacherous and the driving required more of her attention.

"I'm sure that won't happen, *senyora*," she said presently. "Jesus knows everyone by name, no matter where they are. That's what I was taught by the nuns. And the police commander, *Senyor* Mateus, I think he's a good man who will do all he can to help you get the proper headstone."

The woman was slow to respond.

"Kosme wasn't one of the Jesus people," she said. "He believed in the old ways." She checked out the window once more. "I do too, but I add Jesus. They say he sits next to *Maromak*," she said, the Timorese term for God. "In the sky. And talks to him."

Estefana felt relieved the woman was finally conversing and tried to keep her talking.

"Have you always lived here, *senyora*?" she asked.

The woman nodded.

"Since we came from the other side, yes," she said. "Can the window be opened?"

"Yes," said Estefana. "There's a winder under the window on the door. If you work it the glass will come down."

The woman tried to work the contraption which was unfamiliar to her and the glass stayed where it was.

Estefana checked what she was doing.

"The other way," she said. "Try it the other way."

The woman did as she was told and the glass slid down. She let the wind blow in her face for a few seconds and spat out a plug of red saliva that had built up from her chew.

She rolled the window up and sat without speaking for a moment, the ruts in the road buffeting her left and right in the cabin.

"When the *bapa* were here many people died, even those of us who came from over on their side, because there was little food," the woman said and rubbed a hand across her mouth. "The *bapa* soldiers took what little there was. I think about that in my sleep some nights." A second time she wound the window down, spat, and wound it up. "And when the *bapa* left, people were killed in the fighting over that vote," she said, referring to the 1999 referendum on independence.

Estefana waited, wondering why *Senyora* Tavares had started talking about this.

"This land was filled with the spirits of the dead for years. Angry spirits, lost spirits. They complained at night in the trees and on the wind. You could never block out their cries. For spirits, day is night and night is day. That's why they come at night. The land was haunted."

Senyora Tavares rubbed her face roughly with both hands as though trying to erase the memory before clutching the door handle tightly like before.

"People killed all their animals in the ceremonies to please the spirits but it was a long time before they left and joined the ancestors in the world below this one."

"That's interesting," Estefana said. "Why are you telling me this, *senyora*?"

"Because it's even worse now," the woman said. "Much worse."

Estefana glanced across, confused and alarmed.

"Much worse? Why?" asked Estefana.

• • •

The police officers had returned from searching the area where Arturo Cabral was found and had laid out what they'd found on a table in a rear room of the station. There were a dozen plastic water bottles in various states of decay, eight beer bottles, two tubes of cream the nature of which was no longer identifiable from the labels, a host of used instant noodle containers, and two cans of soda scrunched up in the way passing tourists tend to do.

Mateus had driven back to the police station; Carter and Cordero chose to stay on at the health clinic to go over Brooks' instructions again so both nurses understood them clearly. They then walked to the station where an officer told them where they could find the police commander. He was bent over the collection of used containers studying each item closely.

"How was the boy when you left?" Mateus asked.

Carter eyed Cordero before speaking.

"The vials were empty," she said.

"Empty?" said Mateus.

"Empty," Cordero confirmed.

"All of them?"

"There were only two and they were both empty, yes."

"But Brooks said—" he began and Cordero cut him off.

"Brooks noticed the vials," he said. "He mustn't have picked them up. Fomepizole is a colourless liquid, apparently, and so to him they could have appeared full. Same when Carter picked up a vial and handed it to the nurse. They're small vials and easy to regard as full when they're not. We searched for other vials only to find more medicinal bottles and plastic containers were also empty. My guess is they're kept in the cabinet in case an official from Maliana comes to check on the clinic. The official would make a cursory inspection and find everything in order. So the doctor doesn't have extra work to do filling in paperwork for new stock and the official can report everything is fine to the ministry."

"Does Juno know this?" Mateus asked.

"No," said Cordero. "The nurse allowed him in briefly to see his son and quickly ushered him out to the foyer. I suggested she not say anything to keep his hopes alive. He remains there awaiting news."

"And what is the news likely to be if the boy isn't given the appropriate medication?"

"It's too early to say," answered Carter. "The boy's unconscious. The nurses are doing all they can. The head nurse rang Batugade, Maliana and Liquica. None of them have fomepizole. She requested some be sent from Dili but they said it wouldn't get here until tomorrow morning at the earliest."

Mateus straightened and ran a hand through his hair.

"Shit," he said.

"You said it," Carter agreed. "Shit."

She came closer to the table.

"What've you laid out here?" she asked.

Mateus waved a hand over the assortment of items on the table.

"This is everything my officers found in the area where Arturo was picked up."

"And?" asked Carter.

"And I think this plastic water bottle here might be what we're looking for." He picked up a regular sized bottle. The cap had been discarded but the bottom of the bottle still contained the remains of a clear liquid which he swished around gently.

Carter took the bottle from him and sniffed the contents.

"Could be what I smelt on that dead man's lips or I could be talking myself into it. Do you have a lighter somewhere?"

Mateus produced one from the pocket of his trousers and handed it to her.

"And a metal plate or some aluminum foil or something?" she asked.

Mateus handed her one of the cans of soft drink that had been pressed flat.

"This do?"

Carter folded the can to create a small depression and dripped in some of the liquid from the bottle. She moved to the window where the light was brighter and struck the plastic lighter under the metal to generate vapors from the liquid. She brought the lighter up and directed it to the liquid. They could just make out a faint flame that lasted less than a second.

"I'd say that's methanol and a lot of it to ignite like that," she said. "There's no other culprit in this lot?" she asked gesturing to the contents of the table.

Mateus shook his head.

"So we have one man who died from methanol poisoning who in all likelihood came across the border. Another, who lived near the border, dying at much the same time with symptoms consistent with methanol poisoning. We have a teenager in the clinic found several miles away from the dead men showing signs of methanol poisoning." She nodded toward the plastic bottle Mateus had handed her. "And a bottle with a methanol-based solution in it found here in town," she said.

Mateus thrust his hands in his pockets.

"Then we're right about a smuggling operation," he said. "Of toxic liquor."

Cordero wasn't convinced.

"Why would people here be interested in smuggled liquor?" he asked. "Surely there's a lot of locally-made *tua mutin*," he added, referring to a mildly alcoholic palm wine made throughout Timor.

"Yes, and *tua sabu*," said Mateus—a stronger, distilled palm brandy. "But an even stronger spirit, some people will always drink." He pulled up a chair and slumped down into it. "And don't forget the Freitas burial. Gaspa was an important man with many kinfolk. His burial will attract a hundred people or more and go on for days. Local producers would be hard pressed to meet the demand."

"That's if it's intended to be distributed there," said Cordero.

"Juno Cabral has already decided Dario Freitas is the one bringing the stuff here to Balibo," said Mateus. "He could be right. But it could be anyone with connections to suppliers in West Timor and an interest in making money quickly."

Cordero lent across the table.

"Then you need to cancel public gatherings," he said.

"Dario would never agree to another delay of his father's burial and anyhow dozens of people are already here," Mateus said. "We could close the market down but the stall holders would just move somewhere else. It's their livelihood. Try to cancel a cockfight and we'd have a riot on our hands."

"Well put out a public warning not to buy or consume liquor," Cordero said.

"Come on, *maun*," complained Mateus. "Where do you think you are? I've told you there aren't television sets in Balibo, the few radios would be tuned to Indonesian music stations, and no one reads newspapers which come a week late from Dili anyhow. Our only effective public address system is the pulpit Father Francedez uses but he won't be preaching from it until Sunday."

Cordero straightened and thrust his hands in his pockets in frustration.

"Besides," Carter began. "If we're right about a stash of toxic liquor being smuggled in for sale and you cancel any of the gatherings, you may never locate the stuff. It wouldn't go back across the border. It'd be distributed here, eventually. And instead of a lot of people at risk from one big event, you'd place as many people at risk from a whole lot of smaller events over a longer period of time."

Mateus and Cordero exchanged glances but said nothing.

"I've had to deal with a lot of bootlegging on Native American reservations. They're supposed to be alcohol-free but that doesn't stop people smuggling the stuff in. The last thing you want to do is scare the bootleggers off or you'll never find their liquor. They'll just wait it out until you lose interest. You need to find some of the stuff as it's being sold and trace things from there to the rest of the stock and who's supplying it." She noticed Cordero shaking his head. "It's risky, I know, especially when the stuff's toxic. But I think a better plan is to allow the market, the cockfight and the burial to go on and if any of those is where it's meant to be sold we get on top of it when that happens."

"This isn't a Native American reservation," Cordero said, raising his voice. "It's not a confined area—"

"You mean defined," she interrupted him.

"Okay defined, yes. And it's not as though it's an alcohol-free zone like a reservation. Unless you test everyone who's drinking something you're not going to know who's managed to acquire something toxic. And apart from the impossibility of doing that, any attempt to try would expose what you're up to."

"And so your plan is?" she asked him.

"Cancel the public gatherings!" he said. "How do you propose to stop people buying liquor if the idea is to sell it at a market or a cockfight or give it out at a burial?" he asked. "A heavy police presence at any of those things would scare the supplier off."

"A cockfight or a big burial might each warrant some police presence—am I right Mateus?" Carter said.

Mateus nodded.

"So the few officers who would be at those events are told what to keep an eye out for. Plus, nobody in Balibo outside of this building and the health clinic knows you or me or Estefana. There haven't been too many people likely to have even seen us coming or going from the police station in the time we've been here either. So we three mingle in the crowd at each event and once we get a lead on what's going on, and who's behind it, we call in the cavalry."

"You're a woman and so you can't attend a cockfight in this country and you wouldn't exactly be inconspicuous in a crowd of mourners at a Timorese burial," Cordero pointed out.

"You and some male officers can patrol the cockfight. Estefana and I can keep an eye on the market. As for the burial, I could be a curious tourist. There's always a few around. And no one knows I'm with INTERPOL," she replied. "You and I are always dressed in civilian clothes and Estefana can change out of her police uniform."

The softening of the commander's jaw suggested he was gradually coming around to Carter's thinking.

"I don't like it," said Cordero. "It's too risky. Mateus, why don't you organize a search for the contraband?"

Mateus lent against the desk before answering.

"It could be anywhere," Carter suggested.

"That, and I only have so many officers," said Mateus. "Where would we start and how much ground could we cover?"

Carter took up the bottle the liquor had come in and examined it. There was nothing to distinguish it from any other water bottle of the type on either side of the border.

"They'd probably have to taste everything they found to be sure anyhow," she said.

"More than anything else, though," Mateus said, "it wouldn't sit well with the whole notion of community policing we are meant to focus on. Officers searching people's homes on the suspicion they contain something smacks of Indonesian soldiers doing the same during the occupation. I won't have my officers do that." He pushed himself off the desk. "We'll do what *Mana* Carter suggests. I'll carry the blame if anything goes wrong."

"But we'll all carry the regret," Cordero complained.

• • •

"There's a river down here that's *horok*," *Senyora* Taveres said, meaning it was forbidden for people to approach it.

"You mean the Talu?" asked Estefana.

"No," the woman said. "The one that runs into it past Lolitu."

Estefana nodded. The woman resumed her silence. Estefana waited a short time in case Isa Taveres had more to add before venturing a question.

"Why is the river *horok*?" Estefana asked.

"I'm not sure," the woman said. "It's a local thing. A local men's business thing. Some of the women say there are water spirits there. Others say underneath the water is a hole that leads to the underworld. I don't know. Like I told that policeman, I'm from the other side of the border. I'm Wehali."

"So why do you say things are worse for you now?"

"Women have to stay away from men's business that's *horok*," the woman said. She wound down the window a third time and spat the betel quid along with saliva out of her mouth. She didn't wind the window up. "Kosme told me it can be dangerous for women and everyone who lives with them if they go there," she added. "Maybe the river's haunted too."

Estefana glanced across.

"I get out here," the woman said. "I can walk from here. There's no road to my hut."

Estefana pulled to the side of the road.

"You haven't told me why things are worse for you now," she said.

"These things can't be talked about or it causes trouble," the woman said. "How does this door open?"

Estefana leaned across and opened the door. The woman paused before getting out of the seat.

"I've heard that one went to the water," she said not looking at Estefana. She pushed herself out of the seat, slumped back and grabbed the doorframe to heave herself up again. "And the coconut became bitter," she added before trudging off.

Estefana watched her go.

"'One went to the water and the coconut became bitter,'" she repeated. She closed the passenger's door, creased her brow, and swung the SUV around to return to Balibo. She shook her head.

"That makes no sense," she told herself.

11

"You heard *Senyora* Tavares tell the commander she came from a place a day's walk from Laran," said Estefana. "That's in Belu in West Timor. It means she's Wehali."

She had come from taking the woman to the outskirts of Lolitu and was sitting on the edge of her seat now with Carter in the police station. An officer had brought them a dozen sugar bananas, some instant noodles, and three cool water bottles as an improvised lunch.

"Wehali consider themselves the first inhabitants of the island of Timor," Estefana continued. "They say their land was the first to surface from the water that covered the earth in the beginning. The Indonesians brought some of them to where I grew up in Suai, *mana*, just like they brought some here. You remember how close to the border Suai is? I think they brought people to settle along this side of the border so that we would stop thinking there was one people on this side and one on the other."

"That's interesting Estefana except—" said Carter.

"The traditional Wehali use taboo language, *mana*," Estefana continued ignoring the interruption. "When something is secret they disguise it by using special words. When they fear a demon or something might threaten them if they excite it, they refer to it in other ways so it won't think it's being talked about."

"What's this got to do—" Carter tried for some clarity a second time.

"They rarely share the meaning of their taboo language with anyone who isn't Wehali. So I never learned the meanings. When she said 'one went to the water', that probably means someone violated the prohibition on going to the river because it is taboo but she didn't want to name or identify that person out of fear." Estefana frowned. "It's harder to know what she meant by 'the coconut became bitter'. I can't think of any connection. Was that code for the one who went to the river, for the river itself, or a household, or a hamlet? I don't know."

"Well let's put it to one side for the moment," said Carter. "The priority is to find any toxic liquor and prevent a lot of people getting sick and dying. Have something to eat. We have to go."

"Go?" said Estefana.

"Mateus is briefing his officers. Some he'll send to the market, some to the cockfight, and others will attend the burial ceremonies. While he does that he's asked Cordero to speak to Dario Freitas and he wants us to talk to Juno Cabral."

"He spoke to *Senyor* Cabral himself this morning, *mana*," Estefana said.

"True. But when he did, Juno had only just heard the news about his son. He could've been in shock. Mateus says he's had time to calm down a little and wants to know more. After all, if Juno's own son was drinking the liquor there must be a connection of some sort."

Carter picked up a banana.

"Mateus thinks Juno might be less guarded speaking to two women, especially when they're not from here and so aren't part of his police command." She came forward on her chair and handed the banana to Estefana. "I don't have any authority so you're going to have to do the talking. You can tell him I'm with you because INTERPOL has an interest if it's alcohol that's been smuggled across the border."

Estefana took the banana and played with it in her hands.

"I don't know if I can do that, *mana*," she said. "*Senyor* Cabral is an important man. A village head. I would be too nervous to question him."

"You can do this, Estefana. If you get a little tense just tell yourself it's not you questioning Juno—it's the Timorese police and you just happen to be their representative."

• • •

The effect of the incense had long since worn off by the time Cordero entered the store and the odour of stale, imprisoned air was again suffocating. On the positive side, at least someone was visible—*Senyor* Feng, behind his counter, sorting a small pile of coins into their respective denominations.

"*Botarde*," said Cordero, offering the afternoon greeting. "It's me again."

Feng raised his eyes from his work.

"More sugar?" the storekeeper enquired.

Cordero shook his head.

"No. I came to give you this," he said and handed over the joss paper Mateus had taken from *Senyora* Tavares.

"So you are a police officer," said Feng.

"I'm a police *investigator*," said Cordero, emphasizing the distinction.

"How is that different?"

Cordero sighed.

"It's a long story," he said. "And it's not necessary to explain it now. I'm just here helping out the police commander for a few days."

"I thought you were with the police when you first came into my store," Feng said.

"Really? Why?"

"I am an old man, *senyor*," said Feng in his poker face. "I have been able to live a long life because I have learned to recognize people who might cause me trouble. In all the countries where I have lived, they are usually police officers. That's how I know. I can see it in your eyes, hear it in your voice, and feel it in your presence."

Cordero thrust his hands in his pockets and leaned his hip against the counter.

"I also noticed you speaking to the commander yesterday when he pulled up," Feng added. "I didn't think he was interrogating you. And you followed after him."

"You're a clever man, *senyor*."

"There are two types of men in this world: predators and prey. I am of the second kind and so I make a point of staying alert to what's around me."

Feng examined the note in his hand and wandered over to the Buddhist shrine. He put the note in a small red decorative box off to the side.

"Has the commander caught the one who broke into my store?" he asked returning to the counter.

"He's working on it," Cordero replied, knowing full well that Mateus had more pressing concerns.

"There are two notes still missing," Feng said.

"Two, huh," said Cordero. "And that's all that was taken in the break in?"

Feng nodded and folded his arms inside the sleeves of the loose tunic he wore.

"Who would have known the notes were there?" Cordero asked.

Feng shrugged.

"It is no secret that I burn the joss paper twice a year to honor my ancestors," he said. "Many people have seen it."

"And you never lock the notes away?"

"Why would I? They have no real value."

Cordero eased over to the row of plastic bottles along on wall.

"What is interesting is the nature of the break in," said Feng.

"How so?" replied Cordero absently.

"Very few people break into houses or businesses in Balibo," Feng said. "There is little to steal, you see. When they do break in, their efforts are almost always…how shall I put it? Destructive. They break or smash things. But my door was not smashed or broken. It was like whoever came in knew how to open a lock without a key."

"Hmm," Cordero muttered. The break in resulted in the theft of items of little value and in any case it was none of his concern. He bent down and amused himself by inspecting the bottles, his hands pressed into his trouser pockets. Feng watched him and said nothing more about the break in.

"Do you sell liquor?" Cordero asked.

"I have one bottle of *tua mutin*," Feng said. "I have two bottles of *tua sabu* there on the shelf as well," he said and pointed. "All the liquor I sell is made by people in the village. So the locals already have it. It's only someone passing through who might be interested. Few ever are, however. Those bottles you see have gathered much dust."

Cordero straightened.

"The commander suspects a stock of liquor—very strong liquor—has been smuggled into Balibo from across the border," he said and faced Feng once more.

"If you are asking me if I have any, the answer is no," said Feng. "If you are asking me if I know anything about it, the answer is no again."

"What I'm interested in are your thoughts on who might bring a quantity of strong liquor into Balibo and how they might intend to distribute it," said Cordero.

"Why do you think my thoughts would be useful to you?"

"Well you are in the business of having items brought in and selling them," said Cordero and smiled. "I'm not."

"It's not hard to bring things into Balibo if you have the right contacts," Feng said. "I don't have contacts for strong liquor and especially not strong liquor that would be smuggled across the border. As I said earlier, the usual people who have caused me trouble in my life have been police officers. So I keep my business dealings strictly legal so as to avoid any kind of trouble with the police." He began to scoop up the coins he had sorted into small cardboard boxes. "As for distribution, Balibo is a small village. Everyone knows everyone. It's not hard to sell or share things when that is the case."

"There's a market tomorrow, I believe," said Cordero. "And a cockfight. And there is the ceremony and feasting following the Freitas burial. Which of those would you think is best suited to the sale of liquor?"

"They are each as good as the other," said Feng.

"There's always an elaborate ceremony of some sort with the burial of an important man," said Cordero. "Lots of eating, drinking, you know."

Feng shrugged and offered no further opinion.

Cordero nodded. Nothing Feng had said gave rise to suspicion and his lack of interest in the matter didn't strike Cordero as contrived. Could he be trusted? Cordero left the answer to that question open for the moment.

He started to leave but stopped in the doorway when he noticed Bobu ride up outside on a spluttering motorcycle trailing a plume of black smoke. A guitar was slung across his back and the young girl he claimed to be his daughter was perched between him and the handle bars. Both were laughing and neither wore a helmet.

"What do you know about the one that calls himself Bobu?" Cordero put to Feng.

"The clown? It's others who called him that at first. Young boys mostly trying to make fun of him. He won them over. He has that gift. And so he embraced the name." Feng eased over to the doorway and stood beside Cordero. "And I know Dario is paying him to play his guitar and sing at the ceremony for his dead father."

Bobu threw his leg over the rear of the motorcycle and stood, talking to his daughter about something Cordero couldn't hear.

"You say he has a gift that makes him popular," Cordero asked. "What's his secret?"

"Who can fathom the minds of the young," Feng said. He gestured with his chin toward Bobu. "They see him as something their life in this village is not. Colourful, exciting, carefree. Or perhaps he is simply different to them and so interesting."

"Have you ever seen him talking to Arturo Cabral?" Cordero asked.

"I don't make a point of checking on who Bobu talks to and who he doesn't. It's none of my concern."

With that Feng went back to his counter and started to put his boxes of coins away.

Father Francedez pedaled up to the store on a bicycle, one hand pressed down firmly on a hat he was wearing to keep it from blowing off. He dismounted next to Bobu, adjusted his glasses, and pinched the cheek of the girl. The priest and Bobu talked for a few minutes. Cordero couldn't make out what either was saying. Bobu was gesturing wildly and Father Francedez was laughing. It was obvious they knew each other quite well—well enough to share a joke in each other's company at least.

Cordero made a mental note to drop in on the priest on his way back from his visit to the house of Dario Freitas.

12

Estefana had to brake suddenly to avoid driving into a pack of scrawny dogs fighting over a food scrap in the middle of the road. She blew the horn. They ignored her. She edged forward and blew the horn a second time. One of the dogs lifted its head, raised its ears and tore away. Another took the chance distraction to grab the scrap of food and took off in the opposite direction, the other dogs barking and whining as they raced after it.

"Why are there so many stray dogs in this country?" Carter asked.

"To control the cats, *mana*," said Estefana.

"Why are there so many cats then?"

"To control the rats."

Estefana put the vehicle into gear.

"When food is short, there are fewer dogs," she said. "People eat them," she added matter-of-factly.

Carter looked across. Estefana's eyes were fixed on the road.

"And the cats and rats?" Carter asked.

"If food is very short, there are fewer of them as well."

A young girl of eight or nine carrying a baby on her hip walked into the middle of the road just as Estefana was about to accelerate off to the health clinic. Again, she broke suddenly and the girl looked up as though she had the right of way. She came over to their vehicle and peered up through the windows with big, round eyes. She hitched up her shorts, hoisted the baby higher on her hip, and moved on across the front of the vehicle without so much as a word.

"You've certainly got to keep a close eye on things around here," Carter commented.

"Not always," Estefana said as she drove off.

"What was that?" Carter asked.

"*Maun* enjoyed the dinner last night," Estefana said.

"Cordero likes food and he likes gin," said Carter. "So of course he enjoyed himself."

Out of the corner of one eye Carter caught Estefana smiling.

"What?" she asked.

"Nothing, *mana*," Estefana said coyly.

"Come on," Carter said. "I know that look."

"I think he likes you too, *mana*," Estefana said, her eyes fixed firmly on the road.

Carter glanced at her.

"Excuse me?" she said.

"It's in the way he doesn't keep his eye on you," Estefana said.

"What on earth are you talking about Estefana?"

Estefana swerved to avoid a pothole in the middle of the road.

"Well?" Carter insisted when Estefana had straightened the vehicle.

"Josinto and I sometimes walk along the seafront in Dili on hot days," Estefana said. "He doesn't look at the people selling ice-cream, not because he doesn't like ice-cream but because he does. He likes ice-cream very much." She smiled again just a little. "It's the same with *maun* not looking at you, I think."

"You're crazy," said Carter, shifting slightly in her seat.

Estefana was grinning now.

"Maybe you like him a little bit too," she said.

"Oh, and that's in the way I *don't* look at him I suppose," said Carter.

"Yes, *mana*," Estefana replied. "Because maybe it makes you uneasy to look too closely at him."

Carter stared out the passenger's window for a few seconds.

"There's a word I learned in my Tetun language class last week, Estefana," she said. "You should know it. *Lia-bosok*."

Estefana made a face.

"No, I don't think I know that one, *mana*," she said.

"Well, I'm told it's the closest thing the Tetun language has to the English word 'bullshit,'" said Carter. "I'm sure you've heard me say 'bullshit' enough times to know what it means. And that's what all this liking and not looking you're talking about is. Bullshit. I've had men look at me and I've had men not look at me. I can read the meaning of both. And I don't read anything into what Cordero does or doesn't do. I'd be surprised if he ever had any feelings for a woman." She folded her arms tightly across her chest.

"Yes *mana*," Estefana said, and left it at that.

"And as for me," continued Carter, "I'll be off home to Arizona in a couple of months. I don't want anyone or any—wait a minute, is that our man?"

Estefana had driven into the parking space in front of the health clinic. Juno Cabral was pacing back and forth outside the entrance. Estefana blew out a nervous breath. Her brow creased.

"You'll be fine, Estefana," Carter said. "And I'll be with you. Don't get into a funk about it. Just do it."

Estefana cut the engine.

"Funk, *mana*?"

"Yeah. It means—forget it, okay?" said Carter. "Let's go."

They left the SUV and caught up with Juno. His face was long and drawn. Estefana introduced the two of them, haltingly, and in a tense voice said that she needed to ask him a few more questions. He took little notice of what she was saying, instead peering through the door of the clinic at the nurses inside. Estefana explained who Carter was and why she was there. Juno jiggled about and popped his head over her shoulder. Estefana raised her hands slightly in an appeal for help and Carter gestured for her to pose questions. Estefana began by asking Juno if there'd been any improvement in his son's condition. That, finally, grabbed his attention.

"They won't let me near him," he complained, glaring through the door. "They hide themselves away and every time I've tried to see Arturo they gang up and make me come to the front of the clinic or out here. They won't tell me anything either."

Estefana was translating for Carter who suggested Estefana tell Juno she would speak to the nurses once she'd finished her questions. Carter hoped that might make him more likely to open up. When Estefana had made the promise, Juno stopped his pacing. He followed them both into the front room of the clinic and sat down. He lifted his eyes to Estefana as though he was willing to talk. That increased her confidence a little and so she took a seat next to him while Carter moved off to the side so as not to be a distraction.

Estefana rubbed her hands on her trousers, glanced up at Carter, and faced Juno.

"We—I mean two police officers—collected a plastic water bottle on the slope down on the far side of the old fort where your son was found this morning. It contained what we—I mean the police commander—believes is the liquor that your son drank. The liquid that made him sick. It's just a normal plastic bottle and the liquid is clear." She glanced across at Carter before continuing. "Do you know anything about bottles like that?" she asked Juno.

"No."

"Have you seen anything like that in your son's possession lately?"

"No."

"Do you know where Arturo might have come across it?"

Juno took a moment to answer.

"I've no idea," he said.

"Are there any plastic water bottles around your house that you know of, *senyor*?"

"Of course there are. We use a water dispenser in the house. We have plastic bottles we fill sometimes when we go out. Other than those"—he shrugged—"there are no bottles lying around that contain liquid that I know of. Certainly none that contain liquor, I can assure you."

Juno leaned forward and checked down the corridor.

"Have any of Arturo's friends been to the house recently, *senyor*?"

Juno shook his head. Estefana looked up at Carter who nodded her encouragement to keep the questioning going.

"Has Arturo mentioned any friends he's gone to visit recently?"

"No." Juno sat up and faced Estefana. "So, the police commander still thinks this is the result of some kind of smuggling operation?"

"That's what he thinks at the moment," Estefana said. "Do you know anything that might help the police to confirm that, *senyor*?"

"No, nothing," Juno said. He scratched his chest before waving off to the side at nothing in particular. "There are times when people tell me things because I'm the village head and they think I can do something about what they say. People sometimes don't tell me things for the same reason. This is the first I've heard about smuggling, liquor—all of it."

Estefana had been translating the substance of Juno's responses for Carter's benefit. But she had run out of questions and conveyed that to Carter by raising an eyebrow.

"He was quick to lay the blame for his son's condition on someone else when he spoke to Mateus," Carter said. "Ask him why?"

Estefana did so and Juno became quickly agitated.

"Dario Freitas likes to pretend he's an important man," he said. "His father was a traditional nobleman—a leader of standing in the village. Dario thinks people should show him the same respect." Juno scoffed at that. "He forgets the Portuguese made people like his father responsible for collecting taxes and the people hated Gaspa for it. They hated him even more when he did it for the Indonesians."

Juno gazed down the corridor again and then looked back at Estefana.

"Dario inherited some fields around Maliana and he employs workers to raise vegetables there for the markets in Dili," he continued. "That's how he makes his money, and his money is the only reason he has any influence now. It certainly doesn't come from anything to do with his character. So, he organises a big funeral ceremony for old Gaspa to show off what a big man he is. People from all over will gorge themselves for days on the food he'll provide. Don't you think he'll also ply them with liquor? Why are you questioning me and not him?"

"One of our officers is talking to *Senyor* Freitas today," Estefana said. "Do you have any evidence for what you say?"

She anticipated the question might anger him and it did. Juno jumped to his feet.

"My evidence is lying in a bed down there!" he said, pointing down the corridor. "You said you'd speak to the nurse. Well, how about you do that?"

Carter could see there was little to be gained by further questioning and signalled Estefana that she'd done enough.

"I will go now, *senyor*," Estefana said. "Please sit down."

Juno swayed a little before he slumped into his chair. Carter backed away and stared outside through the front door while she waited. Estefana went to find the nurse who had retreated into a back room. The nurse opened the door when she heard it was Estefana knocking and not Juno.

"There's been no change," she said of the boy's condition. "He's pupils are very dilated and his breathing continues to be rapid and shallow. It could go either way. I think he needs that medicine from Dili but it may come too late. I don't want to tell his father that, you understand."

Estefana did. She rejoined Juno in the foyer and told him that Arturo was resting and everything possible was being done for him. Juno said nothing. He leaned forward and buried his face in his hands.

• • •

"I was nervous, *mana*," Estefana said as they made their way back from the health clinic.

"Well, it didn't show, Estefana," Carter replied. "You handled it well."

"Now that's over I am going to do something I'm much more relaxed about doing," Estefana said.

"What's that?"

"I'm going to prepare dinner!"

They stopped at the store so Estefana could buy some tofu, rice and spices to go with the vegetables she could get fresh from a roadside stall. Outside the store Bobu was sitting on an empty wooden crate, strumming his guitar. The girl Josefa was lounging between his legs, an arm dangling over each of his thighs. The sweet smell of burning eucalyptus from a house nearby perfumed the air.

From the SUV, Carter caught the girl's eye. The same stirred and confused feeling she'd had when she first set eyes on the girl returned but only fleetingly. She raised a hand just a little to acknowledge Josefa who returned the gesture with a smile.

The sound of a dog whining nearby distracted the girl. The dog was scrabbling around a slab of broken concrete bordering a gutter off to the side of the store. It was a female, the stretched and enlarged teats suggesting it had recently given birth to a litter despite its own half-starved state. The dog raked at the slab with one paw then another, sniffing at the concrete, and jigging this way and that in search of a better angle to secure what lay underneath. There were blotches of bare skin where its fur had been torn out in fights with other dogs, one ear had been nipped and was bleeding and flies found the spot irresistible.

While Bobu was absorbed by a riff he was trying to master, the girl sat up straight and studied the dog. She stood and searched for something. Carter watched as she took a rake that was propped up for sale at the front of the store, and shook it to test its strength. Slowly she approached the dog, which eyed her and bared its ratty teeth. The girl held the rake across her body and stared down at the dog. The dog snarled briefly before starting to whimper.

The girl approached the concrete slab, lent down and poked the end of the rake under the slab to flick whatever was jammed there out into the open. The dog shimmied and yelped behind her.

The first sweep with the rake produced only twigs and leaves washed under by the runoff from the rain. Next, an empty, crushed plastic water bottle. Finally, the girl managed to flick out a dead rat. She stepped away. The dog considered her, wary about what she might do next. Then it dropped its head suddenly, snatched the rat and ran off with the rat's tail dangling from its jaws. The girl replaced the rake where she had found it and resumed her position between Bobu's legs. She looked at Carter and smiled a second time.

Estefana placed the items she'd purchased on the rear seat of the SUV and climbed in the driver's seat. She noticed Carter's expression.

"Are you alright, *mana*?" she asked.

Carter wriggled in her seat.

"Sure. Why?"

"No reason," said Estefana, not wanting to draw attention to the puzzled look on Carter's face.

• • •

Fidalgo kept a close eye on the hut for a full ten minutes. The old motorcycle that the clown rode was nowhere to be seen, there was no movement around the hut, and there was no smoke from a cooking fire either inside the hut or outside.

He convinced himself there was no one around and drew confidence from that.

The rain would have wet the top of the thatching, yet not soaked right through—it was too short a downpour for that and anyhow the heaviest rain had fallen further east over Balibo. He could ignite the drier fronds on the underside of the thatch and they would smolder rather than burn.

It was what he wanted: no one would get hurt and the result would be dramatic enough to have neighbours wonder who was living here or what might be wrong inside the house. Perhaps it would be terrifying enough to raise questions for the occupants about whether to repair the hut or start anew somewhere else. Either way, Bobu and his daughter would know they weren't wanted in Lolitu and, if they didn't move on, the next time could be much worse than this.

Fidalgo knew the grass around the hut would be damp and so he'd brought dry bark from the sacred house where it was stored inside to light the cauldron. He gripped it tight and held it to his chest as he hobbled toward the hut. He made sure to keep a screen of vegetation between him and the more distant huts just in case someone was cleaning their yard and might chance to see him. When he reached the hut he pressed himself to the bamboo wall just to the left of the entranceway, held his breath while he listened for any sound inside, and slowly let the tension drain from his body.

He examined the fronds under the overhang of the thatch. Too wet here and he realised he was on the western side of the hut— the side from which the storm had come. He dragged his lame foot as quietly as he could around the hut, checking the fronds as he went. At last he found a dry section and smiled his satisfaction.

He lengthened the bark into a fire stick, stroking it until he was sure it was thick enough and strong enough to reach the fronds with its flame. He took a plastic lighter from the pocket of his shorts. He flicked it and the lighter sparked but failed to ignite. Another try. Same result. Perhaps he was more nervous than he thought. He gave the lighter a shake and tried again. A flame caught, just enough to do the job. He lit the bark and rotated the stick until it flared around the tip. He poked the end up into the thatch.

The dry frond caught immediately, an orange flame accompanied by a rich, crackling sound which spread laterally until the wetter fronds reduced the fire to a collection of smoky embers that glowed bright in the light breeze. He moved further around the hut and lit more thatch until his fire stick had burnt down to the edge of his hand. Grey plumes of smoke were swirling around the walls of the hut by now and billowing thick and black over its top. He tossed what was left of the fire stick near the entrance and shuffled off.

Fidalgo hadn't figured on the old woman being asleep inside the hut or a rider on the pony who'd been watching him from within a growth of tall grass off to one side.

13

It was a brisk 30-minute walk from Feng's store to the small estate where Dario Freitas lived on the edge of Balibo. Cordero took 45 minutes, weaving in and out of people making the same trip for Gaspa's burial ceremonies. It was a cavalcade on foot, on motorcycles, and riding in the back of small trucks, but Cordero was in no hurry. If Mateus had felt a sense of urgency about questioning Dario, he would have given Cordero his SUV or arranged a police motorcycle for him to take. He hadn't done either. Perhaps the commander knew it would be quicker to walk; perhaps he too was in no hurry. There was enough doubt still about a supply of toxic liquor finding its way to the mouths of thirsty revellers to allow some comfort in the thought that the assumption may prove wrong. For the moment, then, Cordero pushed the idea aside to enjoy the afternoon sunshine and time alone to consider things other than the problems besetting Balibo.

He passed two shirtless men mixing cement by the side of the road and exchanged a greeting. Further on he inspected a vacant block where weeds grew through the tracks of heavy machinery left idle for want of spare parts. Wisps of smoke carried the sickly-sweet smell of smouldering rubbish through the air. As he waved it away, he noticed across the road an old man humming to himself as he sat with a goat tied on a chain. The man mistook Cordero's fanning for a salutation and raised a hand back. Cordero pushed on, feeling pleased with himself and the world.

Up ahead dozens of people were huddled in clumps outside the compound where he'd been told Dario Freitas lived. Inside were many dozens more. Most were men or children. Some of the older men were bare-chested with a colourful *tais* thrown over one shoulder and a buffalo headpiece—a traditional symbol of strength and security—completing their outfits. Others wore open-necked shirts and trousers which, in rural Timor, constituted formal attire.

Some of the children were being admonished to be quiet and show respect. Most of them were simply bored from standing outside for hours with nothing at all to do. Cordero mingled for a time and saw nothing untoward. This was the solemn period of the burial ritual. When it was completed and Gaspa had been safely buried in the family plot, things would pick up and take on the character of a festival where the consumption of alcohol would be far more likely to occur.

The women were sitting around the coffin of Gaspa Freitas inside the house, demonstrating their grief as best they could by burning candles or mumbling prayers. It was the *lutu* or period of mourning before the burial. During the *lutu* the good deeds of Gaspa Freitas would be recounted by his kinfolk so that his spirit might leave his body satisfied that there had been an appropriate rendering of all he had done in the service of others. He'd been dead for a total of twelve years and so good deeds that couldn't be recalled could be invented because no one was likely to recall enough to dispute them.

The house itself was large by Balibo standards but had seen better days. The white paint on the stucco walls had weathered badly and the Portuguese colonial tile roof was cracking in parts. Cordero approached a man leaning on one of the columns at the entrance portico, offered a greeting, and asked where he could find Dario. The man took a cigarette from his mouth and shrugged. As he did, a young girl emerged from the front door carrying a tray of sliced *bibingka*—a baked rice cake.

"Ask her, *maun*," the man said. "She should know. That's Dario's daughter, Marquita."

The girl appeared to be about ten years old. She made an effort to rush past Cordero but he held a hand out and stopped her. She looked up, a happy expression on her face which Cordero regarded as a little inappropriate for the occasion. He reminded himself that she was too young to have known her grandfather, and she was playing hostess by ferrying snacks of various kinds to guests while her mother was busy preparing an endless supply of more substantial refreshments in the kitchen.

"*Botarde alin*," he said. "You are Marquita?"

"Yes, *senyor*," the girl responded. "Marquita Immaculata Ignacia Freitas," she added as though reciting a well rehearsed phrase.

"Do you know where I can find your father?"

The girl blinked at Cordero with big brown eyes.

"If you need to use the toilet, *senyor*, it is now inside," she said, gesturing with the tray of snacks into the house. "We have a new one. You sit down on it. And when you push a button, water comes out." The girl frowned. "That's what's supposed to happen. My father says the pipes aren't connected yet. So you can sit but there's no water. Only what's in the tub beside the toilet." She fixed him directly with her eyes and in all seriousness asked: "Are your pipes connected, *senyor*?"

Cordero wasn't sure how to answer. He brushed a hand through his hair.

"My pipes? Well, yeah, they're connected," he said to the girl. "It's okay if they're not though—for a while at least. But I don't need to use your toilet. I need to talk to your father."

"He's around the side," she said holding the tray in one hand and pointed to her left with the other. "He has to make sure everything is right for my grandfather's burial tomorrow. He was a *dato*, you know."

"Yes, I know that. Thank you, *alin*," Cordero said. "I'll go find your father there."

Cordero went around the side of the house to find Dario standing under a marquee where the coffin of Gaspa Freitas would be placed for a mortuary ceremony before being taken to the cemetery for burial. There was a table in the centre of the marquee and Dario was considering which *tais* to drape over it from a number a woman held over her arm.

"*Senyor* Freitas," Cordero said. "*Botarde*."

Dario looked up from the *tais* he was holding.

"Ah, the stranger from the Chinaman's store," he said. "Good of you to come. Please, help yourself to some refreshments on the porch."

"Thank you, no," said Cordero. "My name is Vincintino Cordero. I'm a police investigator. I apologize for interrupting this solemn occasion. I'm afraid I need to ask you a few questions."

Dario handed the *tais* he was examining to the woman. He had failed to tell her which covering he wanted over the coffin and the woman showed frustration behind his back at the continuing indecision.

"A police inspector?" he said.

"Police *investigator*," Cordero corrected him.

"Is that why you followed the police commander yesterday?" He put a hand to his chin. "Now that makes sense. What brings you here? Is something wrong?"

"Could we go somewhere private? This won't take long," said Cordero.

"A few questions you say?"

"That's right. I won't take much of your time. If that's okay with you."

"Yes, yes. Of course," said Dario. He asked the woman to lay out the *tais* he'd just seen. She smiled her relief. He told her he'd return shortly. "Follow me," he said to Cordero.

They strolled to an overgrown garden plot at the rear of the house. Aside the gnarled trunk of an avocado tree they stopped, the branches offering shade from the intense sunlight. Dario planted his feet and faced Cordero.

"How can I help?" he asked.

"Have you heard what happened to Arturo Cabral?" Cordero began.

"Arturo? No. I've been busy since last night welcoming guests and preparing the ceremonies. As you can see there is a lot to be done. What's happened to Arturo?"

"He's in the health clinic. He was found staggering around earlier today near the fort. We think he'd drunk some liquor we have reason to believe was toxic."

"That's...that's...," Dario began but had trouble finishing.

"The nurses are doing what they can," Cordero said. "Yesterday, as you know, I followed the police commander down toward the border. A body had been found in a clearing. No one knew who the man was. He could have come from West Timor. We arranged for a pathologist to come from Dili to examine the body. He found the man died from methanol poisoning."

Dario tut-tuttered in disbelief.

"I'd heard a body had been found but, like I said, I've been busy with the arrangements for my father's send-off. I've just come from picking up my supplies from the Chinaman. They should have come days ago. Now I've things to organise here." He stopped himself. "What you're telling me is terrible news."

"We suspect the dead man smuggled liquor from across the border," said Cordero. "Would you know anything about that?"

"About smuggling!" He shook his body as though trying to shake the thought off. 'No! Why should I?"

"You haven't heard anything about a stock of strong liquor that's become available in Balibo?"

"No, I tell you! I've no interest in strong liquor. Why do you think this has anything to do with me?"

Cordero glanced across to what he could see of the crowd in the front of Dario's house.

"You have a large crowd to provide for," he said. "Over several days I suspect."

"My father died the day before the country became independent in 2002. He was a *dato*."

"Yes, you told me that outside the Chinaman's store," replied Cordero. "A nobleman."

"That's right. A nobleman. An important and respected nobleman. And he had a large kinship network. Some of the people he was connected to by birth or by marriage now live on the other side of the border. Others were dispersed all over Timor by the troubles caused by the Indonesians and their militias. So, it has taken time to get everyone together to take part in the proper burial rites. Do you think after all that time and all that effort I would do something illegal to taint my father's reputation much less to place these people in harm?"

"I merely have to ask these questions if only to rule you out of the investigation," said Cordero.

"Rule me out?" said Dario, slapping the sides of his legs as though he'd been gravely insulted.

"I'm a *dato's* son!" he declared.

Cordero kept his voice even.

"It's been suggested that's exactly why you might be involved," he said. "To impress people by hosting a feast with generous amounts of food and drink." He eyed Dario. "Including alcohol. A lot more alcohol than could be sourced locally."

"That's absurd!" Dario said and made to storm away. "Wait a minute," he said and stopped. He came back and stood in front of Cordero. "You said it's been suggested that I'm somehow involved. You didn't say who was doing the suggesting."

Cordero didn't react.

"Well?" Dario edged closer. "I bet I know who. Juno Cabral. Am I right? You said it was his son put in the health clinic this morning. So, who else would you have talked to since? Huh? Who?"

He held Cordero's stare for a long moment.

"What do you know about Juno Cabral?" Dario asked. He waited for an answer, but none came. "Nothing I can see. You're not from here. Well let me educate you."

• • •

Bobu was riding back to Lolitu, his work in Balibo having been done. He was feeling good with the world. Josefa was pressed between him and the handlebars enjoying the wind in her hair. The money Dario would pay for entertaining guests tomorrow night would be enough to allow him and Josefa to leave the border area, leave Balibo entirely, and move to Dili. There was only Umbelina to worry about and that could wait. Things were looking up for the first time since he had come to Lolitu and so he'd decided to go with the feeling and not let complications take anything away.

As the motorcycle clanked its way along the track, Bobu could smell smoke in the air and soon caught sight of the hut. He could see one bamboo wall was blackened and some of the thatch roof above it had collapsed.

"Shit!" he said and accelerated as best he could without causing Josefa to fall.

The boy he knew from a neighbouring hut—Amando—was sitting in the shade of the candle nut tree, his pony tethered to a branch motionless by his side.

"What's happened?" Bobu shouted as he pulled to a stop and eased Josefa off the bike. He didn't wait for a reply. "Stay here," he said to the girl and he rushed inside the hut.

He came out waving a hand across his face and coughing from the smoke inside.

"Where's the old woman? Umbelina?" he yelled to the boy.

"I took her to my house," Amando said, getting to his feet and coming nearer.

"Is she hurt?"

"No. But she doesn't see good and she can't ride a pony. She slid off twice on the way to my hut. I had to push her back up both times."

"What's happened *apá*?" Josefa asked, using the Tetun for daddy. "Where's Umbelina?"

"Umbelina is okay," Bobu said. "Don't worry. Stay here, outside, okay?"

"What about my things inside?" the girl protested.

"Your things are okay," Bobu reassured her. "Let me talk to Amando."

He strode over to the candle nut tree.

"What can you tell me?" Bobu demanded.

The pony stirred and whinnied, and the boy had to calm it. He turned back to Bobu.

"I took the old woman to my hut," he said. "My mother is taking care of her. She wasn't hurt. She was asleep and when I went inside the hut, she didn't know what was happening. My mother told me to come here and wait for you."

"So how did this happen?" Bobu asked. "How did the hut catch on fire?"

The boy hesitated a moment.

"Come on," said Bobu. "We're friends, right? You can tell me."

"A man came out of the bushes over there," Amando said pointing vaguely, "and lit a fire and put it up to the roof."

"You saw him?"

"I was riding by and I saw him. That's why I went in for the old woman when the man ran away and the hut was on fire."

"You're a brave boy, Amando," said Bobu to encourage the boy to tell him more. "A hero in fact."

The boy's chest puffed out, just a little.

"Who was this man? Did you see who it was?" Bobu asked.

The boy dropped his gaze and glanced back at the pony.

"You did, didn't you?" said Bobu.

The boy said nothing.

"Come on, Amando," urged Bobu. "Tell me who it was. We're friends, aren't we?" he said a second time.

The boy circled the dirt with his foot, weighing up his duty as a friend and the possibility that the culprit might come after him for betraying his identity.

Friendship with Bobu finally won.

"It was Fidalgo," the boy said.

"Fidalgo de Queiroz?"

The boy nodded.

"You sure it was him?"

"I'm sure. I know because he has a stiff leg. I watched him burn the hut."

Bobu stared at the hut in silence. Amando and Josefa, who had come over and joined them, both waited for his reaction.

"What are you going to do, *apá*?" asked Josefa.

"Huh?" said Bobu.

"I said what are you going to do?"

Bobu's eyes remained fixed on the hut but he drew the girl in close with one hand.

"Right now we're going to check on Umbelina," he said slowly. "Then I'm going to leave you with Amando for a while and I'm going to talk to Fidalgo."

"You're going to his house?" asked Josefa.

"No," Bobu replied. "It's Friday. I know where to find him!"

• • •

"He worked for the Indonesians," Dario said. "Did you know that?"

Dario had calmed himself. He'd taken a pre-rolled cigarette from his top pocket, lit it and spat out a flake of tobacco that had stuck to his lip.

"I don't mean when they invaded," he said. "I mean when they'd set themselves up to run this country. He took a job as a junior official in the district administration. When they left, he joined the main pro-independence party—Fretilin—because it won enough votes to form government. When Fretilin lost office in 2007, he switched parties and became a member of the ruling coalition. Are you getting the picture? Juno's an opportunist, out for himself and no one else."

He blew smoke out of the side of his mouth away from Cordero.

"The Indonesians use a lot of pesticides in their farming. They use them in planting, harvesting and storage, whether it's rice they're growing or strawberries or oranges. They used them here too, especially around Liquica where they were hoping to grow a lot of rice and on the vegetable farms in Maliana. When they pulled out, they left plenty of the stuff here. Local farmers never liked it. They stopped using it and resumed traditional practices."

He puffed on his cigarette and let blue smoke drift from his mouth as he spoke. Cordero was wondering where Dario was leading with this information.

"How do I know all this? I have land around Maliana and I grow vegetables there which I sell to buyers from Dili. Well, when

Juno was voted village head a couple of years ago, he promised to develop the roads around Balibo—all the way to the border. Said that would make it easier for people to buy and sell in the main markets here. Would allow kids to come from there to school here in Balibo. Have you been on that road?" he asked and gestured in its direction with his cigarette. "Nothing's been done. Juno sent trucks down there pretending he was acting on his election promise. You know what the trucks carried? I bet I do."

He took a last drag before tossing the butt on the ground and pressing it into the soil with his shoe.

"All of the Indonesian pesticide the locals in Maliana wanted removed went in a matter of weeks," Dario said. "But went where? The contractor who was paid by the government claimed the stuff was safely disposed of. They never said how or where. And this being the new Timor, no one bothered to ask." He thrust his hands in his pockets. "You know who the contractor was? I suggest you ask Juno."

"You're implying a lot," said Cordero. "Do you have proof?"

Dario merely scoffed.

"Did anyone investigate what the trucks were doing going to the border?" Cordero asked.

Dario smiled.

"Like I said, this is the new Timor. The Timor of elected village heads with party affiliations all the way to the capital."

"So why are you telling me this?" Cordero asked.

"Because as I said, Juno is interested only in himself. He doesn't care about the people here. He hates it here. The reason he's running for re-election is he wants to convince the party leadership he'd be a good candidate for a higher position. In Liquica or Dili. And he'll do everything he can to get there. Think about it. Why is *his* son in the health clinic for drinking something that made him sick?"

"Do you have evidence that Juno is involved in a smuggling operation?" Cordero said.

"I don't need evidence. I know the man too well."

14

"We have two men out to discredit each other," said Cordero.

They were sitting in the police commander's office where Carter and Estefana had reported on their questioning of Juno Cabral, and Cordero had given an account of his conversation with Dario Freitas. It was very hot and the air was sticky with humidity.

Cordero stood up and walked to the air-conditioner. He was surprised to find it off and so he turned it on. Nothing happened. He banged on the side. The machine made no sound. He banged on the top.

"I've tried that," said Mateus. "It doesn't work."

Cordero ignored the police commander and banged a third time on the front of the machine. That didn't work either. He slumped back down into his chair and wiped sweat from around his neck.

Mateus was drumming his fingers on the desk.

"Their mutual dislike is long standing," he said.

"Why?" asked Cordero.

Mateus shifted his weight.

"Dario sees himself as the rightful traditional authority in Balibo because his father was a noble," he said. "Juno is a product of the new system introduced when East Timor became independent. Village heads are now elected. So there's competition there."

"That's it?"

"No."

Cordero waited.

"What else?" he asked when Mateus didn't elaborate.

Mateus leaned back in his chair.

"Did you happen to meet his daughter Marquita?" he asked.

"As a matter of fact, I did. I talked to her. Nice girl," said Cordero.

Mateus nodded.

"She's Dario's only child," he said. "Not what you'd expect of a traditional Timorese right? Usually, they'd have ten kids. Maybe more."

Mateus rubbed a hand under his chin. Cordero leaned forward in his chair the better to concentrate on what the commander was saying.

"They had a boy also—Angelino," Mateus continued. "He died some years ago. Car accident on the road to Maliana. Next Dario's wife Agueda developed some kind of condition that prevented her having more children. So Marquita is the only one they have. Dario worships her."

"I don't see why that—" Cordero began but Mateus held up a hand to indicate he hadn't yet finished.

"I'm getting to it," he said. "Marquita would be ten or eleven years old now. I'm not sure which. But about 18 months ago she complained to Dario that Juno's son Arturo had"— he paused and shot a glance at Carter and Estefana —"touched her."

"Touched her how?" Carter asked.

"Under her skirt," Mateus said. He waved a hand around at nothing in particular. "Timorese tend to start young, but even so, that is very young. Dario was outraged. He went to see Juno to have Arturo punished. Juno wouldn't hear it. He defended his son and said Marquita must be lying. That only made things worse."

"When I told him Arturo was in the health clinic he didn't sound too upset," Cordero said and bunched his lips in thought.

"No, he wouldn't be," said Mateus. "Dario came here and made a complaint. Well what could I do? Marquita said one thing—or rather Dario did because his daughter wouldn't talk about it with anyone—and Arturo said another. No hard evidence either way.

I tried to get Dario and Juno to talk through the whole business but they refused. Ever since they've been at each other's throats."

"Okay," said Cordero. "That could explain a lot. Aside from that, what about the other things Dario said about Juno switching sides to advance his own interests?"

"Oh, Juno is an opportunist," said Mateus. "No question there. That doesn't make him unique. Take Dario. This burial business with his father has been delayed and delayed in order to draw the biggest crowd he can impress."

The light was fading in the room as the sun sunk behind a line of clouds on the western horizon. Mateus switched on his desk lamp.

"What do you make of the suggestion that Juno was involved in a scheme to dump Indonesian-era pesticides somewhere along the border?" Cordero asked.

The police commander came forward over his desk.

"When he became village head he promised many things," he said. "One was a clean-up of Balibo with volunteers he said he'd organise. The clean-up happened—it just didn't last. Another was a second full time nurse at the health clinic. Well you've seen that he managed to secure that. He talked a lot about improving the roads around here. That was a popular idea except it's not something that can be done at a village level. Trucks off toward the border? I don't know too much about that. It's certainly an isolated area with few inhabitants. So a dumping operation there is plausible but I've never heard of anything like that. I do remember a truck got bogged there and we had to send an officer to organize the locals to dig it out."

"What was the truck doing there?" Cordero asked.

"The driver said he was taking road construction materials to Leohitu. He didn't say what materials or who he was taking them to."

"*Was* he delivering road construction materials?"

Mateus shrugged.

"We didn't follow that up. Why would we? The problem was to get the truck out of the mud and on its way. He'd managed to get lost though. He'd left the road to Leohitu and wound up in the scrub."

"Do you know anything about the pesticide thing?" asked Carter.

Mateus raised a hand as if to say 'Not much'.

"Only that the Indonesians used a lot of it. They wanted to develop East Timor into a food bowl. And the locals hated pesticides. They wanted to continue with traditional farming practices. So when the Indonesians left, yes, there were stocks left over here. Some of the large farms and plantations the Indonesians had created used them for a while but in time most of that was discontinued. I don't know what happened to any leftover stocks. Nothing to do with the police."

"Right," began Cordero. "Consider this. Juno worked for the Indonesians which means he could still have connections with people on the other side of the border. He's up for re-election which means he's got a reason to want to get people onside and handing out free liquor could be a way to do that. And it's his son lying in the health clinic having drunk some of the stuff. That's suggestive."

Mateus nodded.

"Except you don't win votes by poisoning voters," he said.

"True," Cordero conceded, which weakened his suggestion.

"Any update on the boy?" Carter enquired.

"Not that I've heard," Mateus said.

He picked up a sheet of paper and passed it to her.

"My counterpart in Atambua faxed me this a little while ago," he said.

What he'd handed over was a copy of a rap sheet, written in Bahasa Indonesian, and bearing the grainy mugshot of a disheveled man listed as Faisal Jollo.

"Our dead guy?" Carter offered.

"Yes."

Carter inspected the sheet again.

"I can't read Bahasa," she said.

"No," said Mateus as Carter handed the sheet to Estefana who scanned it briefly and passed it on to Cordero. "It says he was convicted of smuggling kerosene across the border. Twice that they know of. Spent two years in prison in Kupang. He's from a village outside Atambua originally. Closer to the border. As far as they know, he went there to live when he was released. I've asked Border Patrol for any information they may have on him. Contacts over here in East Timor and such."

"So his background adds to the suspicion he was smuggling something across the border when he died," said Carter. "And since he died from methanol poisoning that something is likely to be a batch of toxic liquor."

"It's gone from possible to highly probable," agreed Mateus.

"If that's true, and if it's Juno Cabral behind it, surely he'd know not to distribute it now his son's seriously ill," said Carter.

"It could still be *Senyor* Dario behind things," Estefana said. "As *maun* said, there are two men competing for influence not just one."

"You don't impress your kinfolk by poisoning them either," Mateus said to Estefana. "Dario would also know by now the liquor is toxic."

"Either of them could think that Arturo was unlucky and drank from a bad bottle," Cordero suggested. "So the rest of the stuff could still be pushed."

"What about the dead guy out on the border?" said Carter. "He wasn't drinking from the same bottle as Arturo so it's clearly not just one bad bottle."

"We're assuming it is Dario or Juno," said Mateus. "It could be someone else. We just don't know."

"Well I say again that we've got to put a stop to all the social gatherings coming up," said Cordero. "The market, the cockfight, the Freitas burial ceremonies. There must have been a hundred people I saw out there at Dario's place. More are coming. A lot of the men will find their way to the cockfight. It's all too risky!"

"Look, we've been through this," said Carter. "I don't like it anymore than you do. But I've seen what toxic liquor can do. I've seen kids lose their parents and parents lose their kids. I've seen people who weren't killed probably wish they had been because their kidneys are shot and they're on dialysis every couple of days. How close is your nearest dialysis machine?" she asked. No one answered. "Thought so," she said. "So you don't want this stuff to go underground until the focus of the police shifts someplace else."

"Because the stuff won't go away. It'll resurface, you can bet on that, and folks'll end up just as dead only with no one taking much notice because the problem surfaces here and there over time."

Cordero opened his mouth to respond but the police commander cut him off.

"As you say, *mana*, we've been through this and nobody's canceling anything," he said. "I've arranged for officers to attend the market and the cockfight and three to go to Gaspa's funeral on duty but out of uniform. They'll appear to be merely paying their respects to the old man. They've been instructed on what to look for. Another two officers will attend in uniform. Any more than that in uniform might raise questions. I've put Officer Edi Sobado in charge of coordinating the surveillance at Dario's. Of course, the four of us will also attend each event."

"I don't like it," said Cordero. "I don't like it at all."

"You don't have to," Carter countered. "You just have to fall in with the plan."

Cordero stood and made to leave.

"Where are you going?" Carter asked.

"I want to have a talk with Father Francedez," Cordero said.

"Then you shouldn't waste time," said Mateus. "He conducts a novena on Friday nights," he said, referring to a Catholic devotional service. "It's only a small gathering of older parishioners and so he starts early but you should still catch him if you hurry."

"I'm cooking dinner again tonight, *maun*," said Estefana.

"Well, expect me in a little while," he said and tossed Estefana the keys to his vehicle. "Take the SUV. I'll walk back to the guesthouse."

15

Father Francedez was cleaning his reading glasses when he opened the door of his residence to Cordero. Beside the presbytery where he lived was the parish church—which was dedicated to Saint Anthony. It was an impressive structure with a high bell tower complementing the solid concrete nave. By comparison the presbytery next door was small in size and purely functional in design.

"*Bonoitre,*" the priest said, offering a good night greeting with a note of curiosity in his tone.

"*Bonoitre, amu,*" Cordero replied. "My name is Vincintino Cordero. I'm a police investigator. I wonder if I might have a few minutes of your time."

"A police investigator! Oh dear. So this is not a pastoral call?" the priest said.

"No, it's not," said Cordero. "I'm just after a little information. I won't take too much of your time."

"Well you'd best come in," Father Francedez said. "This way please," and he swept his hand toward a small front room just inside the doorway.

The room was dominated by a large wooden table that served as a desk. Behind the desk was a hard-backed chair and in front were two mismatched easy chairs, the stuffing from one popping out from the edge of the cushion that formed the seat. On top of the desk Cordero noticed a Catholic missal which contained the prayers and rites a priest would use over the course of a year, a notepad and pen, and an assortment of official-looking correspondence piled up to the side.

On the wall behind the desk was a framed picture of the late Pope John Paul II around which a small Timorese flag had been draped. On the opposite wall was a photograph of the bishop of Maliana together with one that, from a quick glance, Cordero took to be a much younger Father Francedez at his ordination to the priesthood. The only other furnishing in the room was a small glassed-in cabinet that contained about a dozen leather-bound books of a weighty religious nature.

"Please, take a seat," Father Francedez said, sitting himself behind his desk. "How may I be of help?"

The sun had dropped below the horizon and the room was darkening although the priest made no move to switch on a light. Cordero settled himself in the better of the easy chairs, adjusting to the signature smell of candle wax and spent incense that he remembered from every presbytery he had ever visited.

"Earlier today I noticed you talking to the one they call Bobu," Cordero said. "The fellow who plays the guitar. You were outside *Senyor* Feng's store. I was inside talking to Feng. It looked to me like you know Bobu well. I was wondering what you could tell me about him."

"Is he in any trouble?" asked the priest, coming forward over his desk.

"No, no, nothing like that. We have reason to suspect a supply of liquor has been smuggled across the border and we're just trying to get a sense of how everyone fits in here. In Balibo and the border hamlets I mean. I'm from Dili, you see. I'm not familiar with this place or its people. I'm interested in this Bobu because he doesn't fit in, yet seems to know a lot of people here."

Cordero smiled his best reassuring smile and waited while Father Francedez processed what that rather vague and superficial statement could mean.

"You do know Bobu?" Cordero said to elicit a response. "Well, I mean."

"Oh yes I know him," the priest said, adjusting his reading glasses. "Very well in fact." A glint came into his eye. "No, he doesn't quite fit in as you say."

Father Francedez placed his hands together on the table.

"He's been in prison you know," the priest began.

• • •

"I called my mother, *mana*," Estefana said as she chopped eggplant for the dinner she was preparing with Carter assisting her once more.

"Oh yeah, good. How is she?" Carter asked.

"She has a bad foot, *mana*."

"A bad foot?"

"Yes. It is swollen and she doesn't know why. She said she is going to see a doctor about it. She thinks it could be an infection."

Estefana put the eggplant pieces to one side and placed a mixture of fresh herbs in front of her to rip and chop.

"Is she in any pain?" Carter asked.

"No," said Estefana. "Not really. She never complains so I'm not sure. She says she is worried that it could be something to do with the veins in her leg or maybe her kidneys."

"Well, it's good she's getting it checked," said Carter. "I hope you said hello from me."

"No, *mana*. I didn't say that because you hadn't told me to say that. I didn't tell you I was calling her."

"Right. Okay," said Carter, wiping her cheek with the back of her forearm. "Can you pass me another onion to cut, please?"

Estefana handed across two white onions. She raked the herbs into a bowl and took a red capsicum to slice.

"I called to ask about the Wehali taboo language," Estefana explained. "Remember me saying that I think *Senyora* Tavares was talking in taboo language when she told me about the coconut becoming bitter?"

"Yeah," said Carter vaguely.

"Well, there are Wehali living in Suai and I thought perhaps my mother would know what the reference to a coconut meant."

"And did she?"

"No. But she said she would ask. She knows some of the people who were relocated to Suai by the Indonesians. They didn't want to go back when we became independent, you see. They preferred it here."

"Okay," said Carter. "That's good."

Carter wiped an eye with the back of one hand, took a deep breath and wiped the other eye.

"Are you alright, *mana*?" Estefana asked.

"Yeah. Onions," said Carter. "Cutting them always makes my eyes water."

"My mother taught me to rub the knife with a lemon before I cut the onions," Estefana said.

"I might try that," Carter replied. "Except we have no lemons here now."

They finished preparing the vegetables for cooking.

"I think I will go to the novena tonight, *mana*."

"The novena?"

"Yes. The novena the police commander said Father Francedez conducts every Friday night. I will go and pray that there is nothing seriously wrong with my mother's veins or kidneys and for her foot to heal. I won't go until we finish cooking, of course."

"Mateus said the novena starts early," said Carter. "Will you make it?"

"Well, *maun* has gone to speak to the priest before the novena so I have time. But if I don't, I'll just say a prayer before the statue of the Virgin Mary."

"Would you like me to go with you?"

"No, *mana*, thank you," said Estefana. "I would rather go alone and I won't be gone long."

"So it'll just be me and Cordero here," Carter said and bit her lip. "Are you sure you don't want me to go with you?"

"I'm sure, *mana*. Thank you for the offer."

"I'll put some of the food aside for you," said Carter.

"Thank you."

"Take the SUV," said Carter. "It'll save time."

"But if *maun*—"

"Don't worry about *maun*," Carter stopped her. "Leave him to me."

• • •

"Prison you say. Please go on," Cordero urged the priest.

He crossed his legs and wrapped his hands around the raised knee. He was interested to hear more. Very interested. Father Francedez removed his glasses, squeezed the bridge of his nose, and blinked twice to sharpen his focus.

"Yes," he said. "Prison. That small Gleno prison in Ermera. Apparently, he'd stolen something when he lived in Dili." The priest shook his head slightly. "I don't know the details. I was told he couldn't find work to support himself and his girlfriend and in desperation—well, if you're a policeman you know how it is. Whatever he stole, or whoever he stole from, he was sentenced to three years. After a year or so he broke out and so the time he had to serve was doubled."

"So what's he doing here? I take it he hasn't escaped from prison again."

The priest chuckled at that.

"He came here for his daughter. She's the reason he broke out of prison the first time. To see her. I wouldn't blame him for that. He's not a bad person, really."

"What's the daughter doing here?"

"Fabio's—that's his real name—Fabio's girlfriend came originally from Lolitu, and she moved back there from Dili to live with her mother when Fabio went to prison."

"So you met Bobu—I mean Fabio—through her?"

"Not *met* exactly. Rather I began to know of him. When she brought the daughter to be baptized here in the church. Fabio was in Gleno."

"What's her name?"

"The daughter?"

"No, the mother."

"Rosaria. I think the surname she gave was Maros but I'd have to check on the baptismal certificate. It wasn't Fabio's surname. They weren't married in any official sense."

The priest stared out the window.

"How did you get to know Fabio then?" Cordero asked.

"Following the baptism, Rosario came every month or so to dictate letters to Fabio," the priest said. "She'd never gone to school, you see, and so she couldn't write. Fabio had gone to school and could read and write. Now you would know that there is no postal service to speak of in Timor. I have connections though, through the Church." He flicked a finger toward the correspondence on his desk. "So Rosaria would dictate the letters to me and I would arrange to get them to Fabio in prison. Sometimes he would write to her but he always complained that he wasn't given much paper to write on in prison."

"And these letters—were they just a lover's chit-chat?" asked Cordero.

"More or less. She would always give an account of what was going on in Lolitu and Leohitu, who lived there, what they were doing, you know. I suppose she knew there wasn't much for Fabio to do in prison and so she wanted to provide as much information as she could." The priest smiled. "I don't mind telling you sometimes writing the letters she'd dictate would take up most of my afternoon. Even so...."

"Where is Rosaria now?"

Father Francedez spread his hands.

"I heard she went across the border with a man from West Timor."

"And left her daughter here?"

"Rosaria never fitted in here. She was what some call a 'free spirit'. She wore Dili clothes, not the clothes of a woman from the border region. She refused to work in the garden plots or pluck chickens like other women out that way. She had no motorcycle, but she would arrange a lift with someone every once in a while and come to Balibo to make some money cleaning at the school or working at the market." He wriggled in his chair. "The worst of it was she spoke her mind— whoever she was talking to, and some people didn't like that. At first, she'd say to me that people in Lolitu and Leohitu would ignore her, like they just wanted her to go away. Before long she said they started criticizing her and telling her to do this and not do that. Toward the end she said they were threatening her.

"Threatening her?" Cordero asked. The priest ignored the question.

"She was quite young. And you know what young people are like. Perhaps she left because she was scared. Perhaps she was bored." He shrugged. "Who would know?"

There was a knock on the door.

"Come," said the priest, and a nun popped her head into the room.

"People are arriving for the novena, *amu*," said the nun. "Your vestments have been laid out."

"I'll be there in a moment," the priest said. "Thank you."

Cordero waited until the nun had gone.

"You said Rosaria was being threatened," he said.

"That's what she told me," Father Francedez said. "But you know how the young can exaggerate."

The priest stood to conclude the questioning and Cordero did as well.

"I hope I've been some help," Father Francedez said.

"You have," replied Cordero. "Thank you for your time."

As he rose to leave, Cordero admired the picture of Pope John Paul II.

"A hero of yours?" Cordero asked, gesturing to the picture.

"A hero to all Timorese," said the priest gazing up at the picture. "Do you remember his visit?"

"It was 1989, wasn't it? My family had moved to Australia and I was just a teenager," Cordero said. "Had other things on my mind, you might say. I recall hearing about the visit, nothing much more."

"I remember it well," said the priest. "I was in the seminary. The Pope flew in to Dili from Jakarta. Every country he visited, he would kiss the ground as he stepped off his plane out of respect for the country he was visiting. Every *unique* country."

"Yes, I remember he did that," said Cordero.

"Well he had already done that when he arrived in Jakarta," the priest went on. "If he did it here, he'd be suggesting East Timor was a country in its own right and not part of Indonesia. Everyone at the airport was waiting to see what he would do. The Indonesians would be furious if he kissed the ground on arrival. They made threats, you know, about what would happen to the Church in Indonesia if he did. Even so, Timorese longed for him to recognize our plight and kiss the ground whatever the consequences."

He took a deep breath that raised his shoulders slightly.

"Now at the airport, he didn't kiss the ground. But at an outdoor Mass he celebrated later in front of a hundred thousand Timorese he kissed a crucifix that had been placed on a small cushion on the steps of the altar. It wasn't something he usually did." He turned suddenly to face Cordero. "Do you see the genius in that? The Indonesians couldn't complain because he hadn't kissed the ground but to all those people watching on from a distance it appeared that he had."

He smiled remembering the moment.

"Sometimes what we appear to do," the priest said, "is much more important than what we actually do."

16

The light was fading even on the high mountain tops in Indonesian West Timor to the southwest. The air was still sticky with humidity and frogs had begun their mating calls in the grounds outside the guesthouse.

Inside Cordero was loosening his shirt as he settled into his chair. He'd offered to help serve but the food, plates, and utensils were already laid out on the table. They started on the dish of stir-fried tofu and vegetables exchanging small talk as they ate. The food was tasty, very tasty, and Cordero sat back after eating with a satisfied grin on his face.

"That was a great meal," he said. "I don't know how Estefana does it."

"I helped," said Carter. "It's all in the sauce you prepare. And that means the herbs and spices you mix in. Estefana is teaching me. Her mother showed her how to make different sauces."

"Well you can thank her mother for me," Cordero said.

"And?"

"And Estefana," he added. "And you, of course."

"Estefana's going to make me such a great cook before long that I can't see myself ever enjoying frozen meals in the microwave when I get home," Carter said.

She rose and collected the plates and forks. She put them in a plastic tray off to the side of their table for washing up later. Leftover food she spooned into a serving bowl for Estefana and covered it with a clean plate.

Cordero checked this way and that around the room.

"Do you know where that bottle of gin is that Brooks left?" he asked. "I feel like a drink after such a delicious dinner."

"You read my mind," Carter replied. "I'll get it."

She went into the bedroom she shared with Estefana.

"I didn't want any trouble with that cranky caretaker," she called back from the bedroom, "so I kept the gin under the bed here out of sight just in case she mounted a patrol."

She returned with the gin and a bottle of tonic and lined up two cups side by side on the table. She prepared two generous servings of gin, sat down across from Cordero and handed him a cup. They both took a drink and he coughed at the strength of the mixture.

"I'm glad this stuff's not toxic," he said.

"Me too," she agreed and quickly finished what was left in her cup without a second thought. "Tell me more about what you learned from the priest," she said.

He wriggled into a more comfortable position as she refilled her cup and topped up his although it had barely been touched.

"Well, for starters, Bobu went to prison for theft and his sentence was extended because he tried to escape."

Carter whistled at that and drank some more gin.

"That wouldn't have been so hard to do. Timorese remember the brutality of Indonesian prisons and so our approach is a little more humane. Bobu was put in a small prison in Ermera. I wouldn't be surprised if he was let out each day to work in the coffee plantations nearby. He probably just wandered off one day and didn't come back. May not even have planned it." He took another sip of gin. "It happens."

"Anything else?"

"He met his girlfriend—Rosaria—in Dili. When he was sent to prison, she came home here because she had a small child and no other options. That's why Bobu stole in the first place apparently. To provide for them. So Rosaria would get a ride into Balibo when she could to work in the market or to dictate a letter to Father Francedez who'd arrange for it to be passed on to Bobu in prison. Rosaria never learned to read or write. Bobu can do both."

Carter nodded slightly.

"Apparently she never readjusted to local expectations and was regarded as something of a troublemaker," Cordero continued. "Story is she ran off eventually with a fellow from West Timor."

"And left her daughter?"

"Well," said Cordero. "It happens."

"It happens alright," she said. "My own mother did that, remember?"

He remembered only too well her telling him once that her mother had walked out on her father when she was about five years old. He could see the memory was painful and didn't comment.

"And the priest knows all this how?" she asked, sipping from her cup.

"The priest became acquainted with Rosaria through all the letters she dictated to him. When Bobu was released and came for his daughter, Father Francedez was the only person he actually had any kind of connection to—daughter aside."

"Yes, the daughter," Carter said as much to herself as to him.

"So Bobu and the priest just got on, I guess," Cordero said.

"There's something about that girl," Carter said and lowered her eyes to the table.

"Which girl, Bobu's?"

"Yeah. Bobu's.

"Something? Like what?"

She drained her second cup.

"It hit me when I first set eyes on her. I couldn't work out why. Then I saw her outside the store." She looked up. "Something about her reminds me of Bec—my sister. I don't know. How could that be? She's Timorese. It's weird."

She poured herself another gin and drank greedily from it, coughing this time once it had gone down. She reached for the bottle and stared at her reflection in the glass. Cordero sensed that it was best not say anything about the girl or Bec or to comment on Carter's drinking.

"So do you think he's involved with the liquor and the smuggling?" she said following a long silence. "This Bobu character, I mean, not the priest."

Cordero lifted a hand as if to say 'Who knows?'

"Father Francedez thinks Bobu is a decent guy who genuinely loves his daughter," Cordero said. "He says Bobu came here to take care of her when her mother left." He fiddled with his cup before draining it. "You do meet some interesting characters in prison though and he may still be in contact with some of them."

Carter topped up her cup and refilled his, which was now empty. Close to half the bottle was already gone. Cordero's expression betrayed a little uneasiness.

"What is it?" she asked.

"I may have to stay here tonight too," he said, and waved a hand over his cup. "The gin, you know. These drinks are strong."

"There's plenty of room," said Carter. "Is that all you're so deep in thought about?"

He pulled a face as though trying to avoid an argument.

"Well?" she pressed him.

"I still think we should've shut down the cockfight and the burial ceremonies tomorrow," he said. "I've a bad feeling about letting these things go on."

She ran her thumb under her top lip. He noticed how flushed her face was becoming. He also noticed how she was beginning to slump a little over the table. It was hot, she was probably tired, and she was drinking a lot and fast.

"It's not the cockfight or the burial we need to shut down. It's the smuggling operation and the supply of toxic liquor," she said. "Letting these things go ahead gives us a chance to do that."

He eased back and played with the cup in his hands.

"What if the liquor is not even intended for distribution this weekend?" he said.

"In that case, there'd be no reason to have shut these things down," she replied. She stifled a burp. "And we'd have to work on Plan B."

"Plan B? What's that?"

She drained her cup and poured yet another.

"Plan B?" echoed Carter, slowly standing the bottle back on the table. "Plan B is to work out another plan if Plan A comes to nothing," she said.

They sat without speaking, him sipping at his gin. She edged back in her chair.

There was a 'pop' as the light bulb above them blew. The room was only lit by a second light at the end of the hallway and a weak, watery glow enveloped the room. As she looked up at the ceiling the half light played on her profile which he couldn't help but admire.

"Shit," he said, to get his mind off that, and he stared at the light fitting as well.

"There's a spare," she said. "I noticed it in the cupboard yesterday."

She rose a little unsteadily, went to the cupboard, and felt around inside for the bulb.

"Are you okay there?" he asked.

"Fine," she said.

"You want me to come over?"

"There's the little sucker," she said, ignoring his question.

She came back and dragged her chair just to the side of Cordero.

"I can do it," he said, mindful of how much she'd drunk.

"So can I," she replied.

"You've had—" he began.

"Do you know how many light bulbs I've changed in my life, Cordero?" she asked, pointing the new bulb at him. "I'll tell you. This'll be number eleven. Or twelve. Can't remember exactly. After my father was killed, my stepmother made me do all the chores around the house that he used to do. Sweeping, mopping, taking the trash out. Changing light bulbs was the least of the things she made me do. It's one of the reasons I left home when I did." She rubbed roughly at her nose. "It didn't feel like home anymore. It felt like a labour camp."

She handed him the good bulb and climbed onto the chair.

"So there's nothing you can tell me about goddam light bulbs," she added.

She reached up to the socket in such a way that her blouse crept up her chest exposing her stomach directly in front of

Cordero's face. He couldn't help but notice how taut and flat her stomach was and how unblemished her skin.

The blown bulb was hot to the touch and she swore and blew on her fingers to cool them. The chair bobbled.

"Why don't you let me?" he said.

"Just be patient," she said.

She dug into the pocket of her trousers for a kerchief. That pushed her belt down further exposing more of her stomach and the top of black panties. She wrapped the kerchief around the blown bulb and twisted it free. She handed it to Cordero who juggled it due to the heat before letting it down on the table.

"Hand me the bulb," she said.

He did as she asked, after which he held his hands either side of her body without touching her, without her knowing, just in case she slipped and fell.

She fiddled with the bulb for a few seconds and finally managed to set it. The light came on and the room brightened if only a little.

"There!" she said. When she glanced down she noticed Cordero had turned his face to the far wall. She remembered what Estefana had said about him not looking at her. She dropped her arms.

"Something over there amuse you?" she taunted him. "Jesus maybe?"

"Um, no."

"Friend of yours is he? You're showing him a lot of interest."

"It's just—"

"Just what?" she asked, enjoying his embarrassment.

"You shouldn't make fun of things like that," he said.

"It's just a picture, Cordero."

"It's what it signifies," he said. "Who it signifies."

"He's not here," she replied.

He shifted uncomfortably.

"You think he is? Is that it? Maybe I should make him a gin and tonic," she said. "What do you think?"

He looked up at the picture and then at her. He was becoming more uncertain of the situation. He passed a hand across his face and sniffed. She stepped down off the chair and scraped it across the floor to where she could sit across from him. Her blouse still hung over her belt.

She checked her cup. Took another sip. They were silent a moment. She studied his embarrassment.

"Do you like ice-cream?" she asked.

"What?"

"Ice-cream. You know, chocolate, vanilla, strawberry. Do you like it?"

"Sure I do."

"On a hot day, if you were wandering along the seafront in Dili and you felt like an ice-cream but had no money, would you avoid looking at the ice-cream vendor?"

"I don't know where—"

"Answer the question," she said. "Would you avoid looking at the thing you…let's say desired?"

"Well, maybe I would," he said. "I haven't thought much about it."

She studied him, even though her eyelids were growing heavy now.

"Let me ask you something else," she said.

"Ask? Sure," he replied.

"It's kind of personal," she said.

He drank what remained of the gin in his cup, wiped his mouth and smiled awkwardly.

"Sure," he repeated. "Ask away."

She leaned in on the table.

"What do you think of me?" she said.

He fidgeted with his hands on the table and stared into his empty cup.

"Think of you?"

"That's right, think of me."

"I think that…you're good at what you do," he answered.

"I don't mean that," she said.

He fidgeted some more.

"Well, I think you're a good person too," he said.

"I don't mean that either," she said.

"Well I don't know what you want me to say," Cordero said.

She tilted her head to the side. Her eyes were clearly glazed.

"Do you find me attractive?" she asked.

He stared at her before opening his mouth to speak.

"*Mana! Maun!* I'm back," said Estefana coming down the hall. "I missed the novena but I said my prayers for my mother. Now I'm hungry."

Neither of them had broken eye contact and neither spoke.

"Did I interrupt something?" Estefana asked, puzzled by the look on their faces.

"Not, not at all," slurred Carter. "We were just about to, to—"

She opened a hand as though the gesture would complete the statement.

"To what, *mana?*" Estefana asked.

"Pack it in and go off to bed," said Carter.

• • •

They could hear the rattle of a motorcycle approaching although there were several belonging to people coming and going to Leohitu and Lolitu and they paid it no mind. It was a dark night, only a shadowy half moon trying without success to break through the thin layer of cloud blown in from the across the border. Inside the sacred house they sat in the dim, flickering light provided by the fire in the cauldron.

The sacred house had been built on stilts that rose out of the ground more than the height of a man. The structure atop the stilts took the shape of a huge cow's bell—one small room with a top-heavy peaked roof adorned each side with a goat's skull rather than the buffalo skulls more prosperous communities could afford. The walls were bamboo, the canopy a thick grey thatch. There were no windows or slits, only a single doorway at the front and a ladder led from it to the ground. Every time they entered, they'd raise the ladder so that their deliberations could be conducted without interruption or intrusion.

They were sullen and pensive. Each wore a necklace of needle-sharp eel teeth and their bodies, naked to the waist, were smeared with brown and red and yellow clays and dotted with vegetable dyes. Their shadows, which the flames in the cauldron projected onto the walls, resembled giant shadowy creatures that could have emerged from beneath the slime of the river.

"It would have been better if you'd waited for drier weather," complained Rodrigo. "The whole hut would have gone up in flames and burnt down quickly."

Fidalgo's eyes remained fixed on the floor.

"I didn't want to hurt anyone," he said in a flat voice. "It was just to scare them."

Helio was the first to notice that a motorcycle had pulled up just outside the sacred house, its engine running. He shifted slightly the better to catch the sound.

"To scare them," grumbled Rodrigo. "Lot of good that would do."

"Fidalgo de Queiroz!" yelled a voice from below. "Come out here you bastard!"

Helio looked at Fidalgo who sat upright, jerking his head this way and that, his eyes wide open in fear.

"Come on Fidalgo! I know you're in there!" the voice called.

Helio's son, João, started trembling. The old man put his hand on the boy's thigh to calm him.

"Come out here, you bastard!" demanded the voice.

"It's the clown!" Rodrigo said.

"Bobu?" repeated Fidalgo.

There was no way Bobu could climb into the sacred room. The stilts had been planed smooth and offered no foot or hand holes. Even standing on the saddle of his motorcycle, Bobu could only reach the bottom of the doorway which had been jammed shut. He paced up and down in his anger.

"What will we do?" Fidalgo asked. No one ventured an answer.

A rock hit the door and the thud echoed around the inside of the room.

"Come out you bastard!" Bobu cried.

Another thud as a second rock hit the door, followed by a third. Rodrigo sprang to his feet and rummaged through a bundle in a corner of the room. He returned waving around an old *katana*—the curved, single-edged sword favoured by Japanese troops who had occupied Timor during World War II. It was now regarded as *sacra*—a sacred object—because it had been seized by a local Timorese resistance fighter and used to kill the officer who carried it.

"I'll handle this!" declared Rodrigo, striding toward the doorway.

"I'll come too!" said Fidalgo, although he remained seated holding his bad leg. "We'll demand that he leaves us alone."

"Demand be damned!" Rodrigo called back. "He's a threat to all of us. This has to end! I'll take care of him I tell you and we won't be bothered by him anymore!"

Bang—as yet a fourth rock hit. One of the eel skins dropped from its place on the near wall.

"No!" said Helio, standing and grabbing Rodrigo by the arm. "You two have had your chance and it hasn't worked. Leave this to me."

Bobu was about to hurl a fifth rock when the door creaked open. Helio stood in the shadow of the entranceway and glared down at Bobu.

"Put that rock down!" he ordered. "What do you want?"

Bobu kept his grip on the rock but lowered his hand.

"I don't want you, Helio," said Bobu. "Not just yet. Right now I want that crippled bastard, Fidalgo."

"Why?"

"Why?" repeated Bobu, opening and closing his fingers on the rock. "I'm sure you know why. The bastard tried to burn down my hut. He could've killed my daughter if she'd been asleep. He would've killed Umbelina except someone dragged her free!"

"Umbelina?"

"My daughter's grandmother. Don't waste my time pretending you don't know!" Bobu raised the rock and tried to see around Helio. "Fidalgo!" he shouted.

"Who dragged the grandmother free?" Helio asked.

"What does it matter who it was?" asked Bobu. "Get out of my way!"

"If it doesn't matter, tell me who it was," said Helio.

"A neighbour's boy. That's who. He's the one who said that dog Fidalgo de Queiroz lit the thatch and skulked away like the coward that he is!"

"And you believe a boy?" Helio said.

"Yes, I believe *that* boy. Unlike your lot he's my friend. You've all been at me ever since I came here," said Bobu. "You want me gone. Well fuck you. Fuck all of you! I'll go when I want. You hear me!"

"Leave now," ordered Helio.

"Fuck you!" yelled Bobu.

Rodrigo stood behind Helio.

"Get out of here!" he yelled at Bobu.

"Who's that?" asked Bobu. "Is that Rodrigo? Is that the miserable Rodrigo Duarte? You come down here and I'll take care of you too!"

Helio elbowed Rodrigo back.

"I told you I'd handle this!" he said tetchily. He turned back to Bobu. "You've made your point," he shouted down. "Fidalgo is not coming out. I've told him to stay where he is. Leave now!"

"You're a bastard too, Helio! You're all bastards. You never liked me singing, dancing, laughing because you lot love misery. What is it they call you? Yam-eaters. That's it. Miserable fucking yam-eaters."

Bobu threw the rock he was clutching off to the side and mounted his motorcycle.

"This isn't over! You hear me!" he declared. "I'd gladly wait here all night and day until Fidalgo shows his ugly face but I've got to prepare for a job in Balibo tomorrow night. They're putting Gaspa Freitas in the ground. If it was up to me, it'd be Fidalgo! But I'm not done here. You can count on that. Tell that bastard. I'm not done yet!"

He revved the motorcycle hard to sound his anger. "I may start playing with fire myself, Helio," Bobu shouted. "I may decide to burn down this fucking sacred house of yours! How would you like that, Helio?"

With a spray of mud he spun the bike and spluttered off. Helio watched him go, shut the door to the sacred house, and moved closer to the cauldron around which the others were now standing.

With all the commotion they'd let the fire die down and it was so dark inside the sacred house that it was hard to make out their individual shapes.

"He thinks we want him gone because he laughs and sings?" It was the voice of Fidalgo. "He's crazy. It's not about that at all."

"How did he recognize me?" said Rodrigo stepping forward from the cauldron. "I've never spoken to him. It's like he has special powers. What are we going to do?"

Helio ignored the question, sat, and rubbed his thighs.

"I'll handle this," he said.

The others looked at each other and then at him.

"What will you do?" asked Fidalgo.

"It was my son who was killed," Helio said. "I will extract revenge for Osorio so that his spirit will not roam in anger. I will protect this sacred house. And I will put an end to all of this trouble."

17

"*Uma aluga kuartu nee la'os ita nia uma!*"
The crusty old caretaker was castigating Cordero, saying the guesthouse was not his own personal property, his own home.

"You can't come in here whenever you like!" she went on. "Who do you think you are? You must ask my permission."

"*Senyora*, I only—"

"Don't interrupt me young man!" the woman said. "If I give you permission you have to pay. You think everything is free to take as you want?"

"I—"

"Who knows what you are doing in here with those women!" she broke in. "One is young enough to be your daughter and the other is a foreigner. You should be ashamed of yourself. You know what they say about foreign women, don't you? I'm sure you do and I think that's why you're here!"

The shouting had woken Carter who drifted out of her room bleary-eyed, her hair tangled over sleepy eyes. She was wearing an FBI Academy T-shirt that came half way down her thighs and appeared to be the extent of her sleeping attire. The old woman let out an audible humph and glanced at Cordero as if to say 'See what I told you'.

"What's all the fuss about?" Carter asked in a husky voice.

"The landlady here is reprimanding me for staying another night without telling her," explained Cordero. "She's also asking for ten dollars and I only have five."

"Tell her to put it on my bill and keep your five," Carter said, passing a hand across her forehead and yawning. "You may need it some time."

Cordero did as he was told and the old woman issued another stern 'humph' and stormed out leaving the door ajar. She'd left the usual breakfast tray with fried eggs, bread rolls and coffee on the table although she'd only brought enough for two and made no mention of more for Cordero.

"I didn't sleep too well last night," said Carter pouring herself coffee. She held the jug up as an offer to Cordero.

"Please," he said.

"Why are you up so early?" she said, filling a cup for him.

Down the hall came the sound of roosters in neighbouring yards competing to outdo each other with their cock-a-doodle-do abilities.

"The oil," he said, reaching for the sugar.

"Oil?" she asked and yawned once more.

"Cooking oil, remember? I had to get it for my cousin's wife, Cipriana. She's doing a big cook-up today for some kind of gathering Moises is having tomorrow for the kids. I haven't been back since I bought it so I'll take it this morning before we get to work." He sugared his coffee, sampled the result, and downed it in one swig. "I'll be about twenty minutes."

"Don't rush," said Carter, knuckling her eyes. She slurped her coffee and considered the cold, dried-out eggs with little enthusiasm. "I sure won't."

• • •

Cordero drove slowly through the village. The sunlight was bright through widening breaks in the clouds and the day was heating up. It was market day and people were busy ferrying produce to the stalls and lighting fires to get BBQs going to cook chicken skewers and corn cobs. Through the driver's window he could hear the laughter of children and women shouting to their men to bring more produce, reposition tables, or lay out goods on the ground.

The colourful sights and raucous sounds were not enough to distract him from the events of the night before. Why had Carter asked him if he found her attractive? He did, of course. In fact, he found her very attractive. It wasn't just her physical appearance. It was the way she carried and conducted herself—carried with poise and confidence; conducted in a pragmatic, no-nonsense way. He liked that. He considered those the best qualities in Timorese women while the Western qualities Carter exhibited—brazenness, sassiness, cheekiness—he also found more than a little appealing.

Yet it was more than that. It was her sense of values. At heart she was a decent person—a very decent person—honest, trustworthy, and caring toward others.

Shit! He said to himself. *It sounds like I'm considering her for a job!*

He pulled up suddenly to let two young girls, arm-in-arm, cross the road. One was leading a goat tied to a length of rope.

He drove off and passed a boy not yet a teenager pushing a shoddy wooden cart piled high with coconuts into the center of the village. Another two boys, about the same age and each pushing similar carts, were emerging from a passageway between two cement block houses. Cordero thought nothing of them as he turned onto the gravel road that led to the where his cousin lived.

How could he explain what attracted him to Carter? He'd become used to Western women growing up in Australia. He wasn't troubled by their attitudes or behaviour even if both could jar at times with his own. He'd almost had an Australian girlfriend—Diana—who liked him. But being a member of the tiny East Timorese community in Australia he felt too self-conscious to do anything about it. With Carter he'd come—eventually—to feel relaxed around her, at ease with just being himself. He didn't have to pretend. That was something he hadn't felt with a Western woman before.

She *was* a Western woman, however. And he *was* a Timorese man. Culture and circumstance separated them however much their personalities might complement each other. Besides, she was in East Timor reluctantly—she'd even mentioned going home to the US when she was talking about preparing the meal last night.

So why had she asked if he found her attractive? And why did she not seem embarrassed by the question this morning? Was it because she'd drunk too much gin to remember the night before?

Probably, he thought.

On a downward bend in the gravel road to Moises' house, he almost ran into a young teenager struggling to push his cart of coconuts across the uneven surface of the road. The cart was made of packing crates and one wheel was slightly bigger than the other causing it to wobble as it went along. Cordero hit the brakes. The boy jumped clear of the SUV, the cart lopsiding in the process, and coconuts bounced out all over the road.

Cordero swore under his breath, pulled on his park brake, and stepped out to help regather the load.

"Don't you know to cross a road where you can see what's coming at you?" he said to the boy.

"Don't you know not to drive so fast?" the boy countered. He was wearing a grimy singlet and shorts smeared with grease, his legs just two stacks of thin bones trailing down to dirty bare feet.

"Respect your elders and don't talk back," Cordero said.

"What?" the boy asked, scratching his backside.

"Forget it and just be quiet," said Cordero.

They righted the cart and began to toss the coconuts into it. When the last of the coconuts had been retrieved, Cordero checked up and down the road where the coconuts had rolled.

"Where's your machete?" Cordero asked.

"What?" said the boy.

"Your machete," repeated Cordero. "How are you going to cut the coconuts so people can drink the water inside if you don't have a machete?"

The boy said nothing.

"Well?" Cordero persisted.

"I'll borrow one when I get there," the boy said.

"Get where?"

"The village, where else?" the boy said. He bent double to force his cart into motion, and started off.

"You mean the market?"

"Ah, yeah, the market," the boy said without conviction.

Cordero climbed into his vehicle and drove on. He tried to re-engage with his thoughts about Carter but was distracted by three more boys straining behind assorted carts full of coconuts. Just before he made the house where his cousin lived he noticed another boy pushing coconuts in the direction of the village. He stopped and watched him pass by, cut his engine and stepped out of the vehicle.

"Wait!" he shouted. "Hold on! Wait!"

The boy peered over his shoulder and kept moving.

"Wait!" Cordero repeated. "Stop!"

The boy slowed and Cordero caught up with him. He cast an eye over the cart and its coconuts. He couldn't see a machete or a knife of any kind.

"What's the matter with you?" the boy asked.

"I want to buy a coconut," Cordero said.

The boy stared at him, confused.

"What?"

Cordero pointed into the cart.

"I want to buy one," he repeated.

"They're not for sale," the boy said.

On the side of the road by a stand of bamboo two small children stood gawking at the exchange in silence. One chewed on the neck of a torn T-shirt, the other was busy picking his nose.

"What do you mean they're not for sale?" Cordero asked. "You're not pushing them around for the fun of it are you?"

"I mean I'm selling them later, not now," the boy said.

Cordero rifled through the contents of the cart, suspecting there might be more than coconuts to find inside. There wasn't.

"Why not sell me one now?" he asked. "What's the difference?"

"I don't have any change," the boy said.

"You don't know what sort of money I'm going to give you," said Cordero.

The boy said nothing and made to go on his way.

"Where's your knife to cut the coconuts?" Cordero asked.

The boy stopped, said nothing, and wiped his mouth with his fist.

"I asked you a question," Cordero said.

The boy sniffed and rubbed his nose with his other fist. The dust on his hands and the sweat on his face left streaks of grime across his cheeks.

"Why should I tell you anything?" he asked. "I don't know you."

"I'm a police investigator," Cordero said.

A little colour came into the boy's face.

"A police officer?" he said.

"A police *investigator*," Cordero repeated. "That means I can cause you a lot more trouble if you don't answer my questions."

The boy faced off up the road, avoiding eye contact.

"Don't have a knife," he said.

"How are you going to cut the coconuts?" Cordero asked.

The boy stared at the ground around his feet. He didn't answer.

"Well? Where are you going anyhow?" Cordero asked.

"To the village," the boy said as if it was obvious. "I told you."

"Where in the village?" Cordero asked.

The boy shrugged.

"Around, you know," he mumbled.

"What?"

"Said I'm going around," the boy said in a voice that sounded his annoyance.

"Meaning what?" Cordero asked.

"Meet my friends and decide where we go," he said.

"Lot of your friends selling coconuts today?" Cordero said.

"Lot of people coming to the village," the boy replied. "It's market day and there's a cockfight and a big burial this afternoon and one of those burial feasts tonight. Going to be hot too. People get thirsty."

Cordero studied the boy a moment longer then waved him on his way. He took three steps toward his vehicle when he noticed the two young bystanders staring at him.

"Boo," he sounded and pretended to lunge at them with his arms open.

They ran around behind the screen of bamboo and he could hear them giggling with excitement.

He felt a tinge of excitement too—enough that he forgot for the moment the implications of Carter's question to him the night before.

• • •

"I think I know how the liquor is going to be distributed," Cordero told Carter and Estefana when he'd returned from delivering the oil to his sister-in-law. The two were sitting at the table, the breakfast tray gone. Carter had managed somehow to wash and brush her hair and dress in jeans and a clean T-shirt and was much more lively and alert than she had been forty minutes earlier. Estefana, as usual, was neat and tidy and eager to get to work. She had dressed in casual attire to disguise the fact that she was a police officer in order to patrol incognito as suggested by Mateus. Carter had been telling Estefana what Cordero had learned from the priest about Bobu.

"I passed a whole lot of boys pushing carts full of coconuts into the village," Cordero interrupted them.

"So?" Carter replied.

"A *whole* lot," Cordero repeated.

"So?" Carter said a second time.

"So the ones I stopped and spoke to didn't have knives or machetes, you know, to slice off the tops of the coconuts to get to the water inside. And I offered to buy a coconut off one of the boys. He wouldn't sell it to me. Can you believe that? Passing up a sale?"

"Okay," said Carter slowly as she started to appreciate the significance of each point he made.

"I think whoever has the liquor will use the boys to circulate during the market or the cockfight or maybe even the post-burial feast selling bottles of the stuff. No one will suspect young boys trying to make some money and any transaction will simply be regarded as the sale of some coconut water."

Carter considered that and nodded.

"You could be right," she said.

"I know I'm right," said Cordero. "Like I said I spoke to two of the boys and I told one that I'm a police investigator. That information is likely to get around. So I'll have to be careful about where I go and what I do or I could be seen as acting suspiciously. When you two circulate today and tonight, keep your eyes out for any boy with a coconut cart."

"Markets I understand and cockfights…well, as a woman I guess that's not for me. So tell me more about the feasting tonight following the burial," said Carter. "What's it all about and what can we expect?"

"There's always a feast at a burial like this," said Cordero. "It's to celebrate the fact that the spirit of the dead person has been sent off to the other world and won't bother anyone in this world again. The feasting is also the occasion when relationships within and between families affected by the death are renegotiated. In America you'd talk about obtaining 'closure' as though a death is the end of everything. Here, Timorese regard a death as a new chapter in the same story—for the dead person who is now an ancestor spirit and for those living in this world in terms of how they regard each other."

He grabbed his keys off the table.

"These ceremonies take time. They're not like a fight over a will or anything like that. They must be conducted in a relaxed, friendly way that creates a new sense of harmony among people connected to the dead person. Hence the feasting which can go on for days. I was over at Dario's place yesterday. I caught a glimpse of the food they were preparing. It'll be big, believe me."

"We should go now and tell the police commander about the coconut carts, *maun*," said Estefana. "The market will open soon."

"Of course," he said to Estefana. "We'll go now. My guess is the boys have gone to some secret location to fill the carts with the liquor and get final instructions." He eyed Carter. "You're the one who said we have to catch them in the act to put a stop to any threat of a mass poisoning. So we'll keep a look out for boys with carts and hold our fire until we witness one of them take something from his cart that's clearly not a coconut."

18

Mateus listened closely to Cordero's theory that the illicit liquor would be pedalled by boys concealing the bottles under the coconuts in their carts. It sounded a little impractical—organising all the boys, ensuring they didn't run off with the money they made—but this was Timor and Mateus had seen much stranger things before.

"Could be," was all he said.

They were standing in the police commander's office waiting on the officers rostered on to cover the market and the cockfight. It was not yet 9 o'clock. The temperature was rising, and the room was stuffy with humidity. Cordero felt like giving the air-conditioner another try but let the temptation pass.

"Why else would there be so many boys selling coconuts and all of the ones I stopped selling them without knives or machetes to cut them with?" he put to Mateus to get his mind off the heat.

Mateus opened his hands above the desk. "Maybe they're selling the coconuts to be taken home and eaten," he suggested.

"Nobody has to walk too far from their home to find a coconut in Balibo," Cordero said. "They're sold to people away from their homes so they have something to drink on hot days. Imagine how hot it's going to get later."

There was a tap on the door and Officer Edi Sobado opened it without waiting for permission.

"They're all here, commander," he said.

Mateus rose from his desk.

"Show them in," he said.

Three officers entered the room. One was the young female officer who, along with Edi, had been down near the border when the body of the suspected smuggler had been found. Another was a second junior male officer in a uniform that was too big for his frame. The third was a middle-aged man with an expansive belly that was stretching the button on the bottom of his police shirt. Edi came in last and closed the door behind him.

Mateus dispensed with introductions.

"It's possible that the liquor will be sold from coconut carts," he said. "So keep an eye out for any boys selling coconuts. The stuff could also be hidden behind stacks of vegetables or in the racks of second-hand clothes. A bottle could even be smuggled in by someone pretending to be holding a fighting cock. Keep your eyes open but your hands away from searching things until you have good reason to suspect something. We don't want to warn off whoever might have the liquor. Watch what people are buying and if it looks like it could be liquor, get a good look at whoever is selling it before you do anything else."

Mateus resumed his seat. He picked up his pen and started to tap it on the desk.

"*Mana* Carter and Officer dos Carvalho will cover the market as well," he said before addressing them both. "Stay around the market. Leave the cockfight to me, Cordero and the male officers here. I believe the cockfight starts at midday."

"You're not coming to the market?" Carter asked.

"You and Officer dos Carvalho in civilian clothes will pass largely unnoticed. Other uniformed officers mingling around a market won't look out of place. Cordero and I will check on Arturo Cabral at the clinic and come down when the cockfight is about to begin."

• • •

The market was situated in a block of land set aside behind government buildings where the main road curved around the ruins of the fort and trailed off south to Maliana. A rusty tin-roofed colonnade provided covered space for stalls piled high on concrete tables. Jackfruit, hands of bananas, limes, tomatoes, and neat stacks of onions, chillies, and garlic were on display. In a shady spot at the front of the colonnade cuts of pork hung for sale along with locally caught fish. Elderly women with blank expressions sat waving plastic bags tied to sticks to keep the flies at bay. At the other end, beyond the fresh produce, were racks of second-hand clothes identical to the ones on the headless mannequins lined up outside Feng's nearby store.

Few of the younger women working stalls spoke to each other and none touted for business. Old men squatted just as silently on the concrete steps of the colonnade selling clumps of tobacco that ranged in colour from light tan to near black. On the far side of the colonnade were make-shift tent stalls selling *tais* and Chinese-made flip-flops and hats, the merchants lounging out of the sun. On the other side were fewer tents but a collection of parked motorcycles on which sat men smoking cigarettes. People milled around the market, but few were showing interest in purchasing anything.

"Do you have markets like this where you come from, *mana*?" Estefana asked Carter as they wandered down through the offerings.

Two very young boys ran out in front of them, giggling as they were chased by a third. All were barefoot and dressed in what looked like hand-me-down clothes.

"Well, we have what we call swap meets," Carter said. "They're mostly for used gear people want to sell. You know, tools and electrical or sporting stuff. There are farmers markets which are more like this. Fruit and vegetables, agricultural supplies. I don't go to either much. Maybe I should. It's a good atmosphere here although people aren't buying much or even talking to each other."

"People don't have a lot of money, *mana*. And everybody sees each other all the time," said Estefana. "What's there to talk about?"

Officer Edi Sobado and the female officer were near the parked motorcycles. Edi was cadging a cigarette off one of the men there while his companion was keeping a close watch on those mingling about without obvious purpose. The other two officers were examining the tent stalls, pretending to be interested in what they had for sale while actually trying to detect if liquor was among the items.

So far, they'd seen nothing to suggest it was.

Although the crowd had built up by 11 o'clock, almost two hours of surveillance had revealed nothing. No one had noticed anything suspicious and certainly nothing that would suggest the sale of liquor.

"I'm starting to doubt that this is where the stuff is going to be distributed," Carter said.

"Perhaps it is too early to think about drinking liquor, *mana*," Estefana replied.

"In my experience the time of day has little to do with when people drink once they set their minds to it," Carter said. "But you could be right. The cockfight might be a better bet. Of course, women aren't allowed there."

"It's not that they're not allowed, *mana*," Estefana corrected her. "It's just that the men will stop the fight if a woman approaches. Cockfighting is for men only. Traditionally it is associated with ideas about—" and her voice trailed off.

"Ideas about what?" Carter asked, examining a silk headscarf in Rastafarian colours.

"About," Estefana began but hesitated a second time.

"Go on," urged Carter.

Estefana checked if anyone was close enough to hear, even though she was speaking in English.

"About whether a man who is married, or who wants to get married, has the power to produce children."

"Power?" asked Carter, and Estefana merely raised an eyebrow.

"Is that so?" said Carter.

"You see if your rooster draws blood and wins, it means the ancestors will favour you with many children."

"I must remember that," said Carter. She started off. "So let's do one more lap of the stalls."

Across from a mound of sweet potatoes stood a small girl in a blue dress buying three lose cigarettes from a man in a dirty shirt open at the front.

Carter stopped and put a hand on Estefana to do the same.
"Isn't that Bobu's daughter?" Carter asked.
"I think it is, *mana*," said Estefana.
The girl took the cigarettes and placed some coins into the man's hand. The man squatted back down. The girl put the cigarettes in a pocket in her dress and strode off.
"Come on," Carter said. "Let's see what she's doing buying cigarettes."

• • •

Mateus and Cordero walked to the health clinic. The nurse had merely shrugged when the police commander asked about the boy's condition and she gestured for him and Cordero to follow her to the room where Arturo had been settled.
"Has that medication arrived from Dili?" Mateus asked.
"Not yet," the nurse said.
Juno Cabral was sitting beside his son's bed in the health clinic. A woman Mateus knew to be his wife Osmera, wiping eyes red from crying, was hunched on the other side of the bed. Apart from the bed, the room contained some cabinets stacked with linen and a small side table for preparing medications and dressings across which lay a bright beam of sunlight.
"*Bondia* Juno," Mateus said entering the room. "*Bondia Senyora* Osmera."
The woman took a kerchief from her eyes and merely nodded. Juno didn't acknowledge the greeting.
"Any news on Arturo?" Mateus asked.
"They say he's had seizures and his heart is no good," said Juno. From the strain on his face, the stubble on his chin, and the fact that he was wearing the same clothes he wore the day before, Mateus figured Juno hadn't left the clinic since he first came. He put his hand lightly on the man's shoulder. Juno dropped his face into his hands and took a few stuttering breaths.
Mateus edged closer to the bed and studied the boy. Ordinarily he would have been called handsome: thick, dark curly hair over olive skin and the beginnings of a patrician jaw. Now Arturo's eyes

were squeezed shut, his face had collapsed in on itself, and his lips quivered as he struggled for breath that was barely discernible.

"I wanted him taken to Liquica or Batugade," Juno continued. "Or better than that to the hospital in Dili where he could get proper treatment. They told me he'd never survive the journey and that I should just wait here and pray." He scoffed, whether at the lack of emergency services or the suggestion of prayer was hard to tell.

"Is the doctor back?" Mateus asked, turning to the nurse.

"Tonight or tomorrow," she said uncertainly.

Mateus made no comment.

"Have you called Father Francedez?" he asked Juno.

Osmera blessed herself and started sobbing once more. Juno didn't answer.

"Is there anything you need doing?" Mateus asked. "Anything I can do to help?"

Juno sat up and took a deep breath. He faced Mateus.

"Get the bastard who did this," Juno said. "And hand him over to me!"

• • •

"*Tanba sa ita sosa sigarru, alin?*" Estefana asked the girl.

"*Sira mak hodi apá,*" the girl said.

"She said she bought the cigarettes for her father, *mana.*"

"Ask her where her father is," said Carter.

When Estefana did, the girl pointed in the direction of the fort. She looked up at Carter and smiled.

"My name is Josefa," she said in Tetun. She pointed at Carter. "What is your name."

Carter knew enough from the Tetun classes she'd taken to answer that without Estefana translating.

"My name is Carter," she said in Tetun.

"Kayter?"

"No, Carter."

"Kay—"

"Not Kayter. Carter."

"Carter."

"That's right."

"Carter," the girl repeated.

The girl laughed and her facial expression—the glow in her eyes, the turn of her lips—struck Carter once again.

"Where are you from?" the girl asked. It was another simple question every Tetun learner masters in the first lesson.

Carter crouched down to be at eye level with Josefa.

"I'm from the United States," she said, this time in English.

"The union stakes?" the girl said, in English.

Carter held back a smile.

"No, the United States," she corrected. "You know, America."

"Oh, America!" the girl said and smiled a big, broad smile.

"Is your country beautiful like Timor?" Josefa asked, reverting to Tetun.

Carter appealed to Estefana to resume translation duties.

"I think so," said Carter when she understood the question.

"Do you have buffalos?"

"We have bison," said Carter. "Some people call them buffalos even though they're not like the buffalos you have here in Timor."

"Why not?" the girl asked when Estefana had translated the comment.

"Because they're a different species."

"*Espésie*," explained Estefana in Tetun. "It's like a family of animals."

"Oh," said the girl although her expression suggested it remained a mystery to her.

"And goats?"

"Yes and goats. Just like your goats here," said Carter. "Is your father here for the market today?"

"No," Josefa said. "He has to sing for *Senyor* Dario tonight. I think he is practising. He said he could do that in the fort because no one will be there to disturb him."

"Are you both going to the burial today?" Carter asked.

"No. *Apá* said that would make me sad. We're going to the feast tonight. There'll be lots of food there. More than we have at home."

"*Ita gosta escola?*" Carter asked—"Do you like school?"—exhausting the phrases she'd learned in Tetun.

"I was in school for three years," said the girl with evident pride. "My teacher was *Senyora* Pereira. She was fat and her hair was falling out."

The unflattering description was delivered in all seriousness and Estefana had to restrain the urge to laugh when she translated it.

"Okay," said Carter. "But do you like school now?"

"*Senyora* Pereira went away. Maybe she died. I don't know. The school has no teacher since she went away," the girl said.

"What about here, in Balibo? There must be a school you could go to here."

"It's a very long way from Lolitu to Balibo," Josefa said, a frown on her brow. "*Apá* says I'm too young to walk or catch a microlet on my own and he's too busy to bring me. One day he's going to take me to Dili," she added, brightening, "and he says that when we live there I'll go to school every day. Maybe I'll learn more about your bibons."

"Bisons, not bibons."

The girl giggled.

"Maybe I'll learn English good too!"

A woman puffed her way past balancing a bag of rice on her head and dragging a girl of no more than three years of age by the hand. The woman paid them no mind but the girl stared at them while sucking on her thumb. Josefa offered a tiny wave of her hand to the girl who didn't respond.

"Do you live in Dili?" she asked turning back to Carter.

"Yes."

"Near the beach?"

"Yes, not far from the beach."

"Maybe when I'm living in Dili we could go to the beach together," the girl said.

"Maybe we could," said Carter. "I like swimming at the beach."

"*Apá* once took me to the beach in Liquica," the girl said. "It was fun and we splashed in the little waves. I couldn't go where the waves were big. I can't yet swim, you see, so I had to stay away from deep water. Can you swim?"

"Yep. I can."

"Maybe you could teach me when we go to the beach together in Dili."

"I'd like that," said Carter.

"I must go now," Josefa said. "*Apá* will want his cigarettes."

Carter stood.

"Okay. Good talking to you, Josefa."

"Good talking to you too, Kay—" Carter gave her a disapproving look. "I mean Carter!"

They both laughed.

"She likes her father very much," said Estefana when the girl had run off.

"I liked mine. You liked yours. All girls like their fathers," Carter said. "He's the model for the partner they choose in life. If they're lucky."

19

As Mateus and Cordero were leaving the health clinic, two men barged through the front door. The face of one was covered in blood that spotted down his T-shirt; the other had an arm around the injured man helping him in. They forced their way past Mateus and Cordero and called out for the nurse. She soon came into the foyer, gave the man a quick examination, and helped him to an area where he could be cleaned up and have his injuries dressed. She called over her shoulder for the second man to wait at the front of the clinic in order to fill out the necessary paperwork for the visit.

The man stood, uncertain what to do with himself, and glared at the nurse as she guided his injured friend down the corridor. He spun around, recognized Mateus in his police uniform for the first time, and nodded as he pushed back out through the front door. Mateus and Cordero followed him.

"Accident?" Mateus asked, drawing up to the man.

"Came off his motorcycle," the man said and waved an arm vaguely, "where the road's washed away on the climb up from Batugade."

"That could be a lot of places on that road," quipped Cordero. The man ignored him.

"How did you get here?" asked Mateus.

"Hailed down a construction truck. Dropped us off just up the road."

"Is your friend badly hurt?"

"Head hit the road, I guess. Wasn't wearing a helmet. You know what head wounds can be like." He gazed through the glass panel in the door of the clinic. "I don't think it's too bad. He wasn't knocked unconscious or anything," he said in an attempt to convince himself more than them.

He paced off to the side of the building under the shade of a fig tree. A sign there read: '*Fuma aat ba ita-nia saúde*'—'Smoking is bad for your health'—but the ground beneath the sign was littered with butts. The man patted down his pockets. "You got a cigarette?" he asked Mateus.

"I don't smoke," replied Mateus. "Where are your motorcycles?"

"We had to leave them out on the road. On the side, you know," he answered. "I'll go back for them when my friend is fixed up."

Mateus and Cordero wished him and his friend luck and walked off. They decided to pop into the police station for a coffee before the cockfight. "You wouldn't see too many traffic accidents in what you do I guess," Mateus was saying. "For police like me it's a regular thing. I read a report recently that there are over a thousand injuries on Timorese roads each year and fifty people killed. That's just what's reported. A lot of accidents aren't. And the state of the roads! Why people don't wear helmets is beyond me."

They entered the station and went to the rear room where Mateus set about making coffee.

"Arturo isn't doing well," Cordero said.

"No, he didn't look good at all," agreed Mateus.

"I'm surprised he's lasted this long," Cordero said, dropping into a chair alongside the table in the centre of the room. "You know, given that the guy from West Timor died quickly by all accounts."

"Arturo is younger and so probably stronger and healthier," said Mateus. "And he may not have drunk as much. Who knows? There was some left in the bottle and more could have spilled out when he had a bad reaction."

The coffee made, Mateus brought two cups to the table. He sat and took a cigarette from his pocket, lighting it with his plastic lighter. He took a long drag.

"Something's been bothering me, Mateus," Cordero said, sipping his coffee and eyeing the police commander over the rim of the cup.

"What's that?"

Cordero searched the room. "Is there any sugar?"

"That's what's bothering you?" Mateus said. "Over there," he said, gesturing with his cigarette.

Cordero rose, grabbed the sugar bowl, and sat back down.

"No, that's not what's been bothering me." He sugared his coffee and took another sip, satisfied now with the taste. "Something about you does."

"Me?" said Mateus and half coughed, half laughed.

"Twice now I've heard you tell people that you don't smoke," said Cordero. "But you do."

Mateus' face broke into a broad smile.

"You have me there," he said. "But it's no great mystery."

Cordero waited.

"About a month ago there was another cockfight," Mateus said and took a second drag on his cigarette. "They're illegal in Timor as you would know but they're also a traditional thing and we couldn't put a stop to them if we tried. Anyway, as you also know, people bet on cockfights. Before this particular cockfight, Edi said there was a small rooster everyone would give no chance of winning but that he'd heard was a champion fighter."

He scratched the side of his face lightly with the fingers holding the cigarette. Cordero sipped more of his coffee.

"Well he convinced a few of us to put a bet on," Mateus continued. "As I told you, my officers haven't been paid for a couple of months and so they all need money. Very keen and I admit so was I. Most of us dipped into what little we'd manage to put aside or else borrowed what we could."

He took a last drag on his cigarette, stubbed it out carefully, and pocketed the butt.

"What happened?" Cordero asked.

"The damn thing was torn to pieces," said Mateus. "We lost everything. Graziela—my wife—found out I'd taken some of the money she keeps for emergencies. She was very angry. As a punishment she's restricted me to one package of cigarettes a week rather than the four or five I usually smoke. So I have to ration them and can't afford to be giving any away." He brushed the palms of his hands together. "It's as simple as that."

Mateus finished his coffee and checked his watch. An officer came to the door looking for him.

"Commander," the officer said.

"Yes, what is it?"

"This came from Border Patrol a little while ago. It's an answer to your question about the arrest of that suspected smuggler from West Timor."

The sheet was folded. Mateus put it in his top pocket without looking at it.

"Thanks. I'll check it when I get a chance." He nodded to Cordero. "Time we went," he said and pushed up off his chair.

• • •

On the way to the cockfight they passed Carter and Estefana coming the other way from the market.

"Anything?" Cordero asked.

"Nothing," said Carter. "How is the boy, Arturo?"

"No change," Cordero answered.

"That doesn't sound good," Carter said.

"No."

She faced Mateus.

"Two of your officers have gone on to the cockfight. The woman—Natalia is it?—and the one you call Edi are patrolling the market. Estefana and I are going to get a quick bite to eat before we check if they need us to relieve them."

"Okay," said Mateus. "We'll catch up later."

Mateus and Cordero strolled down through the market, the police commander stopping to chat with stall holders he knew and others who had a complaint about something or other they took the opportunity to make. It was all part of the job, he explained to Cordero, and couldn't be rushed.

Eventually they made their way down a grassy embankment

to the enclosure where the cockfight was to take place. The railing was already swarming with men sitting, standing and hanging off to get a glimpse of the pit while others crowded behind, two and three deep, straining on tiptoe to get a view even though the fighting had yet to begin.

"It'll be a big crowd," Mateus said. "A lot of the men who've come for Gaspa's burial will be here. It's the women who'll do all the mourning until the old man's finally put in the ground this afternoon." He nodded to his two officers who were standing on a rise on the other side of the enclosure. "A big crowd," he repeated.

"Big, hot and thirsty," said Cordero. "Perfect venue for peddling liquor."

"You may be right," Mateus said.

Two rooster handlers strode to the centre of the pit, their fighting cocks held tight in the crook of their arms. One man was middle-aged, his hands calloused and his T-shirt grubby. His opponent was younger, soon to be married, and keen to draw blood in his first contest to establish what Estefana would call his 'power'—his reproductive potential.

The older man's rooster looked menacing with bright orange feathers down its neck and across its back and a green sheen on its powerful thighs. The younger man's rooster was harder to assess. It was held in tight to the man's body with only its pale-yellow head and hackles clearly visible. It was clearly a smaller rooster but whether faster, fiercer, more agile was impossible to say.

The handlers edged the birds closer, encouraging them to peck at each other's combs to incite their hostility. Both handlers took care to avoid contact with the razor-sharp gaffs tied to each bird's left leg as a deadly substitute spur. The crowd started to build, now four and five deep around the pit. The men on the railing began to yell their support to the rooster they were backing, and bets were quickly laid.

• • •

Carter and Estefana re-entered the market with some chicken skewers and rice they had managed to purchase from a street stall just beyond the market. They caught up with officers Edi and Natalia and suggested they get some lunch as well. Edi took no encouraging; Natalia held back a second then followed him to a barbecue stall. Carter and Estefana found some shade under a bougainvillea vine growing between two tented stalls and sat down to eat.

Estefana spotted him first: a teenage boy in a loose pair of old trousers and a soccer jersey wheeling a coconut cart on the far side of the colonnade. He sought out male customers and sidled up to them with an exaggerated display of friendliness. Carter watched his progress as best she could through the vegetable stands and stalls. She saw little evidence the boy was selling any coconuts.

"Let's get closer," Carter suggested. "Keep eating and try to look casual."

They stood by a stall offering a variety of tomatoes for sale, all the time keeping one eye on the boy as he pushed through the crowd.

"*Nuu bee!*" the boy called, meaning coconut water. "*Nuu bee!*"

A man approached the front of the cart and examined its contents, stopping the boy's progress. The boy circled his cart and gestured exuberantly to the man. The man shook his head and made to leave. The boy grabbed his shirt and pulled him back to the cart laughing as he did so. The man took another look at the coconuts before gesturing 'no' with his hand and leaving.

The boy thrust a hand into his pocket then turned the cart around in the direction of the main road. Carter and Estefana followed him at a distance, drifting from stall to stall. Twice the boy looked over his shoulder and each time Carter took hold of something quickly and showed it to Estefana as a ruse. At the road the boy sat down on the edge of his cart, pulled a rag from his pocket and ran it across his brow. He wiped his hands as well.

"Why are you following me?" he called out to Estefana.

Estefana looked at Carter who didn't know what the boy had said in Tetun but guessed he was wise to them.

"I'd say he's done this before," Carter said. "Tell him we're police officers," she added as they walked over to the boy and Carter examined the contents of his cart.

Estefana did as instructed. The boy was unimpressed.

"Show him your badge," said Carter, and Estefana retrieved it from her pocket.

"You don't look like a police officer," the boy said. "They're usually ugly. And she's not Timorese. That badge could be a fake."

"It's not a fake and we are police officers," Estefana said and she thrust her badge under the boy's nose.

"He has a knife here," Carter said. "Maybe he does sell coconut water. Tell him to empty his pockets."

Estefana did. The boy refused.

"You can't make me!" he insisted.

"I'm a police officer," said Estefana in a more severe tone. "Now empty your pockets."

"No!" the boy shouted again.

"Do it now!"

"No! I won't!"

Carter came around and stood over the boy with the kind of scowl on her face she found sometimes worked with boys of a certain age. This proved one of those times.

From deep pockets in the pants he wore, the boy pulled out a lighter, two one-dollar notes, a package of cigarettes, two cell phones, some coins, and a driver's license with a photo on it that clearly wasn't him.

"A good morning's work," said Carter. "For a pickpocket. Ask him his name."

"Abel Xavier," the boy grumbled when Estefana put the question to him.

"I'm not sure that's his real name, *mana*," Estefana said. "Abel Xavier is a famous Portuguese soccer player. And that's the Portuguese national team's jersey he's wearing."

"Ask him again and tell him you'll take him to the police station and put him in a cell if he lies again," Carter said. "And you'll take that jersey off him as well."

Estefana tried a second time.

The boy scratched his chest while he considered his situation. There were two of them, one claiming to be a police officer, and both looking as though they could outrun and outwrestle him. Besides, the jersey was a prized possession.

"Pedro," he said finally. "Pedro Sanchez."

"You believe him?" Carter asked Estefana.

"Could be, yes."

"Ask him where he's from."

"Limahitu," the boy answered.

"It's a small hamlet on the western side of Balibo, *mana*. The side away from the border."

"Ask him why he's here stealing from people."

Estefana put the question to the boy who folded his arms tight across his chest and said nothing. She asked him a second time. Nothing. Carter had seen that kind of defiance in young people many times before on reservations at home. She moved in closer and fixed the boy with a practised menacing stare. He looked at her, at Estefana, and back to Carter.

He was out of options and he knew it.

"My father ran off and left my mother with eight of us to feed," the boy said and Carter noticed his lips tremble ever so slightly. "I'm the oldest. I have to take care of the others the best I can," he added, his voice rising.

Carter softened her glare when Estefana translated the boy's answer. She faced Estefana.

"Well, you're the police officer," she said. "What do you think?"

Estefana studied the boy a moment while he cast his eyes from one to the other.

"It could be true, *mana*," Estefana decided. "Even so, it doesn't excuse what he's doing."

Carter ran a hand over her hair.

"No. It doesn't," she said. "But it's not teenage pickpockets we're after. How about you tell him to return everything he's stolen. Say we'll keep an eye on him while he does it. If there's something he can't return because the person he stole from has left, he's to give it to you. If he does that, he's free to go so long as we don't catch him at it again. Oh, and tell him I want to buy a coconut for one dollar. How's that with you?"

Estefana tried to suppress a smile, only half succeeding.

"I think that is a good plan, *mana*," she said and, turning, began giving instructions to the boy.

20

The referee, a barrel-chested man with a week's growth on his chin and grease all over his workpants, stubbed out his cigarette and joined the two handlers in the centre of the pit. He tucked his shirt roughly into his belt and studied those at the front of the crowd until he was satisfied all bets had been placed. He raised his hand, held it aloft a moment to heighten the tension, and thrust it down to signal the release of the cocks.

The roosters held off, motionless, eyeing each other, necks extended, as the spectators worked themselves into a frenzy encouraging the cock they'd bet on and goading the other. Suddenly the orange cock struck upward from a crouch at its opponent. The gaff affixed to its leg found a mark and sliced through. Feathers—white, not yellow—were torn off the back of the opposing cock and scattered in all directions. Shrills of delight arose from those who had laid money on the orange rooster even as it quickly backed off and its smaller opponent regained its stance.

The yellow feathers had been a ruse. White feathered roosters are considered stronger and fiercer than others and so are harder to lay bets against. Some handlers apply paint or dye to the white feathers to disguise their perceived advantage. It can be a tricky tactic if the white feathered rooster wins and those who bet against it feel cheated. But most of the time only boos and insults are likely to result and this was one of those times.

The smaller rooster, now obviously white feathered, suddenly sprang onto its opponent. That rooster, being larger, was struck by the gaff in the neck. Blood spurt out of the orange rooster and it struggled to stand. Another leap, another strike of the gaff, and the bird was close to death.

"Do you like this kind of thing?" Cordero asked Mateus. "The cockfighting, I mean."

"No, but it's part of the culture we live in," the police commander replied. "I pity the roosters."

"They're valuable and so they're treated well enough," said Cordero.

"Only until the time they're cut to pieces in the arena and chopped up to be eaten," remarked Mateus.

A second cockfight ended in much the same fashion as the first. In the third contest of the day, one of the handlers rescued his rooster, which was clearly losing, before it was seriously injured. Feathers now littered the pit and fluff drifted in a slight breeze above the spectators. Blood lay drying in the dust.

More men were coming down to the cockfight and squeezing into whatever vantage point they could find to watch the contests. For the moment, though, the referee had slipped off to the side of the pit into the sparse shade afforded by a eucalypt tree and was smoking another cigarette.

It was now hot—very hot—and Cordero noticed several of the men buying small bottles of beer from a vender who carried some kind of cool pack on his back. He pointed it out to Mateus, who immediately noticed another vender with a similar pack. Cordero excused himself and went off to buy a beer in order to check if it was, in fact, beer. The first bottle the vendor handed him, Cordero rejected, choosing his own from the pack. The man removed the cap with an opener tied by a cord to his pants and Cordero took a sip.

It was only beer after all.

He finished the bottle, enjoying the cool refreshing taste, and searched out the second vendor, repeating the same approach he used with the first. Again, no strong liquor, only beer.

He strolled over to Mateus.

"It's just cold beer that they're selling," he said.

"I'm not surprised in this heat," said Mateus. "My junior officer wandered by while you were gone. He and the other officer have seen nothing of your coconut carts. In fact, they've seen nothing suspicious at all."

"Nothing, huh?" said Cordero. He put his hands in his pockets and straightened his arms. "Maybe we've thought this whole thing wrong. Maybe the stuff is meant to be sold in kiosks or on request." He faced Mateus. "Maybe there isn't a cache of liquor that's been smuggled across the border at all."

A commotion broke out and caught their attention. Someone was yelling, pushing, shoving. A second man was shouting back in a scuffle others tried to break up. Soon the two men in dispute were whirling through the crowd and trampling over others who were not involved. Punches were thrown. Mateus caught the eye of the older officer patrolling the cockfight and gestured for him to break up the affray. As the officer pushed his way into the melee, Mateus and Cordero strode over to see what all the fuss was about.

"He lost a bet and tried to pay me with this!" yelled one of the men being restrained by the police officer. He forced a hand free of the officer's grip and held up a Hell Bank Note for $1000. "This is shit. I want my money!"

The police commander took the note, examined it, and handed it across to Cordero. Next, he considered the other man. At first the man's face was obscured as he held a rag to a badly bleeding nose. When he took the rag from his face, Mateus recognised who it was.

"You're João Lima," Mateus said. "The son of the elder, Helio Lima."

"I don't care who he is," said the man pushing against the hold the officer had on him. "I want the money he owes me."

"Calm down," said Mateus. "How much does he owe you?"

"Ten dollars!" The man stretched his neck toward João. "Ten!"

"João's from down near the border," Mateus said. "He's not right in the head. Half the time he doesn't know what he's doing. He wouldn't have meant to trick you."

"That's fine but a bet's a bet!"

"Give your name to the officer there," Mateus told him. "We'll see what we can do."

"See what you can do? Bullshit!" the man said.

Mateus hitched up his trousers and fronted the man.

"I told you to calm down," he said. "Do it now or I'll have my officer here take you away."

He took João by the arm and wheeled him from the small group of people who'd gathered to watch the spectacle. João was wiping blood from his mouth and chin.

"Where's he going?" the man who claimed he'd won the bet yelled after him.

"To the police station," Mateus said. "With me. And if you don't shut up and do what I told you to do, you'll be coming too."

· · ·

"Does your father know where you are?" Mateus asked João.

They were in the commander's office. Mateus sat behind his desk, João in a chair in front and Cordero off to the side.

João was staring at the floor, rotating the bloody rag in his hands, and didn't answer.

"You're not in any trouble, João," said Mateus, tilting slightly to one side. "But I need to know what's going on. Does your father know you're here in Balibo?"

João shook his head.

"Why is that?" Mateus asked.

"He went to his garden and on to the sacred house," João said. "So I left."

"And he didn't want you to go with him?"

Again João shook his head.

Mateus caught Cordero's eye.

"That's unusual. Every time I've met Helio, João hasn't been too far away."

"If he lives near the border, why would you know him that well?" Cordero asked.

"His father's an important elder down there. Others respect him and generally do as he says. Community policing is what we do, remember. I have to get to know people like Helio who exercise influence in the hamlets."

Mateus refocused his attention on João.

"How did you get to Balibo, João?" he asked.

João started jiggling his feet. He put his hand on his thighs and rubbed forcefully.

"Stop that, João," said Mateus. "Answer my question. How did you get here?"

João stopped his rubbing and folded his feet under the chair.

"I walked," he said.

"Long way to come on foot," said Mateus.

"I left early. There was nothing else to do."

"No work in the garden?"

"I told you my father went to do that."

"What about around the house? There wasn't anything to do there either?"

"Not today. Nothing."

"And so you came to Balibo to go to the cockfight and lay a bet?"

"No."

"No?"

"I saw the people coming together there and went to see why. That's all. I didn't know what they were doing."

"You tried to lay a bet on a rooster," Mateus said.

"That's what everyone was doing," said João. "So I did too."

Mateus picked up the joss paper.

"With this?"

João nodded. "That's all I had," he said.

"Do you know what this is?" Mateus asked.

João said nothing.

"João! Do you know what this is?" Mateus repeated.

"Money," João said. "It's money."

"How much money?"

João shrugged. "It's money," he repeated. "I don't know how much."

"Where did you get this, João?"

João looked away and started rubbing his thighs once more.

"I told you, you're not in trouble. But this isn't money."

"It is money!" João insisted. "I've seen things like that before."

"It's not money. Can you read what it says here?" Mateus asked. He placed the note in front of João and pointed to the banner which read: 'Hell Bank Note'.

João looked away, embarrassed.

"Well?" Mateus barked.

"I can't read," he said and dropped his eyes.

"No. Okay. Well what it says here is 'This Is Not Real Money'," said Mateus to keep things simple. "Now I've said you're not in trouble but I need to know where you came across this."

João started jiggling and he wrapped his arms around his chest in a gesture that said he was shutting down to further questioning.

"João!" demanded Mateus.

The jiggling continued and the arms wrapped even tighter.

The police commander threw up his hands and sighed.

Cordero, who'd been watching João closely, unfolded his legs, stood, and came toward the desk. He leaned his rump on the desk, his back to the commander and facing João. He picked up the note. João watched him with the corner of one eye, his face kept turned away.

"You know, João, the police commander is right when he tells you that this is not real money. What he didn't tell you is that it's very special. Only special people find notes like this because they're so rare. So you must be a very special person."

João faced him now. His eyes widened and his breathing slowed.

"Now the police commander probably thinks you stole this," Cordero continued in a reassuring voice. "And if you'd stolen it, you wouldn't be a special person, you'd be a thief and the person you stole it from would be the special person. But I don't think you stole it at all. I think you found it. I think you're special. Am I right?"

João nodded in a jerky fashion.

"We have to convince the police commander that I'm right and for that you need to tell him where you found it. Understand? If you don't, he's going to keep thinking that you stole it."

João's foot stopped jiggling as he considered what Cordero

had said. Cordero gave him an encouraging smile. Eventually João unfolded his arms and placed them on either side of his chair.

"It fell out of Osorio's pocket," he said. "I didn't steal it."

"Osorio?" said Cordero.

"His brother I believe," offered Mateus, who was leaning in over the papers on his desk.

"How did Osorio come by it?" asked Cordero.

"I don't know," said João.

"Did you ask him?"

"I couldn't."

"You couldn't? Why not?"

"Because he was dead."

"Dead? How? When?" Mateus intervened.

João looked from Cordero to Mateus.

"A few days ago." He shrugged. "He just became sick and died. I don't know why?"

"You must know why he was sick or how he died," insisted Mateus.

"I don't!" protested João. "I don't!"

Cordero raised a hand for Mateus to ease off.

"How did the note fall out of his pocket if he was dead?" he asked João.

"Helio said Osorio's body was dangerous and he had to be buried straight away. I was helping to carry Osorio out to the grave we'd dug when I noticed the note fall from his pocket." He examined them both. "Does that make me special?"

Cordero looked at Mateus, eyebrows raised.

"Yes it does," said Mateus. "So special that my friend here and I are going to drive you home like the special person you are."

The police commander rose, pocketed the note, and reached for his keys. Cordero pushed himself off the desk and patted João on the shoulder.

Mateus faced Cordero.

"We have plenty of time before Gaspa's burial. I think we should spend a little of it talking to Helio Lima. I want to know how his son came by that note. I want to know what he died from. I want to know if any of this ties in with smuggled liquor."

21

Helio had finished weeding his garden and now sat in the sacred house, alone, the *katana* in his hands. It would require a solid swing of the arm to be effective—either from above the shoulder in a slashing motion or else thrusting forward with the blade coming in directly from just behind his body. The problem was he'd be in a crowd and that might prevent him getting enough room to strike either way. If he'd failed in his first thrust or swing, there'd likely be no chance of a second. He would stand out clearly from the other people and so to try again, or to get away quickly, would be near impossible to do.

He lay the *katana* aside and took the knife he used in the garden out of his waist band. He ran a finger along the blade. It was sharp, very sharp. He'd made sure of that every other day before he took it to work his plot. The knife was much easier to conceal and would do the job if he struck in the right place—the neck, the heart—but the crowd could be a problem then too. Would he be able to get close enough? Would someone see the blade and restrain him before he could stab or slash his target the second or third time that might be necessary?

He put the knife next to the *katana*. *Damn that Fidalgo*, he thought. If he'd waited until things had dried he could've burnt down the hut and that might have convinced them to go. Fidalgo was scared, he was always scared ever since his leg was crushed in a motorcycle accident, and that made him act on impulse but not act well. He—Helio—would have to do what was needed now, but killing someone was a lot harder than setting a hut on fire.

He stood and made his way to the rear corner of the sacred house. He sorted through a pile of old woven cloths, the dust from them catching in his throat as he did. He took a parcel wrapped in leather from the bottom. Like the *katana* it was a relic of the Second World War. But this wasn't a Japanese relic. Helio went back to where he'd been sitting and carefully unfolded the leather. In his hand was an Enfield No2 six-shot revolver—British made and issued to Australian forces when they invaded Timor in December 1941 in a vain attempt at preventing the advancing Japanese seizing the island's airfields.

The story that had been passed down to Helio was that an Australian commando had been captured nearby by a Japanese patrol while scouting for a small band of his comrades attempting to reach the mountains of Bobonaro. There they intended to regroup with their company after it had been routed in a skirmish in Dutch West Timor. The Australian had been wounded, disarmed, tied up, and made to sit on the ground when a Japanese officer came forward. The officer took the man's revolver and went to shoot him in the head. The gun misfired and the Japanese officer was blinded by a spark from the cartridge. The Australian was bayoneted to death but the Japanese patrol had to turn back to Batugade with their injured officer. That meant the other Australians escaped and there were no reprisals against the Timorese who had helped them.

The revolver had removed the threat and that suggested to the local Timorese that it must be *lulik* or sacred. It had been valued as such ever since.

Helio closed his hand around the grip. It felt like it had been molded to the palm of his hand—solid, cool, powerful. He checked the cylinder. It was stiff to rotate at first but with a little persistence it began to function correctly. There were two unspent cartridges in the chambers plus what was left of the one that had misfired, blackened as a result. Helio shook the spent cartridge free and it dropped to the ground. He picked it up and pocketed it. He extracted the live cartridges, rubbed them on his trousers, and examined each one separately. He would have to clean them properly, along with the gun—its barrel, its cylinder, the trigger, the hammer—the way he had seen Indonesian soldiers clean their weapons when they occupied Balibo years before. He hoped that a small amount of cooking oil would serve in place of whatever oil he'd seen the soldiers sometimes use.

He hoped as well that the two unspent cartridges were serviceable.

Helio replaced the knife in his belt. The revolver was easy to conceal, could be fired at close range or from a short distance, and would not expose him immediately. It was the perfect weapon for his purposes.

After Fidalgo's attempt to set his hut on fire Bobu would be alert to further threats. Even so, it would be dark, and only having to point the revolver and pull a trigger meant Helio could move about inconspicuously and withdraw as though he'd never been there. A plan was forming.

• • •

João sat quietly behind Cordero in the police commander's SUV dabbing the rag against his nose as they drove toward the border. Up front, Mateus and Cordero were discussing what they knew—and speculating about what they didn't know.

"Two joss notes from two people down this way," Mateus was saying. "Two people who both died suddenly. That's too much of a coincidence for my liking."

"Perhaps the notes were an identifier of some kind," said Cordero. "You know, the West Timorese guy could have been told to hand the liquor over to someone who showed him the notes. He may not have known anyone around here. And the notes wouldn't implicate anyone seen acting suspiciously. They're not valuable and no one would take much notice of them. Once they'd served their purpose, they could simply be tossed away and no one would be the wiser."

Mateus only grunted by way of a reaction.

"You have a better idea?" Cordero asked.

"Not for the moment, no," admitted Mateus.

As they approached the sacred house Mateus noted that the ladder had been taken up. That meant someone—presumably Helio—was still inside. Mateus pulled up as close to the doorway as he could and they both stepped out. So too did João who sulked off and sat down on a log in the shade of a nearby tree.

Helio had heard the SUV approach. He put the revolver in its leather wrap and replaced the wrap under the layers of cloth. He moved to the door. As he opened it he noticed João wandering off to the side and recognized Mateus from his police uniform. Cordero he didn't know.

"*Botarde senyor*," said Mateus. "I'm the police commander. Mateus Salsinha. This is my colleague Vincintino Cordero. We'd like to have a few words with you."

"What has João done? Is he under arrest?"

"No. He walked into Balibo and we ran into him at the cockfight. We've brought him home. That's all. He's not in any trouble."

"Then we have nothing to talk about," Helio said and went to close the door.

"One moment please, *senyor*," Mateus said. "There is one small matter. May we come inside?"

"This is a sacred house," Helio said. "You are not part of this community. You have no business here."

"No but I am the police commander of this area," said Mateus, his voice a little firmer.

Helio opened the door wider.

"What is this small matter?" he asked.

"João tried to lay a bet at the cockfight using this," Mateus said and handed the joss paper up. Helio bent down and took it, examined it, and handed it back.

"I've never seen that before and I don't know where he would have come by it," he said.

"João said it fell out of the pocket of your son Osorio," said Mateus. "As you and he were taking his body to be buried."

Helio said nothing, his jaw set hard and his expression blank.

"What caused your son's death?" Mateus asked.

"He was sick and he died," said Helio.

"Just like that?"

"Yes. Just like that."

"He wasn't injured in any way?"

"No."

"Was he sick in the weeks or days leading up to his death?"

"No."

Mateus folded his arms and grunted.

"So are you're telling me that there was nothing wrong with him one day and the next he was dead?" he asked.

"Yes," said Helio.

"What was he doing in the days before he died?"

"I didn't keep watch over him. He was a grown man. He lived with his own family. I don't know what he was doing."

"You have any idea?"

"My guess would be he was working in his garden as usual."

"He didn't go anywhere he didn't normally go?" Mateus persisted.

"Not that I know of."

Mateus unfolded his arms and took a step closer.

"You must have known Kosme Tavares. I believe you buried him."

"Kosme? Yes, I knew him."

"He died in much the same way as your son," said Mateus.

Helio didn't react.

"Did they know each other?" asked Mateus.

"Everybody knows everybody else here," Helio said. "It's a small community."

"Did they ever work together? Osorio and Kosme?"

"Everybody helps everybody else out here once in a while. There's nothing unusual about that. I'm not aware of anything specific they did together."

"Kosme had a note similar to this one," Mateus said.

"I know nothing about that note or any other," said Helio.

"Has anybody else died suddenly around here lately?" asked Mateus.

"Not that I've been told about."

Mateus took his cell from his pocket, pulled up the image of the man found dead in nearby bush, and held it up to Helio.

"Do you know this man?"

Helio squinted and studied the image, his brow creased.

"No."

"Never seen him?"

"Never."

Mateus pocketed the cell.

"Why did you bury Osorio so quickly and without the usual rituals?" he asked. "I would have thought that as his father, and as an elder, you would have insisted on them."

"When someone dies like Osorio died, it's reasonable to suspect sorcery is involved," Helio explained. "The body is hot and so dangerous for others to be near and it has to be buried quickly to cool. The rituals for his death will be carried out another time."

"Sorcery? Do you have any reason to suspect a sorcerer?"

"From time-to-time sorcerers are active everywhere," said Helio. "Anyone can learn the black arts and become a sorcerer. Who they are and why they do it is anyone's guess."

Mateus ran a hand under his chin.

"So there's nothing you can tell me about this joss paper?"

"No."

"You mind if I come up and have a look around inside?"

"Look for what?"

"I don't know," said Mateus. "I just want to satisfy myself that everything's as it should be in there."

"Everything is as it should be."

"I'd like to see that for myself."

"As I said, you are not of this community."

"And as I said, I am the police commander. Don't make me force my way in."

Helio wavered between opening the door and slamming it shut. But he didn't want any trouble with the police, not now, and so he relented.

"Whoever that one is can stay where he is," said Helio, gesturing toward Cordero. He lowered the ladder down for Mateus. "You can look but don't touch anything," he said as Mateus climbed past him through the door.

Cordero returned to the SUV to get out of the sun and waited. It only took five minutes before Mateus came back down the ladder and joined him.

"Anything?" Cordero asked.

"Lots of stuff," Mateus said as he climbed in behind the wheel. "No sign of any liquor though."

They watched Helio studying them from the doorway.

"Just a moment," Cordero said to Mateus. He exited the vehicle and walked toward the sacred house. Helio remained standing in the doorway.

"I wonder if you could help me with something else entirely, *senyor*," Cordero said.

"Who are you?" Helio asked.

"I'm a police investigator from Dili. However what I want to ask is a matter that intrigues me as a curious visitor, that's all," said Cordero. "Do you know anything about a road construction project down here?"

"Road construction you say?" Helio sniffed.

"That's correct," said Cordero.

"The last people to build roads here were the Indonesians," said Helio. "That was twenty years ago."

"There weren't trucks bringing road construction materials down this way about eighteen months ago?"

"Not that I know."

"The police commander told me that a heavy truck was bogged once around that time near Lolitu and that locals had to be called on to help dig it out of the mud," said Cordero.

"A big truck, yes. I remember that. Whether it carried road construction materials or not, I don't know. I haven't seen anything like that in Lolitu or Leohitu or anywhere else around here."

"Were you one of the men who dug that truck out of the mud?" Cordero asked.

"No. I was busy in my garden when it happened."

"Do you know anyone around here who was involved?"

"He was," said Helio and he lifted his chin toward João. "He may not think too well but he is strong like a buffalo."

Cordero looked at João and back to Helio.

"Do you mind if we borrow João? Just for a short time? He's not in any trouble. He may be able to help us with something, that's all. We'll bring him back here, I promise," Cordero said.

• • •

"I think we're wasting our time here, Estefana," Carter said. "And I'm feeling the beginnings of a headache. Between you and me, I think I drank too much gin last night."

"Perhaps you should go to the guesthouse and lie down for a while, *mana*," said Estefana. "It's very hot now and the burial is not for another four hours."

"What will you do?"

"I'll stay here at the market for another hour or two. I'll talk to that young female police officer. Afterwards I'll go to the church."

"The church?"

"Yes, *mana*, the church. I missed the novena last night and so I should say more prayers for my mother's foot."

"Yes, of course, the foot," said Carter.

"When I finish the prayers I'll call my mother to ask if she has been able to find out anything concerning the taboo language I told you about. I won't call until after I say the prayers so that when I tell her I said them, she'll be happy."

"Okay," said Carter. "I'll walk to the guesthouse and see you when you get back."

"Drink lots of water, *mana*," said Estefana. "It will help to clear your head."

"Thanks Estefana," said Carter. "This isn't the first hangover I've ever had and it's unlikely to be my last. A little lie down and I'll be fine."

• • •

They drove the way they had come, João sitting by himself once more and occasionally dabbing his nose but saying nothing. Cordero was hoping for something—anything—that might help explain the joss paper, the liquor, and the strange, untimely deaths. As they passed the turn off on their left Mateus threw a quick glance at João and back at Cordero. He didn't conceal his skepticism.

"You think he has any idea—" Mateus began but he was cut off.

"There!" João shouted, and he pointed to a rough track off through the trees to their right.

"Are you sure?" Mateus asked.

"I think so," said João.

"Think so?" repeated Mateus.

"Yes."

Mateus brought the SUV to a stop. He huffed, and gingerly edged the vehicle off the road and toward the trees. They thudded their way across tufted grass and clumps of rocks for thirty yards. João grew more doubtful.

"No, not here," he said eventually.

"What?" Mateus jerked to a stop, threw his arm over the back of the driver's seat and twisted around to João. "Do you remember where the truck broke down or not, João, because we have more important things to do than drive you around all day?"

"I thought it was there," said João, staring out of the window to avoid the commander's glare. He placed the rag to his face to hide his embarrassment. "I was wrong."

"Yes, you were," agreed Mateus. He straightened himself behind the wheel. "Let's go back and drop him off to his father."

"Why not try a little further?" asked Cordero.

"Why not? Because he's an idiot," said Mateus.

They lurched back onto the road and drove toward the sacred house. Before long they passed the track to Lolitu.

"There!" João shouted again.

Mateus slowed the vehicle to a crawl.

"There! There!" insisted João, jabbing his finger on the glass of the window. "I'm sure this time."

"It's on the opposite side of the road from your last call, João," Cordero pointed out.

"I was confused. I don't often ride in a vehicle and I can't tell which side is which," João explained.

Cordero noticed Mateus raise his eyebrows.

"Alright, one last time," the police commander said. He backed up onto a bare patch of earth beside the road. Slowly and cautiously he urged the vehicle forward.

"I think I can make out what's left of ruts caused some time ago by a heavy vehicle," said Cordero.

"Where?" asked Mateus.

Cordero pointed.

"I see them," said Mateus. "The grass has grown over most of it."

They were jostled from side to side on the rough terrain until they came upon a wide pit of mud stretching across the track. Mateus came to a stop.

"Is this where the truck was stuck?" Cordero asked João.

João was looking this way and that.

"I think so, yes," he answered. "Yes. I remember that palm tree over there. It's bent like a banana."

"Which way was the truck facing when you dug it out?" Cordero asked.

"That way," said João, his thumb extended toward the back window.

"Was the truck empty?" Cordero asked.

"There was a driver," said João.

"I mean in the tray. Was there anything in the tray of the truck?"

"I didn't see anything. No. But it was hard to push out of the mud."

Cordero turned to Mateus.

"I'd like to know where that truck was coming from to get here in that position," he said.

"Long time ago," said Mateus.

"It can't hurt to look," said Cordero. "We've come this far. Let's check it out."

Mateus nodded doubtfully.

"We'd better leave the vehicle here," he said, cutting the engine and opening his door to exit. "Wait here, João."

They trudged off through tall grass and spindly acacia trees following a line of old grooves in the turf cut by what appeared to be truck tyres. Mateus figured they were heading in the direction of a tributary of the Talu River.

"It runs below the ridge on which Lolitu's perched and snakes its way to the forest fringe of Leohitu before hitting the border," he was saying. Cordero was only half listening to Mateus: he was concentrating instead on what he could hear—and not hear—around him.

As they approached a rock shelf just above a bank of the tributary the tyre grooves spread out left and right of the line they had been on. The impressions were chaotic as though the truck circled, reversed onto the rock, and drove back in the direction from which it came. Cordero made his way down off the shelf onto the bank of the tributary. Mateus remained standing atop the rock watching Cordero scramble along through thick brush. The police commander fished through his pockets for a cigarette, found one, and lit it.

Before long, Cordero made his way back to Mateus and stood, wiping the dirt off his hands, looking out over the water below them.

"Anything?" the commander asked.

Cordero passed a hand across the river.

"Nothing," Cordero said.

"Oh well," Mateus muttered.

"That's the point," said Cordero. "You can see a sway of dead vegetation close to the side of the river here and out where the current strikes the opposite bank."

"Could've been caused by a torrent coming down after heavy rain," said Mateus.

"Maybe," said Cordero. "Except there's no sign of re-growth."

"Maybe too soon for re-growth," said Mateus, taking his last puff before tossing the butt to the ground and stamping on it.

"Yeah, could be," agreed Cordero.

The butt Mateus dropped had not been fully extinguished when he'd trod on it. Cordero gazed a moment at the wisp of smoke the butt produced and stomped on it himself.

"There's something else," he said.

"What?"

"The silence," said Cordero. "No signs of life. No frogs, no birds, no insects."

Mateus faced him.

"I think this river's dead," Cordero said.

22

Cordero picked up his vehicle from the police station and was driving to the guesthouse when he spotted Estefana heading in the same direction. It was hard to avoid her: a group of young children clustered beside, behind and in front of her like she was a female Timorese Pied Piper.

"Estefana!" Cordero called, pulling up next to the diminutive throng.

"*Botarde, maun,*" she replied.

"Where have you been?"

Estefana began to say something and her words were lost in the boisterous banter of the children. She had to shoosh them before she could answer.

"I went to the church to pray for my mother and then I called her to see how things were going with her foot."

"Her foot?"

The children began to cloy at Estefana and she told them to behave and let her speak to her friend in the vehicle.

"It's a long story, *maun,*" she said.

"Where's *Mana* Carter?" Cordero asked.

"She went to the guesthouse to lie down for a while," Estefana said. "She said she had a headache because she drank too much gin last night."

That surprised Cordero.

"She said that? That she'd drunk too much gin?"

"Yes *maun*. I'm going to the guesthouse now to tell her what my mother said about the Wehali taboo—"

"No time for that now, Estefana," said Cordero cutting her off. "I need you to do an important job for me."

The children were pushing and shoving each other and giggling loudly and Estefana had to settle them down a second time. She pointed to Cordero and told them he was a police investigator. If they didn't settle down, he might have to get out and deal with them.

"He doesn't look like a policeman," said one of the cheekier boys. He was no more than eight years old, shirtless and shoeless. His hair was a tangle and there were smears of grease across his tiny chest.

Cordero had heard the remark.

"I get that a lot," he said to the boy. "But I am. Okay?"

"Where's your badge?" another boy, all of perhaps ten years of age, had the audacity to ask.

Cordero was running out of patience. He brushed a hand across his face.

"It's under my seat with my handcuffs for boys who ask too many questions. Now on your way or I'll get out, tie you up, and put you in jail."

The boys consulted each other wordlessly. As one they all decided to run off and had scattered in seconds.

"Where have you been, *maun*?" Estefana asked.

"I went with Mateus to Lolitu," Cordero said. "We talked to one of the elders in the sacred house—Helio Lima. I think his son was poisoned by the liquor too. That's another story."

He disengaged the gears and yanked on his park brake.

"I need you to go to the police station. Mateus has gone home to dress for Gaspa's burial. Now listen carefully. There's only a junior officer manning the station and whoever it is will expect you. I need you to ring the Ministry of Agriculture and Fisheries in Dili. Get all the information you can from them on the disposal of Indonesian-era pesticides from Maliana about 18 months to two years ago. What was disposed of, by whom, and where? Also, how much the contract was worth and anything else you can find out. Give them the number of Mateus' office phone if they need to call you back. That will sound much more official than a cell number. Tell them it's urgent. We need that information today."

He checked his watch.

"It's almost 4pm now. They'll close for the day. And unless you get onto someone soon, you know how they're likely to pack up early, especially on a Saturday. So can you do that, please? Can you get that information for me?"

"Yes, *maun*. I'll go now."

"Meet up with me at the cemetery when you have that information. I'll pick up *Mana* Carter and take her there for the burial. Hurry now."

He put the SUV into gear and began to drive off.

"Oh, and Estefana!" he jerked to a stop and called out. "Tell whoever you are talking to at MAF that they should test the river water and the soil either side of a tributary of the Talu River just below the hamlet of Lolitu. Tell them we suspect major pesticide contamination flowing along that tributary into the Talu."

• • •

The officer on duty at the police station was the young female—Natalia. As one of the junior officers, and a female, she'd been left to mind the station while the men had been rostered on to do the 'real' policework of surveillance at the post-burial festivities for Gaspa Freitas. The two exchanged a greeting and Estefana was shown into the police commander's office.

"When did you finish at the market?" Estefana asked absently as she took a seat behind the desk.

"About an hour ago," said Natalia. "Edi— Officer Sobado—didn't come back from lunch. Said he had things to do for tonight. I stayed on a while longer," she added and shrugged. "Someone had to."

"I'd better make this call before I lose any more time," said Estefana.

She checked the number in her contact list and dialed. After eight rings someone finally picked up the phone at the other end. Estefana introduced herself and explained why she was phoning.

She was told the person she would need to speak to had just left the office.

"This is an urgent police matter," Estefana said in the most imposing voice she could manage. "You'll have to get him."

The person at the other end must have said it was too late or too hard and went to hang up.

Estefana wasn't about to stand for that. Emboldened by the praise Carter had heaped on her over her interrogation of Juno Cabral, she gripped the handset more firmly.

"Unless you do what I'm asking," she began and made a cheeky face to Natalia, "I'll send someone there to arrest you on Monday for obstructing a police operation."

The person at the other end quickly said that would not be necessary and agreed to do as Estefana instructed. She asked for a cell number and Estefana, remembering what Cordero had told her, gave the police commander's landline number instead. She then hung up to wait.

With nothing better to do, Natalia had remained in the room. Estefana looked up and blew out a breath.

"Phew," she uttered.

"Phew indeed," said Natalia.

"Are you upset that *Mana* Carter and I left you to handle the market?" Estefana asked to fill in time.

"No, not at all," said Natalia. "You aren't local police officers. It was a job for me and Edi. He should't have left like he did but that's Edi. He's always thinking of himself and doesn't care much about anybody else."

The phone on the desk rang and Estefana quickly picked it up.

"Officer dos Carvalho?" a new person on the other end of the line asked.

"Yes," said Estefana and she repeated why she was calling.

"My name is Marco. I coordinate MAF's field activities in Bobonaro district. I was just leaving for the day when I was called back from the car park," he said. "Do you know what time it is?"

"I do but this is an urgent police matter," Estefana insisted. "We need that information right away."

She heard what she took to be a grumble at the other end.

"Our computers are down today," said Marco. "I'd have to look up that information in the paper files."

"Would you do that for me now, please?"

"Do you appreciate how long that could take?" asked Marco.

"Do you appreciate how urgent it is for us to get that information?" Estefana countered.

Another suggestion of a grumble.

"*Extremely* urgent," she emphasized.

"What's this about?" Marco asked.

"I can't go into that now," said Estefana. "There's no time. Just get the information I've asked for—please."

"Okay. I'll ring you back when I have something," said Marco with an audible sigh.

Estefana replaced the phone, her eyes fixed on it a moment.

"I'm impressed," said Natalia. "That was quite a performance. You want a coffee?"

"I think I need one to calm my nerves," Estefana said.

• • •

Cordero arrived at the guesthouse and went straight into the dining area where Carter was sitting, pen in hand and with a notebook in front of her. She had changed out of her T-shirt into a soft blue blouse which she figured was more appropriate to wear to a burial.

"Hi," he said.

"Hi."

"What're you doing?" Cordero asked.

"I've a report to write on border management, remember? For INTERPOL. That's why I'm here. Not nearly as much fun as chasing bootleggers but I guess it has to be done," she replied.

He nodded, threw his keys on the table and slumped into a chair.

"You still have doubts?" she asked.

"About the liquor?" he asked. "Well, there was nothing but beer being sold at the cockfight."

"Or at the market," she added.

"So—" he began without adding more.

Carter placed her pen on the table next to the notebook.

"Aren't you forgetting the guy Brooks confirmed died from methanol poisoning?" she asked.

"I'm not forgetting anybody," he said. "But that's one bottle."

"Then here's Arturo Cabral."

"Okay, two bottles," he said.

"That fellow whose wife came to town with the joss paper?"

"Kosme Tavares?" Cordero said.

"Sounds like he could have been poisoned in the same way," Carter pointed out.

Cordero folded his arms and leaned over the table.

"He may have drunk from the same bottle as the first dead guy," he said.

"How likely is that?" she asked.

"Well no bottle was found near the first dead guy," he said.

"He could have drunk the contents anywhere, tossed the bottle, and stumbled on until the methanol hit him," she said.

"Sounds to me like you *want* to make this a bootlegging operation," he complained.

"Sounds to me like you don't," she countered.

She held his gaze until he gave in and lowered his eyes.

"Okay, you win," he said. "Three bottles."

"It's not about winning," she corrected him. "It's about protecting the community."

"Yes, of course, you're right. So three bottles." He started spinning the keys on the table. "Maybe four."

"Four?"

"A fellow showed up at the cockfight with more joss paper. Tried to place a bet with it." He sniffed. "He was illiterate and soft in the head. Came from out Lolitu way. Said the note fell out of his brother's pocket when he was carrying him off to be buried a few days ago." He looked up. "The brother had been healthy until he wasn't and died."

"Interesting," she said. "Four bottles then. Sounds like liquor aplenty to me."

Cordero let his keys alone and sat back.

"Turns out this fellow was one of the locals who had to dig a construction truck out of the mud about eighteen months ago," said Cordero. "It'd got bogged above a small river near Lolitu. I walked along the banks. I swear it'd been contaminated by something. I've asked Estefana to call the Ministry of Agriculture and Fisheries—MAF we call it—and find out all she can about the disposal of pesticides from Maliana a while back. She's at the police station now."

"Our priority is the liquor here and now, not a possible pesticide dumping a year, year and a half, ago," she said.

"Could be connected," Cordero complained.

"How?"

Cordero didn't know and so he had no answer for that. Carter closed her notebook.

"Are you feeling alright?" he asked.

"Yeah why?"

"Estefana said you had a headache," he said. "Said you thought you might have drunk too much gin last night."

"Estefana talks too much," she said.

"Do you remember what you were talking about last night?" he asked.

He leaned forward.

"Do you?" she shot back.

He vacillated between asking what he wanted to ask and not pushing his luck.

"You were telling me how often your stepmother made you change light bulbs," he decided to say.

"*That's* what you remember?" She pushed her chair away from the table and stood. "We have a burial to go to," she said. "So let's go."

• • •

Marco—the Bobonaro regional coordinator for MAF—phoned back after 40 minutes. Estefana grabbed the phone, a pen and paper handy to write down anything useful he had to say.

"Do you know how many boxes I had to go through to get this information?" Marco asked, annoyed.

"No," said Estefana abruptly.

"And how many files in each of those boxes? I'm supposed to be at my brother-in-law's for a party to honor his father. My wife will not be happy with me."

"Then why don't you get to the point? Tell me what you've found and you can be on your way," Estefana replied.

"You police think you're the only ones with important jobs," Marco said, clearly not finished with his complaining.

"I'm waiting," said Estefana.

Marco groaned just loud enough that she could hear before telling her as much as he could of what she wanted to know.

"Uh-huh. Right. Yes. Okay. Are you sure about that last bit?" she asked.

"Do you really need to ask me that?" said Marco.

"One last thing," said Estefana. "We think MAF should test the waters of a tributary of the Talu River in the area around Lolitu. We suspect there may have been pesticide contamination in the area."

"Pesticide contamination?"

"That's right," said Estefana. "That's what we suspect."

"So the police are specialists in environmental science now, are they?" asked Marco with a huff before hung up.

23

Gaspa Freitas' wooden coffin was carried to the marquee by four men dressed in *tais mane*—the traditional male sarong. Each man wore ankle bells and a feathered headdress. Instead of laying the coffin down they stood it upright against the table on which were set flowers and a collection of candles. The coffin was newly purchased for the burial by Dario and its red lacquered finish reflected the flickering candle flames and the lowering rays of the setting sun. Those gathered in the yard of Dario's house pushed and shoved from the front and sides of the marquee to get a good view of what was happening. Carter and Cordero hung back, watching for anything or anyone suspicious while keeping an eye on the rites by which Gaspa's body would be laid to rest and his spirit finally consigned to the underworld.

From loudspeakers attached to two palm trees either side of the house came a scratchy version of the East Timorese national anthem. While it played, one of the pallbearers went inside the house and came out with a large, framed portrait of a smiling Gaspa taken several years before his death. In the photograph he wore a prominent silver disc around his neck, symbolising his status as a *dato* or village nobleman. The portrait was mounted on an easel next to the coffin as the other three pallbearers began to unscrew the lid.

"How long's he been dead?" asked Carter.

"Ten, twelve years," said Cordero.

"They must be kidding," she responded.

The recording was shut off before the anthem had finished. There was a hushed, expectant silence followed by a wave of moans and yowls as the coffin lid was removed and the crowd caught sight of what remained of the body of Gaspa after more than a decade above ground in the tropical heat and humidity. The casket had been perfumed beforehand which was just as well as strong odours were released with the enclosed air. Some of the women clasped their hands behind their heads to indicate the despair they felt, others bent double in pain while still more reached out as though they could touch the body from afar. How much was mere theatrics and how much genuine grief was impossible to say.

A skull, the jaw fallen into a hideous guffaw, stared with empty eye sockets from the plush lining of the funerary box. Teeth had dropped from the upper jaw and a wisp of dried hair blew in the breeze across what once had been a face. What remained of Gaspa's body—dried out leathery muscle around bones that had long ago become hollow and brittle as they fossilised—had been wrapped in a fresh *tais mane* around which the same silver disc from the portrait had been strung. Fingernails and toenails were long, hard and brown like claws and the remnant debris from parched skin and sinew was stirred into tiny dust devils by the inrush of cooler air.

The rumbling from the crowd died down as near relatives made their way to the coffin to pay their respects to what remained of Gaspa and to hang rosary beds like garlands on the frame around his portrait. When that was done and the last had paid their respects, Dario stepped forward. He too wore a *tais mane* but with trouser legs visible where the wrap ended halfway down his calves. He stood with his back to the mourners and removed the disc from the corpse of his father. He placed the disc on the table with a show of reverence befitting a sacred icon and picked up several *tais* and shawls that had been brought there, placing them carefully inside the coffin.

"That's so Gaspa won't feel the need to revisit the house in search of clothing," Cordero whispered to Carter. "You know, at night or in the cooler months," he added.

"I think he'll need more than clothing if he ever revisits," Carter commented, tilting her head toward him.

When Dario was done, he stepped aside. Space was made for the coffin on the table, and Gaspa's corpse was laid out horizontally and sealed inside the coffin for good. One of the pallbearers approached wielding a long ceremonial sword with goat hair affixed to the handle. He uttered some words which Cordero could not catch from where he stood, raised the sword and brought it down in a precise and dramatic action to stop just above the coffin.

"A traditional act symbolising protection," Cordero explained.

The other pallbearers now grabbed the side handles of the coffin, lifted it off the table, and began to carry it in the procession to the cemetery.

Carter and Cordero waited until the tail end of the line of kinfolk and friends and kept a respectable distance between themselves and the mourners.

"You seem to know a lot about traditional burial practices," Carter said.

"Only what my parents taught me and what I've learned here since," said Cordero. "Yet I find them and the thinking that informs them interesting. Don't you? Among your Native Americans, I mean?"

She shaded her eyes from what was left of the setting sun which had angled the light directly across the landscape.

"Different ways of viewing the world and our place in it do interest me," she admitted. "Take my first month meeting Navajos. An old shaman invited me to take a sweat. To learn something about the people I'd be working with. So I thought 'Why not?'" She looked at him. "You know what a sweat lodge is?"

"I saw one in a movie once," said Cordero. "All dark, no air, hot rocks causing the heat to rise and the sweat to flow. I get the general idea."

"Right. Well, a traditional sweat is divided into parts," she continued, as they started off behind the procession. "Drumming, chanting, and whatnot and at the end of each part, when you're about to pass out, the shaman opens a flap in the covering that seals the lodge to let cool air in to revive you. The whole thing works on the stress the heat puts on your body. You know, light-headedness and how that affects your thinking."

He was nodding, wondering where this was going. Up ahead some of the mourners began singing hymns; others began reciting the Litany of the Saints—an ancient prayer of the Church in which the names of saints, martyrs, angels, and prophets are recited and they are petitioned to pray for the faithful and the deceased.

"Just before the final part," Carter continued, raising her voice above the din, "the shaman says the Great Spirit's here with us. Said I could speak to it if I wanted. So to be polite, you know, I start thinking of anything I needed. Answer: nothing. So I talk about my sister Bec—she was still missing. Last I mention my uncle and auntie whose farm was about to be foreclosed."

The singing and chanting grew louder at the gates of the cemetery. Carter and Cordero stopped and waited until everyone had settled inside.

"Then it was the shaman's turn," she said. "He spoke about the earth, his tribe, his chief's wife's mother. All sorts of things except himself or things directly related to him. You get the picture. Gringos think about themselves and that's the wrong order of things. We approach things from the inside out rather than the outside in."

Cordero smiled at that.

The last members of the crowd were positioning themselves around the gravesite.

"Let me tell you a story," Cordero said. "Years ago, a Portuguese engineer came here to build a bridge over a river down south. He had a glass eye, but few people knew about it. Well, he put together a workforce from a nearby village, took them to the site, and explained that the approaches on both sides of the river had to be cleared of trees and boulders as a first step. When he finished, he left to arrange more supplies."

Cordero put both hands in his pockets. They were winding their own way through the headstones now.

"When he returned, nothing'd been done and everyone was asleep under the trees. He called them together and repeated the instructions. Then he left again. When he returned, same thing—nothing done. Finally he'd had enough. So he called them again, took his glass eye out and put it on a stump. He told the villagers it was a magic eye that'd keep watch on them while he was away. He left a third time. When he came back, someone had placed an old tin can over the eye."

They stopped a short distance from the Freitas family burial plot. A crumbling cement angel towered over the cracked and weathered headstones of ancient members of the Freitas family and two more recent decorative crosses—one marking the grave of Gaspa's wife, the other afixed with a photograph of Dario's son, Angelino, encased in a plastic frame. A hole had been dug to accommodate Gaspa next to his wife and the old man's coffin was laid by its side.

Standing over the grave was Father Francedez in his black funereal vestments clutching a slimmed-down Tetun version of the *Order of Christian Funerals* in one hand and adjusting his glasses with the other. Dario stood just behind him within view of all present.

"The moral of your story being?" asked Carter.

"The engineer tried to use the villagers' superstition to get the better of them. But they were too imaginative to allow that. You're about to see the much the same thing happen here."

The priest read aloud the prayers for the dead. Occasionally he would stop and reach for his aspergillum—the perforated metal ball used for sprinkling holy water over the coffin. When he was finished he made the sign of the cross over the casket and over the assembled kinfolk. He stepped away and what remained of Gaspa was lowered into the grave.

"Watch now," said Cordero.

Slowly, the crowd of mourners dispersed. They slipped away from the grave, some hand in hand, others strolling casually through the cemetery and onto the road that led back to Dario's house. Fathers carried babies in their arms; small children held their mothers' hands and sucked on their fingers or tried to grab blades of grass. The expression on the faces of the children reflected boredom more than anything else.

"See?"

"I don't get it," said Carter. "See what?"

"In times past they would run from the graveside as fast as they could. Stampede almost. You see, when the Portuguese introduced cemeteries, *sidade mate* we call them—cities of the dead—Timorese would fear that so many bodies in the one place would mean the area was full of the spirits of people buried away from their homes and angry about that. These days mourners wait to light their candles on the grave and once that's done they leave calmly. Not because they no longer believe in spirits. They do. But now in their minds the priest exercises a greater, restraining, power over spirits with holy water and a prayer book."

"So the priest is the rusty old tin can covering the glass eye?" she ventured.

"Something like that, yeah."

He glanced at her.

"It's a case of viewing things from a different angle. Like your shaman," he said.

Estefana was running up the road to the cemetery gates. She met them panting heavily.

"*Maun!*" she called. "I did what you asked."

"And what did you find out?"

She bent over her knees to catch her breath before answering.

"I had someone at the ministry check the records. A company by the name of Mallibo was contracted to collect the pesticide in Maliana, ship it to Tasi Tolu, and arrange a barge to take it to Kupang."

"Tasi Tolu is the port just outside Dili," Cordero explained to Carter. "Go on," he said to Estefana.

"The contract was for nearly three thousand dollars," Estefana said, straightening. "I was able to call the two companies in Tasi Tolu that deal with barges. Their offices don't close until 6pm. Neither of the companies had any record of Mallibo contracting with them to hire a barge and only one company had arranged barges to Kupang in the last two years. None of their barges carried pesticide out. Each was only sent to bring new motor vehicles back here."

"So the ministry has no record of the barges being organized or the pesticides being delivered to Kupang?"

"Not that could be found, no," replied Estefana.

"Did that strike whoever you spoke to at the ministry as unusual?"

"No. I was told many people working for the ministry are poorly trained. Also, the ministry has so much work to do and so many contracts going on that things get lost all the time. So nobody was likely to have checked up."

"Good work, Estefana," said Cordero.

"That's not all," she said. She took another deep breath. "I couldn't find any information about Mallibo. You know, who owns the company and that sort of thing. I tried their office in Maliana and no one answered the phone. I was sitting at the desk tapping my pencil over my notes when Officer Natalia came back into the room with coffee."

"Officer Natalia?"

"She's that young officer," Estefana explained. "The one who was in the police commander's office with *Senyora* Tavares and the funny bank note."

"Right, okay."

"She asked what was worrying me. We'd talked before while I was waiting for the ministry to ring back. I said I was trying to figure out this company, Mallibo. She laughed. I asked her why. She said it was a contraction of Maliana-Balibo. She said it was owned by José dos Silva."

Cordero's expression indicated the name meant nothing to him.

"He's Juno Cabral's brother-in-law," said Estefana.

"Really? Juno's wife's brother?"

"No. Juno's sister's husband. That's how Natalia knows. She's friends with Juno's sister."

Cordero whistled softly as Mateus emerged from among the crowd of the mourners.

"I've been looking for you," the police commander said. "Have any of you seen Officer Edi Sobado?"

As one they shook their heads.

"We've been hearing some interesting things about pesticide removal contracts, barges or the lack of them, and people related to Juno Cabral," said Cordero.

"And here comes the man himself to answer some questions," Carter interrupted him. "But he doesn't look happy."

24

In fact, Juno Cabral was furious. The flesh under his eyes was swollen and the eyes themselves red from lack of sleep and pent-up emotion. His hair was unkempt and his clothes hung loose on his body as though it was wasting away. Even so, his jaw was set firm and his teeth were clenched. He stormed past Cordero and the others paying them no mind until Mateus called on him to stop.

Juno spun around on his heels and glared at Mateus.

"Where's Dario Freitas?" he asked in a shrill voice. "Where's that bastard?"

"What are you doing here, Juno?" Mateus said calmly.

Juno edged closer to the police commander. His face was contorted and the tracks of dried tears could be seen on his cheeks. He went to speak but nothing at first came out of his mouth.

Then it did.

"He's dead! My son is dead!"

"Arturo? When?" Mateus asked.

Juno brushed a hand roughly across his eyes.

"An hour ago," he said. "I never had a chance to tell him I love him. I never had a chance to say goodbye. He never regained consciousness. Now he's gone." He wiped his face once more. "He was only 14 years old!" His voice deepened to a growl. "I'll make that bastard pay! You'll see. I'll make him pay!"

Juno started off into the cemetery. Mateus grabbed his arm and pulled him back.

"Let me go!" he demanded, and he tried to shake off the police commander.

"I'm sorry to hear about Arturo," Mateus said, taking a firmer hold of Juno's arm. "He was a good boy. But you need to calm down. We've no evidence that Dario is associated with any toxic liquor. No evidence. And at the moment no clear reason to suspect he is. I have police officers covering the festivities Dario's hosting tonight. If he's involved, we'll discover it and I'll deal with him. I give you my word on that. You must leave things to the police, Juno. Surely as village headman you know that."

Juno tried again to shake free of the commander's grip.

"I know my son is dead! That's all I know!"

"Don't let your grief turn into rage, Juno," Mateus urged, letting go of his arm. "When has that ever done any good?"

"Arturo is dead!" Juno repeated. He slumped to his knees as though anger had been the only thing holding him together and he was now drained even of that. He put both hands to his chest and began to sob.

Mateus patted Juno on the shoulder.

"I have my vehicle parked just down the road there," he said to Cordero. "I'll drive him home or else things might get out of hand. Keep an eye out and if you see Edi tell him to go to the police station right away and wait for me there."

"Estefana has some information she needs to pass on to you," Cordero said. He glanced down at Juno. "It's about what we found at the river this morning."

"It can wait," said Mateus. He placed a hand under Juno's shoulder and helped him to his feet. "This is more important at the moment."

Mateus led Juno away. Carter, Cordero and Estefana watched them go. The last few stragglers were heading off to Dario's house.

"We'd best go," said Carter. "If the idea is to distribute or sell this stuff tonight, Arturo won't be the last to die."

"I hope Mateus has done a good job of briefing his officers," said Cordero.

"I don't doubt he has," said Carter. "He knows what he's doing."

"Then I hope his officers are up to the job," he said.

"Why do you say that?"

"No pay, no incentive, remember?" Cordero quickened his pace. "We three will just have to make sure we have the whole feast covered."

· · ·

At Dario's house, people were milling around in groups talking quietly in front of the marquee. Off to the side of the house, some of the men were barbecuing two pigs and a goat while women came and went from inside the house carrying trays of salad and cooked rice. Some of the food would be offered to the spirits of Gaspa's ancestors to eat and, once this was seen to be done, shared out among the guests. For the moment, however, all eyes were on Dario, who sat under the marquee along with representatives of his kinship group and those of his mother who had predeceased Gaspa by five years.

Dario and the others were exchanging gifts—fabrics of various kinds, small bags of rice, jars of cooking oil. They were small, symbolic gifts—the more substantial gifts of buffalos, pigs, and goats had been exchanged on the occasion of the actual deaths of Gaspa and his wife. Marriage created webs of obligations and claims between the lineage group of the husband and that of his wife: the exchange of gifts was meant to resolve any outstanding debts and release both sides from any further responsibilities toward one another.

Once the gifts were exchanged, Dario signalled for a number of brass gongs and traditional drums to sound. The cacophony was deafening and lasted several minutes until it had caught the attention of those gathered and they had fallen silent. As the noise died down, another sound could be heard—much softer and melodious. A man came forward from the behind the marquee. He was playing a *kafu'i*—a traditional wooden flute popular in this part of Timor.

The *kafu'i* was used to call buffalos, scare birds away from crops, or simply soothe a worker who'd spent long, exhausting hours in the fields. Its purpose here, following the din of the drums and gongs, was to hint at a new beginning. That much became obvious when Dario rose, approached the table, and took the metal disc that had hung around his father's neck in life and, for a short time, in his coffin. Dario placed it around his own neck and turned to face the crowd. His face reflected a smug pride. He said nothing—he didn't have to. He stretched out his hands so that everyone could see clearly that he was claiming the title of *dato* or nobleman now for himself.

Carter, Cordero and Estefana had spread themselves out on the fringe of the crowd where there was a little more movement taking place. Some of the men were angling to be first in line for food; some of the women were herding children back from the unlit parts of the estate to where lanterns dispelled the darkness from the grounds. Cordero noticed crates of cold beer and the mild palm wine *tua mutin* being carried out of the house and placed near the food tables. He intercepted one of the men carrying a crate and inspected the drinks. He opened a couple of random bottles and was relieved to see there was no suggestion of anything particularly strong among the offerings.

When Cordero looked up, he saw Bobu's daughter, Josefa, dragging Dario's daughter, Marquita, by the hand to the side of the house. Apparently the two had become best friends in the sudden fashion that children sometimes do. Marquita was giggling and Josefa was saying something to urge her on, the only word of which Cordero caught was '*apá*'. Cordero noticed a guitar swinging on the back of someone in the shadows. He couldn't see the face but figured it had to be Bobu—Josefa would be taking Marquita to meet him—and he was involved in a dispute with a boy who was gesturing wildly over a coconut cart.

Cordero poked his head above the people around him searching for his colleagues. He saw Estefana not too far off and called out to her over the chatter of people making their way to the barbecue pits and trellises covered with food. She didn't hear him over the noise. For a moment his view of Estefana was blocked by a group of women pushing past. He called a second time, much louder. This time she heard him.

"Come over here now! Get *Mana* Carter! Hurry!" he said, pointing to the side of the house.

Cordero charged off to inspect the coconut cart and find out what the argument was about. He had to elbow his way through people pushing forward to grab food, ignoring their complaints as he did. Finally he was behind Bobu, who he recognized clearly now, and facing the boy he'd tried to buy a coconut from earlier in the day—the boy to whom he'd confided he was a police investigator. When the boy saw Cordero, his eyes flared and he grabbed hold of his cart to rush away.

Cordero pushed Bobu aside, reached out a hand and grabbed hold of the cart. That brought the boy to a stop. Bobu started to back away but Josefa had reached him and had her arms around his legs so that it was hard for him to move. Marquita had come up as well and was also blocking his way.

"Stay where you are, Bobu," Cordero ordered. "I want a word with you." He turned to the boy. "Well now," he said, looking down into the cart. "What have we here?"

"There's nothing in there, *maun*, just coconuts," the boy was saying. He shifted between Cordero and the cart, trying to block Cordero's view.

"He was bringing that stuff into the ceremony and I tried to stop him," Bobu claimed.

"Bullshit!" the boy countered. "You promised to pay me when I sold it!"

"Why would I do that?" Bobu said and pulled out his pockets. "I have no money."

Cordero nudged the boy aside. He reached down into the coconuts and retrieved two bottles of clear liquid from beneath them. As he did Estefana and Carter shouldered their way through the crowd.

"What's up?" asked Carter.

"This," Cordero said, holding up the bottles. "Strange looking coconuts."

Carter and Estefana stared down into the cart. The boy tried to run. Estefana shot out a hand and managed to grab hold of him by his T-shirt. She hauled him back. Carter pulled another bottle from under the coconuts. Cordero clamped one bottle under his arm and unscrewed the cap on the other. He put his nose to the top.

"If I'm not mistaken, I'd say that's our smuggled liquor wouldn't you?" he said to Carter and held the bottle out for her to sniff.

She nodded. "So where's the rest of it?" she asked.

Cordero put the question to Bobu. He shrugged.

"I'd think about cooperating if I were you," Cordero said.

Bobu's face showed no emotion and he remained tight-lipped. Cordero tried the boy.

"I'm guessing you haven't sold anything yet so you're not in any trouble," he said in an attempt to elicit the boy's cooperation. "But if you don't tell me what I want to know Officer Estefana here will take you to the police station and put you in a cell."

Estefana tugged on the T-shirt so the boy knew he couldn't get away. His mouth opened and closed as he swallowed hard but he said nothing. Another tug and the boy looked up at Estefana and back to Cordero.

"Well?" said Cordero.

"The fort! It's in the fort," the boy said. He pointed to Bobu. "That's where he put it. He said no one'd go there because of the spirits of all the dead people there. The ones killed fighting the *bapa*. The ones the *bapa* tortured." He tried shaking free of Estefana but had no luck. "But he owes me. I did everything he told me to do."

Cordero looked to Bobu. He held his daughter in close as though he was about to be separated from her again and sent back to prison.

Two of the drummers from the marquee squeezed between Bobu and Cordero, laughing to each other as they went. Bobu said something but Cordero couldn't catch what it was. There was a bang! And another!

Cordero spun around to his left and then his right. Out of the crowd came a man beating a large gong as he play-acted with a friend. Cordero turned back, bumping into Father Francedez as he did and knocking the priest's glasses to the ground.

"What—!" the priest began.

"Sorry *amu*," said Cordero. "Stand back. You might tread on them. I'll find them."

The priest stepped back to clear a space on the ground. Cordero went down on one knee and was feeling for the glasses in the darkness.

Helio had weaved his way through the crowd, eyes locked on his target. From under the sarong bunched around his waist he took the revolver. In the same motion he cocked it and fired. The bullet flew low, hit one of the metal wheels on the coconut cart and ricocheted into Marquita. She gave a yelp and watched in horror as blood spurted from the side of her arm.

People momentarily froze in place while they tried to work out what had happened. Ears were ringing with the sound of the shot and a choking smell of cordite infused the air. Within seconds the silence was split by yelling and screaming, along with a frenzied pushing and shoving to get away.

Helio knew he only had one cartridge left. The cylinder in the revolver was stiff but he managed to move it with the fingers of his free hand. Women ran in front of him, men behind. Off to the side Father Francedez held his hands to his mouth in shock. Helio ducked and dodged in the chaos to get a clear shot, pointed the weapon and fired again.

But Cordero had flung himself in the path of the bullet. It struck him with the impact of a hammer blow beneath the rib cage on the left side. He clutched his stomach, stumbled, and stared down at his shirt which was staining with blood. He lifted his head, recognizing Helio as he merged back into the crowd, and turned toward Carter.

She was screaming something he couldn't hear.

His legs gave out and he collapsed like a pillar of dried sand.

• • •

People were scrambling in all directions and the squeals of children pierced the air. Carter fell to her knees beside Cordero, reached an arm around his shoulders, and eased him as gently as she could flat to the ground.

"Tino," she said softly under the shrieks and crying.

Father Francedez came forward and stretched out a hand, a helpless expression on his face. Carter ignored the priest and searched out Estefana. She caught sight of her tending to Marquita who was screaming in agony. Estefana had released the boy with the coconut cart: he stood frozen, mouth open in shock, making no effort now to run away.

"Get help, Estefana!" Carter shouted . "Quickly!"

Estefana said something to Bobu and took off toward the house. Carter focused again on Cordero. He was clutching his wound, the blood seeping through his fingers.

"Shit!" he mumbled, his eyes shut tight in pain.

"Don't try to talk," Carter urged him. "Help's coming. You'll be alright."

Father Francedez calmed himself and took a kerchief from his pocket. He forced it into Cordero's hands in an attempt to staunch the bleeding. It made no discernible difference. The priest said something to Carter, but she didn't understand what he was saying in Tetun.

"Not again!" she protested, but Father Francedez couldn't understand her English either. "I won't let him!"

Cordero raised a bloody hand. Carter seized it and held it firmly.

"Hold on," she said. "I'm here."

Another officer rushed forward with Estefana who, after a quick check of Cordero, went back to the girl she'd left momentarily in Bobu's care.

The officer edged Father Francedez aside and crouched beside Cordero, inspecting his wound but avoiding the question on Carter's face.

The Hilux owned by Dario Freitas soon rumbled through a clump of people—another officer who'd somehow managed to commandeer the vehicle at the wheel. The headlights split the darkness and onlookers drew in their breaths at the sight of the man clutching his stomach on the ground and Dario's daughter bleeding and screaming off to the side. The driver jumped from the vehicle and ordered everyone back.

The two officers lifted Cordero gingerly into the back seat of the Hilux.

"We're taking you to the clinic now," Carter told him although Cordero had lost consciousness. "I'll stay with you."

Carter popped her head over the roof of the Hilux to check on Estefana. She was bringing Marquita, sniffling and moaning, to the vehicle in her arms.

Estefana settled the girl into the front passenger's seat.

"I think she'll be alright, *mana*," Estefana said. "But she is in pain and frightened. How is *maun*?"

Carter met her eyes but said nothing. The officer scurried back into the driver's seat and slammed the door. Carter climbed in next to Cordero and Estefana noticed her touch the side of his face before comforting Marquita.

The first officer who'd arrived at the scene of the shooting came up hurriedly to the Hilux. He was carrying a revolver in the palms of his hands.

"Someone handed this in just now," he told Estefana, holding his hands out as in an offering. "I think it was the pistol that was used. It was tossed on the ground over there," he added, lifting his chin off to the side.

"They're going to the health clinic," Estefana told him. "So take it to the police station along with Bobu. I'll take care of his daughter."

25

"They gave him a shot of morphine," Carter was saying. She was wringing her hands and, her eyes moist, avoiding the gaze of Mateus. "At least they had that in stock. They're short of everything as you know. He was lucky."

She wiped her eyes with her hand and Mateus shifted uncomfortably in his chair.

"He wasn't making much sense when I left," she continued. "In and out of consciousness, you know. The nurse said the bullet passed through the side of his stomach and out again but didn't hit anything too important. That's what she said. 'Too important'. Goddam it! He could've been killed!" She sucked in air and calmed herself. "I'll get him to Dili as soon as he's able. I'll have a doctor check him properly."

Mateus and Carter were sitting in the police commander's office. It had gone 9 o'clock and they were both trying to fathom the events of the evening.

"The local doctor should be here tomorrow," Mateus said.

"Right," she scoffed. "I want Tino double checked, maybe even in Darwin or Singapore."

Mateus allowed the comment to pass. It was typical of Westerners to doubt any but their own in times of crisis.

"And the girl, Marquita?" he asked.

Carter wiped her nose this time.

"The bullet must have shattered when it hit the metal wheel of the cart. She was hit by a fragment. The nurse was able to extract it and stitch her up. Pretty straightforward. She'll be fine. They're keeping her in only as a precaution."

Mateus was tempted to say 'So no trip to Darwin or Singapore for the Timorese girl' but he resisted and merely uttered "Hmm".

There was a tap on the door.

"Enter," Mateus said.

An officer poked his head in and asked if the police commander was ready to question the one who called himself Bobu. Mateus took a deep breath, sat erect, and said he was.

"Do you want to stay for this?" he asked Carter.

"Yes, please," she said and eased back in her chair. "There's nothing I can do at the clinic until Tino's head clears and when it does, he'll want to know everything."

"Okay," said Mateus. "I'll translate the gist of what he has to say for himself."

Bobu was brought into the commander's office and sat down in a chair facing Mateus. Carter remained seated off to the side and Bobu ignored her.

"Where's my daughter?" Bobu demanded to know.

"Officer Estefana dos Carvalho is driving Josefa home," Mateus said. "That's her name isn't it? Josefa? You don't need to worry about her."

"What do you mean I don't need to worry? She could have been killed!" Bobu said.

"Yes, but she wasn't," Mateus said. "You could have been killed too. That's what interests me. Your daughter will be fine."

Bobu stretched his legs and crossed them at the ankles. Police interrogations were obviously nothing new to him.

"My guitar? Where's it?" he asked.

"Safely put away. You won't need it for a while."

Mateus took a cigarette from his shirt pocket and lit it. He took a long drag and blew smoke out of the side of his mouth.

"Hey! You told me you didn't smoke," said Bobu, his tone indignant.

Mateus stared at him.

"I lied."

"You got one for me?" asked Bobu.

"No."

Mateus took another drag, stubbed the cigarette out in an ashtray, and leaned forward across his desk.

"I don't have time to play games, Bobu. It's my time to ask the questions and your time to answer," he said. "Let's start with what can you tell me about your role in this smuggling operation."

"I'm not involved in any smuggling operation," Bobu insisted and shrugged the thought away demonstrably. "You've got me all wrong."

"I'm told the boy with the liquor in his cart was arguing with you about payment," said Mateus. "Are you denying that you two had an arrangement?"

Bobu turned away and didn't respond to the question.

"If you're smart, you'll cooperate," Mateus said. "You have a record. Another conviction in connection with smuggled liquor—liquor that has resulted in the deaths of four people—could see you spend the next decade or more behind bars."

"What are you talking about? What four people?"

"Three down near the border and one here in Balibo," said Mateus. "I'm sure someone who gets around as much as you heard the news."

Bobu disentangled his arms and lifted his eyes to the ceiling.

"Are you prepared to go to prison for ten, fifteen years?" Mateus asked.

Bobu stayed silent.

"Think of your daughter," Mateus added.

Bobu's shoulders slumped a little at that thought and he cast his eyes to the floor. He still said nothing.

"Let me tell you what I think happened," Mateus began. "You were approached by Officer Eduardo Sobado to make a little money on the side by selling bootlegged liquor."

Mateus noticed Bobu's eyes twitch at the mention of Edi.

"Your role was to get the liquor from down on the border, bring it up to Balibo, and organise the boys to sell it at the ceremony after Gaspa Freitas' burial," Mateus continued. "Am I right so far?"

There was more fidgeting from Bobu and a few moments without a response before he chose to answer.

"No," was all he said.

"No?" Mateus echoed.

"I didn't have anything to do with a smuggling operation and I wasn't going to make any money," Bobu insisted. "And I don't know anything about four people who you say died from drinking that stuff."

"Then tell me what you do know," said Mateus.

More silence from Bobu. Mateus translated the gist of the conversation for Carter's benefit. Bobu became aware of her for the first time.

"Who's she and why's she here?" he asked.

"She's with INTERPOL. They don't take too kindly to smuggling operations," said Mateus.

"I told you I don't know anything about smuggling," Bobu complained.

"And I told you to tell me what you do know," replied Mateus.

Bobu started jiggling his feet. He bit a fingernail while he thought through his situation. He put his hand in his lap, shook his head, and drew his legs in.

"Sobado knew I'd been in prison," he said. "Don't ask me how. He just knew. He caught me smoking a joint one day. Here, in town. Shit!" he said dismissively. "Who cares about a lousy joint? Lots of Timorese smoke marijuana. It's not like I was growing it or selling it."

He paused.

"Go on," said Mateus.

Bobu shifted uneasily.

"Sobada told me he'd arrest me and send me back to prison unless I did what he told me to do."

Mateus showed no surprise at that.

"And that was?" he asked.

"He told me he'd got a stack of liquor. He didn't say from where. He'd used your SUV to bring it into Balibo."

Bobu faced Mateus directly and sneered at the thought of the police commander's vehicle being used to haul contraband. Mateus sniffed at the statement and nothing more.

"I was supposed to stash it someplace safe, out of sight," Bobu continued. "I chose the fort. No one goes in there because of the stupid fear of spirits haunting the place and there are plenty of places to stash stuff in the ruins where no one would ever find it. Sobado knew I was friends with a lot of the boys in Balibo. I'm the clown around here, remember? The entertainer. So he said to organise the boys to sell the liquor. They were supposed to get a cut when the money started coming in. None of that had anything to do with me."

"So you were being blackmailed?" Mateus put to him.

"You could say that, yeah."

"Whose idea was it to conceal the liquor in the carts?"

"Mine." Bobu smiled. "Not bad, huh? Until that other one—the one who was shot tonight—figured it out." He leaned forward in his chair. "How is he, by the way? He saved those kids from getting hurt."

"He'll live," was all Mateus said.

"And the other girl? The one who got shot?"

"She'll live too. The wound was only superficial."

Mateus folded his arms.

"So why were you arguing with the boy with the cart?" he asked.

"Sobado called the whole thing off. Twice. The liquor was supposed to be sold at the cockfight. You and the other officers were all over that. So he decided to try at the burial ceremony. You were all over that too. Even put him in charge!"

Bobu laughed at that.

"The fact that people had died from drinking it didn't stop him?" asked Mateus.

"I told you I know nothing about that," said Bobu. "As for Sobado, he was prepared to sell the stuff on two occasions. So if he knew about people who'd died from drinking the liquor, it didn't bother him."

"Go on," said Mateus.

"So he couldn't go on with the plan tonight either. I went to the fort and told the boys it was off. That one—Arlo's his name,

I think—got shitty because he wanted the money. Decided to try and sell stuff on his own. We were arguing because I was trying to stop him."

"The officers I sent to the fort tonight found about five dozen bottles," said Mateus. "Is that all there is?"

"Sounds about right, yeah."

"So when Sobado called it off the second time, everything was just going to be left there? In the fort?" asked Mateus.

"Sobado told me to move the liquor to some place the boys wouldn't know about and we'd try some other time. *We!*" he repeated and sneered at that. "I was due to perform for Dario Freitas so that had to wait."

Mateus placed his elbows on the armrests of his chair and formed a triangle with his fingers. He studied Bobu for a long moment.

"Why did Helio Lima try to kill you?" he asked.

Bobu shrugged the question off.

"He's crazy, that's why," he said. "They're all crazy that lot. They sit there in the sacred house being crazy with each other. Helio, his idiot son, Rodrigo Duarte, and Fidalgo de Queiroz. He tried to burn my hut down, for fuck's sake!"

He turned to Carter and apologized for his language.

"Fidalgo tried to burn your hut down?" Mateus asked.

"Uh-huh."

"When?"

"Earlier." He leaned forward. "That's why I'm worried about Josefa. You say she's been taken there?"

"With Officer dos Carvalho, yes. Your daughter will be fine. The officer will make sure your daughter's safe. And I have police officers between here and Lolitu searching for Helio. He'll be too busy trying to get away to get up to any more trouble. And he dropped the revolver," he added, nodding to the handgun on the desk.

Bobu loosened up a little.

"So why try to burn your hut down and why try to shoot you?" Mateus asked again.

"They've been against me ever since I arrived in Lolitu," Bobu said. "Don't like my kind, whatever that is."

"Have you done anything to cause them to dislike you?"

"*Despise*, not dislike," insisted Bobu.

"Okay, despise," agreed Matues. "Have you caused it?"

"No. I haven't done anything I can think of. I haven't tried to challenge them or anything—well, not until they tried to burn down my hut. Maybe they just don't like the songs I sing," Bobu said sarcastically.

"You haven't argued with Helio?" Mateus asked.

"No."

"Or João Lima?"

"No."

"You know Helio's other son, Osorio, is dead. You know anything about that?"

"I didn't know he was dead," said Bobu. "So how would I?"

"And you can think of no reason, no specific reason, why Helio would want to kill you?"

"How many times do I have to say 'No, I don't'?"

Mateus studied Bobu for a long moment.

"You have anything more to say?" he asked.

Bobu shook his head.

Mateus translated the gist of the conversation while still watching Bobu. He turned and raised an eyebrow in Carter's direction. There was nothing she wanted to ask.

"Vasco!" Mateus called and the officer who'd brought Bobu into the room returned. "Take *Senyor* Fábio Aparcio, or Bobu as he prefers to be called, to his cell. I'll decide what to do with him later."

Bobu rose, wiped his hands down the front of his jeans, and eyed what was left of the cigarette Mateus had stubbed out in the ashtray on his desk.

"Help yourself," said Mateus.

Bobu picked up the stub, lit it with the commander's lighter, and was led out leaving a trail of smoke behind him. Mateus took a deep breath and exhaled slowly.

"How did you know about Officer Sobado?" Carter asked.

"Edi?" Mateus sniffed. "My officers haven't been paid for months due to the budget being locked up as I told you. So we're all short of money. As I was telling Cordero, Edi persuaded some of us to bet on a rooster in a cockfight several weeks ago. Foolishly even I went along with it." He raised and lowered a hand. "Well we lost. I don't know how much Edi lost. I know he was sure this rooster would win so I'm guessing a lot. Probably borrowed it. So he'd have a strong incentive to try and make money quickly."

He stood, circled the desk, and leaned against it.

"When we were out examining that first body—the smuggler from West Timor—I asked Edi if the dead man had anything in his pockets. He said 'No'. Said people out in the border area had no use for papers because they couldn't read. *Kaladi*—yam-eaters, remember? That started me thinking it could've been Edi who stole the joss paper from Feng. Wouldn't be hard for a police officer to break into the store. Probably deceived the smuggler and his accomplices into thinking they were being paid real money to bring the liquor across. None of them could have read the disclaimer on the notes that they weren't real money and Edi would have to use something like that because he had no money of his own. When he said the dead guy from West Timor didn't have anything in his pockets, I bet he'd taken some joss paper out of his pocket before we got there. Edi also gets on well with officers from Border Patrol. He would have known when it was safe for someone to come across the border and not be seen."

"Why did you put Sobado in charge of the officers on the lookout for liquor at Dario's?" Carter asked.

"At that stage it wasn't even a suspicion I had," said Mateus. "It was what you call in English a hunch. I couldn't be open about it because, as I've told you, my officers haven't been paid so my hold over them is weak. If I'd suggested one of them was guilty of something and that proved wrong, my authority would be further weakened. Besides, I liked your approach of letting things happen in order to catch people in the act."

"But at the cemetery you said you wanted Sobado to come back here and you appeared pretty confident he was guilty just now when you questioned Bobu," Carter said. "What convinced you?"

Mateus took a slip of paper out of his shirt pocket.

"When we went to inspect that body near the border I asked Edi if he knew the dead man. He said 'No'. When I obtained the man's name and record from my Indonesian counterpart, I made some enquiries with Border Patrol about the man's arrest for smuggling kerosene a few years ago. I'd forgotten about the reply until I changed my clothes to go to Gaspa's burial. This fell out of my shirt pocket."

He unfolded the paper and held it aloft.

"The East Timorese officer who escorted our smuggler back to West Timor was Eduardo Sobado, working at the time out of Batugade. So he knew the man, knew he was into smuggling, and would have had contact details for him." He put the paper on his desk. "And now I have Bobu's statement which seals Edi's fate."

"Where's Sobado now?" she asked.

"I'm told he was coming back to the station when they were bringing Bobu in," said Mateus. "He would have figured Bobu would cooperate in the hope of avoiding another prison term. He was last seen taking a motorcycle from outside and riding off. He won't get far. I've alerted police in Maliana and Batugade."

Mateus swiveled around and picked up the revolver. He forced open the jammed cylinder and inspected the chambers inside.

"This thing must be seventy years old," he said. "Maybe more. Cordite for a propellant! Good thing it hasn't been used in all that time or we could have had two fatalities to deal with—one of them being your friend Cordero."

Carter stood, came across and inspected the handgun Mateus was holding.

"Good thing Helio only had two cartridges and wasn't a practiced shooter," she added. "Sometimes the stars just line up in your favor."

She made for the door.

"Where are you going?" Mateus asked.

"You have everything under control here," she said. "I'm going to play nurse for a while."

As she opened the door to leave she encountered a police officer coming to speak to Mateus. She moved aside.

"There's someone to see you, commander," the officer said.

"Can't it wait?" complained Mateus.

"No sir. He says it's urgent," the officer replied.

"Who is it?" Mateus asked.

"Says his name's Fidalgo de Queiroz. From down near Lolitu."

26

Carter stepped back from the door and resumed her seat. She figured Cordero would only just be emerging from a morphine-induced drowsiness and she could delay visiting him a little longer. Besides, what this man had to say just might explain the events that had almost resulted in his death plus that of Dario's daughter, Marquita, and Cordero would want to know the details.

Fidalgo de Queiroz limped into the room, eyes downcast, carrying a bill cap in his hands. He surveyed the office, Mateus, and Carter, and lumbered to a stop at the desk of the police commander. He stood there, silent and apprehensive, turning the bill cap around in his fingers.

"Are you here to confess to trying to burn down the hut where the one called Bobu lives?" Mateus asked.

"No," said Fidalgo.

"You did try to burn it down, am I right?"

That was met with a shrug from Fidalgo.

"What have you come to tell me then?" said Mateus. "Out with it."

Fidalgo stopped fiddling with his cap and glanced across at Carter.

"She's a colleague from Dili," said Mateus. "That's all you need to know. Now tell me why you're here or get out and let me get on with my job. We'll deal with the hut business another time. I've more important things to worry about now."

"I came to stop someone getting hurt, maybe even killed," Fidalgo said in a voice so soft Mateus could hardly hear him.

"What? I didn't get that. Speak up," he said.

"I said I came to stop people getting hurt," repeated Fidalgo.
"Why do you think someone might get hurt?" Mateus asked.
"Helio," Fidalgo said.
"What? Who? Speak up."
"Helio Lima," said Fidalgo. "I think he might hurt somebody tonight. Maybe at that big burial ceremony where people are gathered. They don't know me there and they'd be too busy to listen to me anyhow. So I came here. To you."

He had Mateus' attention now.

"Take a seat," the police commander said.

Fidalgo's eyes flicked from side to side. He reached for a chair and sat, his bad leg stretched out in front. He rested his cap in his lap, glanced again at Carter, and didn't seem to know what to do with his hands.

"You're a bit late," Mateus said. "Helio did try to hurt some people tonight. He shot Dario Freitas' little girl and a police colleague of mine from Dili."

Fidalgo looked up, eyes wide, mouth open. He quickly bent over his thighs and shook his head.

"Are they…dead?" he asked.

"Thankfully no," said Mateus. "The girl's wound was superficial. The police investigator was shot in the stomach. He'll live."

"What about the one called Bobu?" Fidalgo asked.

"What about him?" Mateus said.

"Was he injured?"

"No."

"Where is he?"

"If you must know, he's in a cell. He was involved in smuggling liquor into the country. Liquor that was poison. Liquor that resulted in the death of several people."

Fidalgo lifted his eyes.

"And Helio?" he asked.

"My officers are searching for him now."

Fidalgo noticed the revolver on Mateus' desk.

"That?" he said and pointed with his cap.

"What about that?" Mateus asked.

"It's from our sacred house. Is that the gun Helio used?"

"As far as we know, yes." Mateus moved the revolver out of reach of Fidalgo and leaned over the desk. "I think it's time you told me what's been going on."

Fidalgo adjusted his position and took hold of his bad leg with both hands.

"Come on," said Mateus. "I don't have all night."

"Helio and me are members of the same clan," Fidalgo began. "There aren't many of us left, maybe twenty. Some moved across the border with the *bapa*; others were killed by the *bapa* militia when they fled back across later. We are the elders—Helio, me and Rodrigo Duarte. We keep the traditions alive and protect the sacred places."

"What clan is this?" Mateus asked.

"The eel clan," said Fidalgo.

"I've never heard of it."

"You're not supposed to. Not unless you're born into it."

"Why's it called the eel clan?"

Fidalgo straightened his bad leg and put his cap back in his lap.

"Our first ancestor was called Ali-iku," he said, a nickname meaning 'Ali the tail'. "He lived a long time ago."

"What's this got to do with anything?" asked Mateus, impatient now.

"I'm trying to tell you," said Fidalgo.

"Okay, go on. I'm listening," said Mateus, folding his arms across his chest.

Fidalgo then related his clan's foundation myth. This Ali-iku was the youngest of four brothers. They all lived on a ridge above a river that flows into the Talu, near Lolitu. One day the brothers told Ali-iku to go to the river and fetch water. When he went there he saw the water was muddy because a big eel had been swimming in it. He told the brothers the water was no good to drink and why.

"They told him to catch the eel, kill it and cook it to eat," Fidalgo said, acting out the actions with his hands.

Carter couldn't follow what was being said and so far Mateus had only told her that Fidalgo had come to warn him about Helio. She could see Mateus' interest had been aroused and figured that what he was being told was key to understanding the night's events. She sat there patiently, not wanting to move or make a sound least she spook Fidalgo and interrupt what Mateus was learning.

The story went that Ali-iku walked back to the river and caught the eel, put it in a pot, and started to cook it.

"But it spoke to Ali-iku," said Fidalgo. "It told him: 'When the sun goes down, we both become eels.'"

Fidalgo related how Ali-iku took the eel out of the pot and told his brothers what it had said to him. They told him he was crazy and to put it back on to cook. He did. After they'd eaten, they all went swimming with their children. The brothers drowned and Ali-iku's body started to look like the body of an eel.

"Just before his head became the head of an eel," Fidalgo said, "Ali-iku taught the children songs and told them what they should do and not do. The last thing was to never eat an eel. Then Ali-iku smashed himself on a rock and slid into the water."

Fidalgo stopped, opened mouth. Mateus was watching him intently.

"Ali-iku is our ancestor and we are his descendants who must keep the rules he gave us," Fidalgo said. "We must also keep that river sacred because that is where the spirit of Ali-iku lives."

It was a story Mateus had never heard and he'd yet to see how it related to the trouble Helio had caused. But he could sense it somehow did. He asked Fidalgo to explain it.

"Eels shed their skins," Fidalgo said. "As they grow bigger. Out there, in the pool on the river where they used to live."

"Used to?" said Mateus, curious about the past tense.

"They stopped shedding skins about a year or more ago," said Fidalgo. "One day Osorio—Helio's first-born son—saw a woman swimming in that river even though it was taboo for anyone, especially a woman, to go near there."

Fidalgo glanced quickly at Carter and blushed.

"She wore no clothes," he whispered. "Helio warned her but she did it again and a second time Osorio saw her. This second time he went there with Kosme Taveres. After this time, the eels started to wash up dead on the banks of the river. Rodrigo Duarte said we must stop that woman and he and I went to see her. There was an argument and Rodrigo pushed the woman over. She hit her head on the rocks and fell into the river. She never came up."

"Okay but—" Mateus began.

"Kosme and Osorio died because they saw the woman naked!" Fidalgo said. "Don't you see? And this Bobu came and threatened us in the sacred house where we keep the totems of the eel. We don't know where he came from but he lives with the daughter of the woman who went into the river. Helio thinks her spirit has taken his form to seek revenge."

"I told you this Bobu character was involved in a smuggling operation," Mateus told him. "What was being smuggled was liquor from West Timor that was made with methanol. Methanol is a poison. We suspect Kosme and Osorio were involved in bringing it across and that they probably drank some to celebrate when they made it without being caught. That's what killed them. Poisoned liquor. It wasn't the spirit of a dead woman."

Fidalgo began trembling after hearing that. He put his cap on, pulled it down so that his eyes were almost blocked, and lent over to recover himself. Mateus considered him for a moment before translating the gist of the story to Carter.

"I've heard similar origin stories," he told her when he'd finished relating Fidalgo's account. "They're attempts to explain and justify where the rules of a clan come from."

"I get that," said Carter, nodding. "We haven't had a chance to tell you something. Cordero had Estefana phone the Ministry of Agriculture today and make enquiries into what Dario Freitas had said about the removal of Indonesian-era pesticides from Maliana. She was told a contract worth about three thousand dollars was given to a haulage company connected to Juno Cabral through his sister's husband to remove the pesticide and have it sent to Indonesia. There is no record of that being done or of the haulage company ever hiring a barge. You put that together with what Cordero found when you and he went out to the river and I'd say there's a strong case for the pesticide having been dumped. Tell him that. Tell him the eels were likely killed by pesticide poisoning rather than a woman swimming naked in the river."

"We only have his word that the woman was killed," said Mateus. "If we're talking about Bobu's girlfriend, the story I heard was she ran off with someone from the other side of the border. This could just be an attempt to deal with a dispute within the clan by implicating some of its elders in a killing. I've seen that kind of thing before. Until we have a body or some hard evidence…" and he left the rest unsaid.

Mateus asked Fidalgo if he knew anything about the smuggling operation. He didn't. He asked if had any idea where Helio would have run to. Fidalgo thought a moment and suggested he might have gone to where Osorio was buried or to the sacred house but he said he was only guessing.

Carter stood to leave.

"I still need hard evidence," repeated Mateus.

"You look for your evidence," she said. "I'm not with the police, remember. Besides, I've had a gutful of stories about women being blamed for some catastrophe that befalls men."

27

"Dario didn't know anything had happened," Carter was saying. "He was too busy showing his silver disc to people and being congratulated for taking on his father's mantle. That all changed when someone rushed over and told him his daughter'd been shot. I think it was the priest."

She was sitting on the edge of her seat next to Cordero's bed in the health clinic. He was groggy but coming around.

"A police officer had taken Dario's Hilux to bring you here. So, Dario borrowed a motorcycle and went straight to the health clinic to see his daughter. Marquita, right? I only caught him out of the corner of my eye as I was leaving. I'm not sure how long he stayed."

"Any sign of Helio?" Cordero asked in a weak, raspy voice.

"He merged back into the crowd. One second there; the next second gone. He could have hung around or he could have fled straight away. It was chaos, Tino," Carter answered. "Estefana was terrific, by the way. She took care of Marquita and Bobu's daughter Josefa and she made sure Bobu didn't go anywhere until one of the officers took charge of him. Oh, and she also kept an eye on you, of course."

She was talking without stopping for a breath. He was finding it a struggle to keep up.

"Estefana said she'd drive Josefa home. She did all of that on her own initiative. She's becoming a very impressive police officer. The nurse here checked you out and gave you a shot of morphine. I wanted to stay but they insisted I go. It was frantic here. So I went to the police station. Mateus questioned Bobu. He admitted he was involved in attempts to sell the liquor. Said he was being threatened by that Edi Sobado character that he'd send him to prison for smoking dope if he didn't do what he was told. Mateus thinks Sobado dreamt up the smuggling caper to make some fast bucks. He—Sobado that is—took off when he saw them hauling Bobu in."

Cordero tried to lift himself up in the bed. The pain from the wound was too much and he gave up. She jumped up, eased him forward, and fluffed his pillows.

"Another guy from down there—Fidalgo something—came in and told Mateus what this was all about. Eels. Can you believe that?" She sat down. "He and Helio were part of an eel clan and when the pesticide killed all the eels in the river, they blamed Bobu's girlfriend. Mateus asked this guy, Fidalgo, if he knew where Helio might go. He said Helio was avenging his son's death so he might go to the son's gravesite. I think it's near Leohitu where his ancestors are buried. Or, he said, he might go to the sacred house out there. Helio is the chief elder, as you probably know. Anyhow Mateus has sent some officers out that way. He's going himself too I think. And he's informed Border Patrol to keep an eye out in case Helio tries to cross the border. He says—"

"Do you know you haven't stopped talking since you came here?" Cordero said.

She paused at that.

"Well I—"

"Is there any water?" he asked.

She took a tumbler off the side table, poured some water into a glass, and supported him with a hand behind his back as he leaned forward to sip a little.

A nurse entered the room.

"How are you feeling *inspetór*?" she asked.

"A little better, thank you," said Cordero.

The nurse examined the wound.

"The doctor will be here tomorrow morning," the nurse said. "I'll make sure he sees you first thing and check the stitches we put in." She leaned over and whispered: "You might want to have things checked a second time in Dili. Just in case."

"What about the girl, Marquita?" Cordero asked.

"She's doing fine. It was a superficial wound. It's just that it bled a lot. You know what kids are like when they see blood. We're keeping her in just to keep an eye on her. Shock, you know. Her father has seen her but he had to go back and reassure his guests that everything was okay. Her mother is with her now."

The nurse fluffed the pillows that Carter had just fluffed and left the room.

"Now I know you're not well, Tino," said Carter.

"What? Why?" he asked.

"I have a limited knowledge of Tetun but the nurse called you *inspetór* and you didn't correct her," Carter explained. "You're an *investigadór* or have you forgotten?"

He tried a smile at that but it quickly turned into more of a grimace from the pain.

"The gowns they give you to wear in hospitals and health clinics have a way of leveling out everybody's status," he said, his voice a little stronger now.

She laughed at that—a nervous laugh that wasn't really warranted by the comment.

"I appreciate all the information," Cordero said, "but there's really only one thing I want to know."

"One thing? What's that?" she asked, coming forward in her chair.

• • •

"Do you think Marquita will be alright?" Josefa asked. She was sitting in the passenger's seat of Cordero's SUV as Estefana turned off the road to Leohitu and onto the track to Lolitu. Josefa was so small she had to sit up straight and stretch her neck to see through the windscreen over the dashboard.

"I'm sure she will be," said Estefana. "I don't think she was badly hurt. The wound looked superficial to me. We'll have to see what they say at the clinic but I wouldn't worry."

"I like Marquita," said Josefa. "She's fun and she showed me lots of things around her house." She grew suddenly pensive. "What's going to happen to my dad?"

Estefana glanced quickly sideways at the girl.

"Well—"

"Is he in trouble?" Josefa asked, interrupting Estefana. Her voice was wavering. "Will they send him to prison like before?"

"I don't know, Josefa. All I can say is—"

"He's not a bad man," insisted Josefa. "I know he didn't want to have anything to do with those boys and whatever was in the bottles. He said he had to organize something with them or he could be sent back to prison." She gazed up at Estefana, eyes watery. "I don't want him to go to prison. I want him to stay with me."

"Let's wait and see what the police commander thinks once he's talked to your father," Estefana said. "Maybe things won't end up that bad for him."

Josefa was unconvinced.

"I wish my mum was here," she said. "She'd know what to do."

"What happened to your mother?" Estefana asked.

Josefa lowered her head.

"She went away," was all she said.

Estefana studied the girl as best she could while negotiating the track.

"Oh?"

"They never liked her here," Josefa added. "They called who *buat-aat*," she said, meaning the evil one.

"That's terrible," Estefana said. "Why did they call her that?"

"They didn't like that she was different. The clothes she wore, the way she did her hair, the songs she used to sing, and how she'd dance with me under the trees. They said it wasn't the way a woman should behave."

"Well that doesn't make her evil," Estefana said. "She sounds like fun to me."

Josefa held tight to the webbing of the seatbelt to steady herself as the SUV bounced across a particularly rocky stretch of ground.

"They didn't like that she swam in the river," she said and turned her face toward the passenger's window. "She didn't wear clothes."

"She didn't wear clothes?"

"No. Not when she swam."

Estefana waited.

"They warned her that the part of the river where she swam was *horok*," Josefa said and paused.

"I heard that," said Estefana. "There's a curse on anyone going there without permission, right? Something about men's business."

"Something like that I guess. I don't know. Anyway she didn't listen," the girl said. "My mum always did whatever she wanted to do and never let anyone tell her different. She told me that's how I should live too."

"How soon after the warning did your mum go away?" Estefana asked.

Josefa frowned trying to remember.

"The first warning?" she asked.

"How many were there?" asked Estefana.

Josefa shrugged.

"Maybe three or four."

"Okay then how long after the last warning did your mum go away?"

"Two, three weeks I guess. It was about the time my school teacher, *Senyora* Pereira, left the school and so I had to stay home with Umbelina all the time. Pretty soon my dad came and that was better."

Josefa fell silent once more.

"It's funny though," she said after a moment.

"What's funny?" Estefana asked.

"My mum had this beautiful bracelet she said my dad gave her when they were in Dili. She loved it because it reminded her of him. She kept it in a bright blue box. You could see the bracelet in a little window on the lid. She loved it so much she wouldn't let anyone touch it. No one. Not even me! Even Umbelina never opened that box."

"What's funny about that?" Estefana asked.

"When she went away she left it here. It's inside the hut. I think she left it because she'll come back one day."

Estefana chewed her bottom lip.

"Who were the people warning your mum to stay away from the river?" she asked.

"I don't know their names. The one with the gun tonight? I think he was one of them. I think I recognized him. I only saw him for a second. I was worried about Marquita."

Their vehicle hit a crater in the track and they were both bumped up from their seats. Josefa giggled. "Do that again!" she pleaded.

"No way," said Estefana.

They drove on past the hut where the boy with the pony lived. Josefa turned and put her hands to the window as if she could touch the hut as it passed by.

"Amando lives there," she said. "He's my friend."

"Your hut's just up here isn't it?" Estefana asked.

"There," Josefa said and pointed.

It was very dark now and Estefana was barely able to make out the shape of the hut in the gloom of Lolitu which lacked street lights, even electricity in the huts.

"Your grandmother will be there, right?" she asked.

The girl shook her head.

"I think she's at Amando's," she said.

"What? Why?" Estefana asked. "Is she sick?"

"No."

"Well why is she there? Is she visiting the people there?"

"No."

Estefana pulled up outside Josefa's hut and left the engine running. In the headlights she could see that part of one side wall of the hut had been scorched and the thatch above it burned.

"Did you have a fire here, Josefa?" she asked.

Josefa stretched up and gazed through the windshield.

"Someone tried to burn it," she said matter-of-factly.

"What? Who?"

Josefa ignored the questions.

"Amando took Umbelina to his hut because of the fire. Umbelina doesn't see too good. And she was scared." Josefa examined her hands. "I wasn't scared. And neither was my dad."

"I can't leave you here alone," said Estefana. "I'll take you back to Balibo."

"I'll be alright," Josefa said.

"No you won't. If I'd known there was no one here to look after you I wouldn't have brought you."

"No! I tell you I'll be okay. I've stayed here before by myself."

"That doesn't matter," said Estefana.

"It does matter! I'm not going back! I'm not!"

Estefana thought a moment.

"Okay. What if I take you to that other hut where your grandmother is?"

"I'll just wait until you leave and come back here. I want to get things for my dad."

"You don't have any light," Estefana said.

"There's a flashlight inside," the girl responded.

"And what if someone comes and tries to burn your hut down like before?"

"No one will come. My dad said he warned them there'd be big trouble if they did. And the police would have caught the man who shot Marquita by now. I can always go to Amando's hut if I get scared. But I won't get scared. I'll be fine."

Estefana was conflicted. She could force the issue and take Josefa to a safer place and risk her running off or she could leave her to her wits here and at least know where she was. She looked at the girl whose determination to have her own way was obvious in her expression. Josefa's mother had taught her well.

"Let me check inside the hut," Estefana said.

She took a flashlight from the glovebox, stepped out of the vehicle, the engine idling, and approached the hut. She slid the door open, shined the flashlight inside and ran the beam around the hut. A smell left by the burning thatch and bamboo struck her. But there was no immediate sign that the hut had been ransacked or the inside damaged.

"Police," she yelled. "Anybody there?"

There was no response.

She slipped inside the hut and checked more closely. When

she was satisfied it was empty, she returned and switched off the flashlight.

"Okay," she said to the girl through the driver's window. "You sure you have your own flashlight inside?"

Josefa nodded enthusiastically.

"I shouldn't be doing this," Estefana said to herself as much as Josefa. She looked back at the hut and out into the darkness. "You could still be in danger."

"I'll be okay. Promise," said Josefa.

Estefana hesitated.

"What if you take my cell?" she asked. "*Mana* Carter's number is in there. You can call her if there is any problem."

"My dad says the cell doesn't work in Lolitu," Josefa said. "And I wouldn't know how to use it anyway."

"I could show you," said Estefana. "It's not hard."

"No. Like I said, it won't work here. I don't want it. Just let me go inside. I'll be okay."

Estefana checked her cell—no bars, no coverage. She tried to call Carter just to check. Nothing. She sighed and surveyed the area although she couldn't make anything out beyond the beam of the headlights.

"Alright," she said in a tone bordering on defeat. "You can go in now."

With that Josefa jumped out of the vehicle and tore off inside the hut.

• • •

"Come on. What is it you're so desperate to know?" Carter pestered him.

"Not desperate," said Cordero. "Curious."

"Okay, curious. What is it?"

He grimaced as he pushed himself up in the bed, took three sharp breaths, and waited for the pain to ease.

"Why didn't you go after the shooter?"

"What?"

"I said, why didn't you go after the shooter? I know you well enough to know that every bone in your body would have been telling you to get the bastard. Except you didn't. You stayed with me. Why?"

She looked down, she looked up, ran her fingers through her hair.

"I don't have any police jurisdiction here, remember?"

"Good try, but since when has that stopped you?"

She tried for a more plausible answer.

"There was a crowd, Tino. It was bedlam," she said. "That means—"

"I know what 'bedlam' means. I also know it'd take more than a crowd of people to stop you acting on your police instincts. So try again."

• • •

She's headstrong that girl, Estefana was thinking to herself as she drove back from Lolitu. Why is it she—Estefana—could interrogate a village head and demand action from a relatively senior government bureaucrat but couldn't stand up to a small girl?

She shook her head and considered turning back. The police probably had caught the shooter by now and she worried about Cordero, who she considered a friend as well as a colleague. She didn't know how serious his wound was. She hadn't gone to the health clinic with the others. He could be dying. She had to get back!

But she had to admire Josefa. She was fearless and determined for one so young. Her mother would be proud of her.

The mother.

Why would Josefa's mother leave a precious bracelet in the hut like that and run off?

Why wouldn't she have taken the girl with her or at the very least kept in contact?

Eucalyptus trees presented ghostly shapes in the headlights along the road back to Balibo. They caused Estefana to shudder and darken the suspicions she was forming.

Josefa's mother had been warned off for swimming naked in a taboo stretch of the river. Warned off! Could that have made her so angry that she simply up and left? Or did she choose to defy those warning her and so they took things further? Much further. Is that why the bracelet was still in the hut? Bobu was in prison when Josefa's mother went missing but Josefa was there in Lolitu. Could those who'd taken issue with her mother because she'd violated a superstition now suspect Josefa was a danger because she bore a grudge? Was that the connection to the 'coconut' reference in the taboo language *Senyora* Tavares had used?

Estefana drove into Balibo and headed straight for the police station. She needed to satisfy herself that the shooter had indeed been caught and so Josefa was safe.

• • •

"Well?" he said as she stalled.

Carter was standing now and began pacing by the bed. Suddenly she stopped, looked up at the ceiling and sniffed.

"I just couldn't—" she started to say and stopped.

He could see her struggling with something.

"Just couldn't what?" he asked.

She shook her head, holding back tears, and looked away.

"What were you were thinking?" he tried.

"I don't know what I was thinking," she said turning sharply. She wiped a hand across her face. "Let's not worry about it now, alright? You need to get some rest. I'll join the hunt for the bad guy since that's all you think me capable of doing."

As she made for the door, Estefana burst in.

"*Mana!*" she said. She corrected herself. "*Maun!*"

"He's fine," said Carter answering the question before Estefana had a chance to ask it. "They've pumped him full of morphine and he's not making much sense but he's fine."

"We need to talk, *mana!*" Estefana said.

"Okay, not in here," said Carter as she led Estefana into the foyer. "Let's leave the patient to lick his wounds in peace."

28

"I don't think that man meant to shoot Bobu," Estefana said.

"Uh-huh." Carter was distracted and showing little interest.

"*Mana!*"

"Sorry. What did you say?"

They were standing outside in the corridor, Carter staring at the door to the room where Cordero had been put.

"I said I don't think that man meant to shoot Bobu, *mana*," Estefana repeated.

Carter faced Estefana.

"Well, he fired twice," she said. "He knew what he was trying to do."

"Yes, *mana*," Estefana said. "But I don't think Bobu was the one he was trying to kill."

"What on earth are you talking about, Estefana?" she said. "He fired two shots at Bobu. If Tino hadn't have put himself in the way, Bobu would likely be dead."

Estefana's expression hardened.

"Both shots were fired low, *mana*," she said. "The first hit the cart, remember, and then hit Dario's daughter in the arm. She's only short. The second bullet hit *maun* in the stomach."

"The revolver was old and could have misfired," said Carter. "And I doubt the guy had fired many handguns. His hands were probably shaking. The recoil might have surprised him. Put him off. Affected his aim."

The nurse strode by and entered the room where Marquita was resting with her mother beside the bed. Estefana lifted her eyes toward the ceiling in frustration.

"Okay so who do you think he was trying to shoot?" Carter asked, more to humour Estefana than anything.

"Josefa," Estefana replied.

"The girl? What possible—"

"Do you remember me telling you about taboo language, *mana*? And how I would ask my mother if she could find out what *Senyora* Tavarese meant when she told me about how the coconut became bitter?"

"Yeah, so?"

"Well I called my mother this morning. I tried to tell you but *maun* said there were more urgent things to be done and sent me to the police station. So I didn't get the chance to tell you. My mother spoke to a woman she knows who is Wehali like *Senyora* Tavares. She asked her what a bitter coconut meant. In taboo language."

"Okay," said Carter in a slow, drawn-out fashion.

"It refers to a young one, *mana*. A child. A child who has descended from someone and has become evil."

"Well that hardly—"

Estefana raised her hands.

"When I took Josefa home, she told me things," she said.

"Calm down a minute. What things?"

"She told me how people down where she lived didn't like her mother. Traditional people. When her mother came back from Dili she didn't fit in like before. They saw her as someone out to make trouble by defying customary rules for how women should behave."

"Okay."

"Wait, *mana*. Josefa's mother used to swim in a river near Lolitu. It was *horok*—that means off limits, out of bounds. And she used to swim there without any clothes on. Some of the traditional men must have seen her because they warned her not to do that. But she wouldn't listen."

The nurse came out of Marquita's room with a bundle of old bandages in her hand. She excused herself as she slipped past Carter and Estefana.

"Yeah I heard that story tonight from someone at the police station," said Carter.

"Right. Well people don't usually learn to swim away from the coast in Timor. She must have learned when she was in Dili," Estefana added. "And she decided to keep swimming here, despite what everyone said."

"Okay," Carter said a third time.

"Everyone was told Josefa's mother ran off with someone from West Timor and left her daughter. I don't think she ran off, *mana*. I think she was killed."

Carter was still not convinced.

"That doesn't prove—" she began.

"Josefa said her mother had a bracelet. It was given to her by Bobu when they were in Dili and she cherished it because it reminded her of him when he was in prison. She valued the bracelet so much she wouldn't let Josefa touch it. It's in the hut, *mana*! Why would she run off to West Timor and leave her bracelet in the hut?"

"A new man, a new start?" suggested Carter.

"I don't think she was like that, *mana*. If she kept the bracelet Bobu had given her with so much care for so long I don't think she would just forget him that easily. And what about all the letters to him *maun* said she transcribed to Father Francedez?"

Carter began pacing, arms folded tight across her chest.

"So how do you get from all of this to thinking Josefa was the intended target of the shooting?"

"If her mother was killed it would have been what we call a *mate mean*—a red death. They're deaths where the victim dies violently. You must perform a ritual to appease the spirit or else they seek revenge. If she was killed, her body would have been hidden, quickly and without any ritual being performed."

Estefana was pacing alongside Carter now.

"The spirits of people who die violently can take hold of the children of the dead person and manipulate others through them," she continued. "I think Helio believes Josefa has been possessed by the spirit of her murdered mother. *Maun* told me

Helio's son is dead and may have been poisoned like Arturo. Helio wouldn't understand what killed his son. The reason for his death would be a mystery to him. He may think Josefa's mother's spirit is responsible. Maybe it was the son who saw her swimming in the river."

"It was," Carter interrupted. "We've just learned that from somebody who lives down there and knows Helio. In fact, everything you say fits with the story he told Mateus."

"So Helio could now believe he will be the next victim. Bobu was only an instrument of revenge. The real source is Josefa."

They stood still and Carter bit at a fingernail while she weighed up everything Estefana had said.

"*Mana*?" Estefana said, impatient for a reaction.

"Just a minute," insisted Carter.

She thrust her hands in her pockets, took three slow paces forward and retraced her steps.

"You took Josefa home?" Carter asked.

"Yes *mana*. There was no one there at her hut. Someone had tried to burn it down a few days ago. Josefa's grandmother had been taken in by neighbours and I wanted Josefa to go there as well. She refused. She said if I took her there, she'd just go to her own hut when I had gone. She wanted to collect things for her father. I wanted to leave my cell with her but there is no coverage in Lolitu. There's no way to contact her."

"So she's there alone?"

"Yes, *mana*. I couldn't do anything to stop her and I hadn't figured everything out until I got back here in Balibo."

"We have to tell Mateus," Carter said.

"I went to the police station before coming here," said Estefana. "I was told Helio has not yet been captured which scared me. Mateus has gone to Leohitu to find him. Leohitu not Lolitu! And the commander wasn't answering his cell. I tried several times. There may be no service where he is either. Only one officer's on duty at the station and he has to keep an eye on the ones in the cells. There's no one to protect Josefa."

"How long will it take us to get to her?" Carter asked.

"About thirty minutes. It is a rough road, remember, and it is dark."

"And how long would it take Helio if he's on foot?"

"He'd have to think the police would be on the road. He probably knows a way through the forest and the grassland. That would be slow on foot. I'd say it would take him about two hours. Maybe a little less."

"Then we've wasted enough time," said Carter. "Let's go."

"*Mana*, if Helio is there we have no weapons," said Estefana. "He's tried to kill once."

"He dropped the revolver at Dario's place. So he's unarmed. Anyhow we'll work something out. Let's just get going!"

29

"I hope I'm right about this, *mana*," said Estefana.

There was a moment's silence.

"You and I both," replied Carter.

"How is *maun*? I didn't ask," said Estefana.

"Annoying," said Carter.

"Annoying?"

"He asks too many questions."

Estefana shot Carter a glance, not knowing what to make of that remark.

"But the wound? Is it serious?"

"The wound? No. He'll live to keep annoying me."

Again, Estefana looked across.

"Are you angry with him, *mana*?"

"Yes. No! Maybe. I don't know," said Carter.

"He's interested in the case. He could have been killed. Maybe that's why he asks so many questions."

"He wouldn't have been shot if he hadn't thrown himself in front of the shooter," said Carter, gripping the grab handle above the passenger's door.

"If he hadn't done that, Josefa or Marquita could have been killed."

"I know," said Carter. "That's what makes it so irritating."

"*Mana*?"

"We call it crazy brave. Cordero was crazy brave to take the bullet intended for someone else. How much longer to the hut?"

"The track to Lolitu is just up ahead. Not far. Another ten minutes. Maybe less."

"Can you step on it?"

"Step on what, *mana*?"

"It means go faster," explained Carter.

"The road is not safe. But I'll try."

The buffeting in the SUV grew worse. Carter and Estefana were knocking against each other one second and bouncing off the doors the next. The sound of rocks striking the undercarriage was like a Gatling gun.

"It's just down here, *mana*."

They passed the hut that Estefana pointed out was where the boy with the pony lived and where Josefa's grandmother had been taken. Soon they could make out the outline of Josefa's hut on the fringe of the beam from their headlights.

"There it is," Estefana said and slowed. "Should I pull up here and turn off the lights?"

"No. If he's in there we should announce our presence. It may make him think twice about what he's doing."

Estefana came to a stop just outside the entrance to the hut. The door was partly open but there was no light coming from inside.

"You have a flashlight?" Carter asked.

"There's one in there," said Estefana, pointing to the glove box.

Carter took it and opened her door.

"I'll go in first. You cover me."

She jumped from the passenger's seat, quickly scanned the area, and ran to the hut. Without stopping, she put her shoulder to the door and rushed in, angling the flashlight like a weapon in her hand. Estefana was right behind her, using the torch on her cell as a source of light. The smell of the fire lingered in the empty hut.

"Josefa!" Estefana called.

No response.

Carter was startled by a sound like a footstep off to her right. She shone the flashlight but could see nothing. There was a scurry. She moved the beam to discover a gecko on the floor staring at her as though she was violating its space. An empty hut, a door ajar—of course, she thought, in these parts that would be an open invitation to lizards, rodents, maybe even scorpions.

"Josefa! It's me, Officer Estefana. There's nothing to be afraid of. Come out if you're hiding."

More silence.

There was a crude bed in the main section of the hut next to a table, two plastic chairs, and some makeshift cupboards. A length of wood fashioned into a walking stick lay on the unmade bedding. Carter flung aside a curtain that partitioned off a section of the hut. Behind the curtain were two single bedrolls on a mat that covered the ground. Neither had been slept in and the area was clean and tidy. Estefana slid through the curtain past Carter. She scanned the area slowly with the light from her cell.

Carter retraced her steps to the main area. She aimed the flashlight at a bench on which were stacked some pots, a wok, and plates and bowls. To one side was a sparse collection of canned goods. Above the bench an assortment of vegetables were tied in a string bag and hung from a beam to keep out of the reach of rats. Under the bench was a large plastic container of water. Nothing showed any sign of having been disturbed.

"Doesn't look like anything's been touched," said Carter. "No sign of a struggle. Let's check outside."

"Wait, *mana*," said Estefana, who remained in the area behind the curtain.

She shifted across to a stack of crates made into a small side table next to one of the bedrolls. She brought her cell down closer to the top crate to focus the light from the phone's torch.

"Come look, *mana*!" she said.

Carter slid behind the curtain. Estefana was pointing to a small blue jewellery box, opened and empty.

"That's the box Josefa described where her mother kept the bracelet," Estefana said. "But there's no bracelet there!"

Carter drew closer and examined the box.

"She said no one touched the bracelet. Not her, not Bobu," Estefana said.

"Well, someone's touched it now," said Carter.

"Who would have done that?"

"Could someone have stolen it?" Carter asked. "You said her grandmother had gone to a neighbour's place and Josefa and Bobu were at Dario's. Could someone have come by this evening and taken it?"

"People don't steal from huts, *mana*. They're all neighbours."

"What about someone passing this way from across the border?" suggested Carter.

"I don't think it's that." Estefana straightened. "Why would people cross the river at night? I think Josefa took it."

"You said she was not allowed to touch it," Carter reminded her.

"Yes. But she also thought her mother had left it and would return for it one day," said Estefana. "There's no sign of a struggle as you say, and the door is open. What if someone came and told Josefa her mother had returned? She could have been excited and took the bracelet to give to her mother as a welcome home present."

"Your imagination is really working overtime now, Estefana," Carter said.

"What other explanation is there, *mana*?"

"Okay, let's say you're right," said Carter. "And let's say Josefa has been the intended victim all along. If Helio Lima took her, where would he go with her?"

"Maybe to where her mother was killed," Estefana ventured. "To kill her at the same place might be his way to deal with the red death and somehow send the spirit of her mother to the next world." They both stared at the empty bracelet box. "But where could that place be?" asked Estefana.

"You said her mother had violated some prohibited area along the river," Carter said.

"Yes. An area that was *horok*."

"Where is that?"

Estefana shrugged.

"I don't know. It could be anywhere."

"It has to be somewhere near here," said Carter. "Her mother didn't own a motorcycle and so she couldn't have gone too far."

"We don't know where to look. We'd never find it in the dark."

"What about that hut we passed a little way along the track? Where you said the grandmother was taken. Somebody in there might know," said Carter.

Estefana brightened.

"We could try there, *mana!*"

• • •

The door to the hut was closed but pale-yellow rays from a kerosene lamp shone through the cracks in the wall. A pony tethered off to the side stirred as they approached the front. Estefana knocked on the door.

"Hello. Is anybody in there, please?" she said.

At first, there was no reaction.

"Hello," Estefana repeated more loudly and knocked more forcefully.

"Who is it?" someone asked. The speaker sounded like a child.

"My name is Estefana. I'm a police officer. I need some information."

The door creaked open a fraction. A boy stood in the dim light. He examined Estefana and shifted his attention to Carter.

"Who's she?" he asked.

"She's a police officer too," said Estefana. "She doesn't speak Tetun."

"How can she be a police officer if she doesn't speak Tetun?" the boy asked. "And she's not Timorese."

"It's a long story," said Estefana. "Are your parents home?"

"No."

"Who is it, Amando?" a faltering woman's voice sounded from deep inside the hut.

"It's alright, *senyora*. It's just the police," said the boy.

"The police! Is it about the fire?" the woman asked. Estefana thought it must be Umbelina speaking.

"I don't think so, *senyora*. One of them doesn't speak Tetun."

"Oh!"

"Go back to sleep," the boy said.

He turned back to Estefana.

"Where are your parents?" she asked.

"They're at the burial. For Gaspa Freitas."

"The burial?"

"My father knows Dario. He's worked for him many times and so he was invited. They could be gone all night. Why are you here?"

"Is there any other adult here?" Estefana asked.

"Yes. Umbelina."

"I mean beside her," Estefana said.

"No. I'm in charge."

"So you are Amando?"

"Yes."

"And you're Josefa's friend?"

"Yes."

"Have you seen Josefa tonight?"

"No. Why? What's happened to her?"

There was a rustling from inside.

"Did I hear someone mention Josefa? Is something wrong? Is she alright?" It was the old woman again.

"Can you step outside for a minute?" Estefana asked Amando. "Just so we aren't disturbed."

"Everything's alright, Umbelina," Amando called back inside the hut. "Just go to sleep. I'll take care of everything. I'm just going outside for a while. Not far."

"To Pancho?" the woman asked.

"Yes, to Pancho," Amando replied.

Amando stepped outside and eased the door shut behind him. They were standing in the dark now and Estefana couldn't read the boy's expression.

"We think Josefa may be in danger," Estefana told him.

"Danger? Again?"

"What do you mean again?" asked Estefana.

"They tried to burn down her hut!" said Amando.

"Yes, I know. I took her there earlier tonight."

"She went to the burial too. With Bobu. Why would you bring her home?"

"There was a bit of trouble at the burial feast."

"Trouble? What trouble?"

"Somebody became angry and started a fight. It's not important."

"Where's Bobu? Why didn't he bring Josefa home?"

"Bobu's helping the police sort out the trouble so I drove Josefa home and she insisted on going to her own hut. She isn't there now. I just checked."

"If you drove her home earlier, why are you here checking now?"

"Because I want to make sure she's safe. We think someone may have taken her away and we need to know where."

"What do you mean taken her away? Who?" asked Amando.

"We don't know," said Estefana. "That's why we're here."

"Well I don't know where she's gone," Amando said. "Why would I?"

"Of course you don't know," said Estefana. "That's not what I'm here to ask."

"What are you here for then?" said Amando, becoming impatient.

"I need to know which part of the river is *horok*," said Estefana.

The boy said nothing for a moment.

"Josefa may have been taken there by someone who wants to harm her," Estefana added.

"Why would someone take her there?" Amando asked.

"I don't know. It's just the most likely place. Do you know where it is?"

Once more the boy went silent. Estefana couldn't see whether it was through fear, suspicion, or some knowledge of the prohibition he was reluctant to divulge.

"You're Josefa's friend, Amando. You must help her. If someone tried to burn down her hut, just think what they might do if they got their hands on her."

"Why do people want to hurt her?" Amando complained.

"I don't know," Estefana said. "But I want to help her. Will you help me help her?"

Estefana had no idea what Amando was thinking but she hoped that it was a decision to assist.

"It's where the eels lived," he said.

"The area that's *horok*? Is that what you mean?"

Amando nodded but Estefana couldn't see the motion clearly.

"Is it, Amando?"

"Yes!" he said.

"And where's that?"

"Down from the ridge through the trees," he said.

"Can I drive there?" she asked.

"There's no road."

Estefana gave Carter a much-shortened version of the conversation.

"Ask him if he'll take us," Carter said.

Estefana put it to Amando.

Instead of answering, the boy went back inside the hut. Estefana made to follow him. Carter put a hand out to stop her.

"Wait," she said.

"I'll only be gone a little while," Estefana heard the boy say. She figured he was addressing Umbelina. He came back out, a blanket folded in his arms.

"We'll take Pancho," Amando said.

"Pancho?"

"My pony. He knows the way even in the dark."

30

Timorese ponies are small—Pancho was only eleven hands high—but are known for their exceptional strength and agility. Amando was tiny, Estefana slight, and Carter carried no more than an ounce of fat on her entire body. Amando held Pancho by a rope he'd tied around the pony's neck and the women climbed onto the blanket he'd thrown over the pony's back to act as a saddle. He mounted last behind the pony's withers. Estefana grabbed Amando around his thin waist and Carter did the same to Estefana. Their feet hung loose just off the ground.

Pancho bridled at first but soon settled down and did what Amando asked of him. They bobbed up and down as the pony cantered along. It was faster than walking if bumpy and uncomfortable. Even so Pancho somehow knew where he was going without much direction from Amando. He made his way through the forest cover as though he could sense where each tree was to avoid and they'd soon reached the top of the hill behind the boy's hut.

"It's down there," said Amando, pointing although neither Estefana nor Carter could make anything out in the dark thicket of trees and shrubs.

Pancho was sure-footed, if slower, making his way down toward the near bank. Approaching it he stopped and refused to go any further despite Amando's gentle prodding with his feet on both sides of his belly.

"He knows it's not safe from here with three on his back," Amando said. "There's a track you can follow," and again he pointed. Carter slipped from the back of the pony as did Estefana.

Carter couldn't see anything that resembled a track and reached for the light. It wasn't there.

"I think I lost the flashlight," Carter said. "It must have slipped out of my belt when we climbed on the pony."

"My cell's running low on battery too, *mana*," said Estefana.

They both searched around in the shadows for a track without success.

"There!" Amando called, noticing their confusion. "Through those trees. It's not far now to the river. I'll stay here with Pancho until you come back." With that, Amando jumped off Pancho and sought out a place where he could sit. "You will find Josefa?" he asked. "Promise!"

"If she's where we think she is, we'll find her," said Estefana. "Thanks for all your help, Amando."

"Pancho did most of it," said the boy.

"Well thanks to Pancho too, of course."

Carter and Estefana began to feel their way down what Amando had generously called a track. The brush was thick and added to the difficulty of navigating in darkness. They'd gone forty yards when Estefana made a poor choice of a foothold, slipped, and nearly plunged over a drop. Carter was lucky to grab hold of her arm and heave her onto solid ground. Estefana slid down onto her backside to catch her breath.

"Sorry, *mana*," she said. "And thank you."

"Don't mention it," said Carter.

Just as Estefana made to get up, a half-moon broke through the swirl of clouds and cast a dim light across the ridge and over to the opposite bank. The river took on a silvery shimmer as it snaked its way beneath them.

"Quickly, Estefana, while we have some light let's get down to the riverbank," said Carter.

They scrambled over boulders and through the thickets. Down below them on a rock ledge overlooking the water they heard voices—one shrill and clear, the other deep, gruff and hard to make out.

"Josefa," mouthed Carter without sounding the name.

Estefana nodded.

Carter prodded Estefana down in a crouch behind a growth of fishbone fern. It was almost as tall as Estefana and thick with fronds so that it provided a screen to conceal them.

"You talk to Helio," Carter whispered. "I'll try to outflank him and see if I can take him down."

"I not sure I can do that, *mana*," said Estefana. "I've never done anything like that before."

"Yes you can do it," Carter insisted. "Remember when you were nervous about questioning Juno Cabral? You did that just fine and you'll do just fine now."

"What will I say?"

"Keep him busy. That's all you have to do. I need him distracted. Ask him what he thinks he's doing to a small child and why. Whatever he says, just question it. Okay?"

Carter didn't give Estefana time to object. She tapped her on the shoulder, rose and was gone into the darkness.

Estefana took a deep breath and made her way closer to where the voices were originating. A pallid glow from a lantern sitting atop the rock lit up the tiny form of Josefa and illuminated the legs of the man and a long-bladed *katana* he held against them.

"No! You lied!" Josefa was screaming. "You lied!"

The deeper voice said something but Estefana couldn't make out what it was.

"You're a bad man. You lied to me. My mother's not here. Let me go! I want to go home, you hear!"

This time a growl came from the deeper voice, loud and insistent.

"No! Don't you touch me! I'm going home!" cried the young girl.

Estefana was close enough now to make out the shape of the man but the moon was swallowed by clouds again before she could see his face.

"Stop what you're doing!" she shouted. "Let the girl go! I'm a police officer!"

The man was startled and spun around wildly. His head bobbed this way and that as he tried to make out who'd called to him in the darkness.

"Who's there?" he said. "Who?"

"I'm Officer Estefana dos Carvalho. I'm ordering you to put that *katana* down and let the girl come to me."

Josefa tried to run past the man. He extended his free hand and pushed her closer to the edge of the overhang. She slipped but he pulled her up by the hair. She screamed in pain.

"Let her go!" ordered Estefana.

"I don't know who you are!" the man yelled. "This is none of your business. Go!"

"I'm a police officer!" Estefana declared again. "Let the girl come to me!"

The man waited a moment, ducking and weaving as he tried again to see who was shouting at him.

"If you thought you could overpower me you wouldn't be hiding," he called. "So go before I come after you!"

"I'm not going anywhere until you've released that girl!" Estefana yelled. "Why have you brought her here?"

The man picked up the lantern and edged forward a little in the direction from which the voice was coming. Estefana crouched down beneath the brush and the light drifted over branches and leaves above her.

"Estefana!" cried Josefa. "Tell him to let me go! He said he'd take me to my mother. He lied! He's a bad man!"

The girl tried to push past the man a second time. He stopped her with the *katana*.

"Put that *katana* down!" Estefana shouted at him.

"Show yourself!" the man yelled again.

Carter had made her way to the far edge of the overhang without being seen or heard. She was ten yards from the man—too far to rush him if he decided to strike the girl and too far to avoid being struck herself unless Estefana managed to create a big enough distraction. Carter could only hope that she would.

Suddenly Estefana stood and moved to a small clearing directly in front of the man. It was dangerous but she couldn't think of anything else to do to help Josefa.

"Why did you bring that girl here?" she asked, trying hard to keep a calm and even tone in her voice.

"Because she's possessed!" the man hissed in answer. "She's trying to kill us all!"

"Don't be silly!" said Estefana. "She's only a child!"

The man shuffled his feet on the rock and waved the *katana* through the air. His face was still hooded in darkness.

"She's the spirit of her mother! She's come back to extract her revenge!"

Carter didn't understand what was being said but she could see that the man was growing more desperate and whatever Estefana was saying could provoke him to lash out at her or at Josefa at any moment.

"What revenge? For what?" Estefana said, remembering Carter's advice to keep asking questions—any questions—to keep the man distracted.

"For what was done to her! Here!" the man screamed.

"And what was that?" Estefana demanded to know.

The man lurched toward Estefana, the *katana* raised. Josefa saw her chance. She pulled free of the man and leapt off the rock and into the river. A slight splash could be heard as her tiny body hit the water.

Carter rushed in, knocking the man with her shoulder and ramming him onto the hard surface of the ledge. The *katana* flew from his hand, rattled off the rock and slid into the undergrowth. Carter remembered Josefa couldn't swim. She ignored the prone man trusting Estefana could deal with him now he was unarmed and winded. She kicked off her boots, slipped out of her pants, and tore off her blouse.

She knew she could break her neck on jagged rocks below that might be hidden in the dark or, more likely, damage her back or her legs and not survive the water. But the girl was in danger. She had no choice.

By luck the pool below where she'd jumped was clear of obstacles and deep enough to absorb her plunge. Carter came up gasping for air, hair covering her face. She brushed it aside, treading water. She could see nothing in the darkness and only guess where Josefa might have gone. A strong current was running through the centre of the river and Carter thought the girl might have been sucked into it. She swam out from the bank before realizing she too was being propelled downstream in the process.

She stopped swimming to listen. Something hit against her leg—a submerged branch. *Why are there always damn submerged branches in rivers?* she thought to herself. *Could Josefa have been caught in one and pulled under?*

The current was moving her away from where Josefa had hit the water. Carter twisted, frantically trying to catch a sign of the girl or a sound that would tell her where she was. She knew there was little time to have any chance of saving Josefa from drowning.

"Over there, *mana*!" cried Estefana from the ledge. Carter couldn't see in the darkness to where Estefana was pointing.

"Where?" Carter yelled.

Estefana couldn't see Carter either. She was guessing her location from the noise she made in the water just as she guessed where Josefa was from the coughs and splashing she could hear from the ledge.

"Twenty yards down river from where you jumped in but on the other side!" Estefana called. "She's struggling in the current! Hurry, *mana*!"

Carter swam off with little confidence about where she was heading. After what she guessed was twenty yards she stopped and realised she'd gone more like thirty in the current. She started back, working harder this time, her arms aching and her lungs burning for air.

She stopped, treading water, aware that she would be drawn quickly down stream again if she wasn't swimming, wasn't fighting the current as hard as she could. But she had to orient herself somehow. She had to find the girl.

She heard a gurgling and a thrashing of arms in water. She pushed herself with a strong, quick breaststroke closer to it. And there, just a little beyond her, was Josefa, going under, coming up, struggling. She was clinging to an exposed limb of another submerged branch.

Thank God for damn submerged branches, Carter thought to herself this time.

"It's me, Carter!" she said as she swam toward the girl.

"K...Kayter!" the girl screamed. But then she was gone.

Carter dived down knowing she would see nothing in the dark, murky water, but hoping she could feel for the girl. She came up for air and went straight back down. She felt something like hair to the touch and next her hand caught hold of a skinny arm. She lifted Josefa up and broke through the surface of the water. Josefa was listless, unconscious.

Carter rolled the girl onto her back. She put one arm around her chest and paddled hard with the current across to the side of the river where Estefana had scrambled down to the edge. Estefana helped lift Josefa out of the water and laid her down on the bank. She was still unresponsive.

Carter climbed out of the water.

"*Mana!*" Estefana pleaded but could say no more.

Carter could see why.

"Stand aside," she said.

She crouched down, called Josefa's name and squeezed her shoulders. No response. She opened the girl's mouth and checked that her airways were clear. She placed an ear to Josefa's mouth but could detect no breathing. She put one hand on the other and performed fifteen fast chest compressions, trying to moderate her strength due to the girl's slight torso. She opened Josefa's mouth, squeezed the girl's nostrils shut with her fingers, and blew two strong breaths into Josefa.

She eased back. Josefa didn't move. Carter lent over and repeated the drill a second time. Still nothing. She knew she was running out of time, the girl out of life. She tried again. After two much harder compressions Josefa coughed up a mouthful of water, swung her arms uncontrollably as she grappled for air, turned on her side and retched violently.

Carter kept a hand on the girl's shoulder until she'd begun to settle down. She noticed the girl was clutching something in her hands against her chest. She took a closer look in the dim light. The bracelet was wrapped around Josefa's fingers.

"*Mana!*" Estefana said, this time in a tone of relief.

"She'll be alright," Carter said, her eyes fixed firmly on Josefa.

"She will," agreed Estefana. "She will be alright!"

"Where is he?" Carter asked Estefana.

"I don't know, *mana*. He got up, pushed past me and ran away," Estefana replied.

"Sit here with her while I get some clothes on," Carter said.

She hurried off to find her pants, blouse and boots. Josefa sat up, spat, and wiped her face with the back of her arm.

"Are you okay?" Estefana asked.

The girl could only nod. She tried to get up.

"Just rest a minute," Estefana told her, pressing down on Josefa's shoulder. "You've been through a big ordeal. Rest a little."

Josefa didn't argue. She coughed to clear the last bit of saliva obstructing her breathing and sucked in air.

"Where's Carter?" she asked.

"She's just gone to get dressed. She'll be here soon." Estefana rubbed the girl's back. "Why did you jump into the river, Josefa?"

"He had a big knife," Josefa said, brushing the wet hair either side of her eyes. "He was going to kill me. My mother used to swim here so I thought I'd be safer in the river."

The girl wiped her face again, this time with the back of the hand that held the bracelet.

"You brought your mother's bracelet," Estefana said by way of a question.

"That man said my mother had come back. He said he was taking me to meet her because she'd hurt her foot and couldn't walk far. I was excited about seeing her after all this time. I wanted to give the bracelet to her to welcome her home." She turned her face up. Estefana could see her eyes were moist but not from the water in the river. "But he lied to me. She's not coming home, is she?"

"I don't think so, Josefa," Estefana said. "But I know she'd be very proud of you for what you did."

"But what did I do?" Josefa asked.

"You escaped from the bad man, you went into the river like your mother used to do, and you've come back alive," said Estefana.

Carter re-emerged, dressed but damp still. The buttons had been ripped off her blouse and so she'd simply tied the ends over her belly to compensate. She sat on the rocks and put her boots on unlaced, figuring Helio had gone and there'd be no more excitement for the night. She'd picked up the lantern that had been left on the ledge and under its yellow light they were able to find their way up the track toward where Amando was waiting. He was sitting next to Pancho, a body slumped on the ground on the other side of the pony.

"What happened?" Estefana asked.

Amando was smiling broadly when he saw Josefa was okay.

"What?" he said.

"I asked what happened to him," Estefana said gesturing toward the man.

"He came up the track in the dark and knocked into Pancho," Amando said. "Pancho doesn't like it when someone he doesn't know touches him. He kicked. I think he kicked the man in the chest or something. Anyway he hasn't moved since. Why is Josefa and that foreign lady all wet?"

Carter took the lantern over to check on the prone figure who had wanted to kill Josefa. She rolled him over.

It wasn't the shooter.

It wasn't Helio Lima.

31

"Helio came back to the sacred house and we arrested him there," Mateus said. "He wasn't Catholic, but it was almost like he'd come to confess. Or maybe just to tell Rodrigo Duarte that he hadn't been able to kill the girl. Either way he didn't put up any resistance. I don't think his heart was in it from the start."

It was mid morning Sunday and they were sitting in the police commander's office drinking strong coffee. He had returned from his home where he'd gone to have breakfast with his wife: Carter and Estefana had come from the guesthouse where they'd changed clothes and took the opportunity to rest up after taking Rodrigo from the river near Lolitu to the police station. The sun was shining through the window which was half open allowing in a pleasant, cooling breeze and the scent of lantana.

"We talked for a while outside the sacred house," Mateus continued. "Rodrigo must have come and hidden in the shadows when he saw my SUV. He would have heard me tell Helio that Josefa had been taken to her hut. Once we left with Helio, Rodrigo would have climbed into the sacred house, taken the *katana* and the lantern, and gone off to finish the job himself."

"Estefana and I couldn't quite figure why Josefa would have gone anywhere with Helio," said Carter. "After all, she'd seen him shoot Marquita and Cordero."

"Hmm," agreed Mateus. "She didn't know Rodrigo. He'd never met her. So when he fronted her hut, said he'd take her to meet her mother, she probably jumped at the chance."

"Do you know exactly what happened to Josefa's mother?" Carter asked.

"Pretty much what Fidalgo had said," Mateus said. "Helio told me she was disliked as soon as she came back to Lolitu. Seeing her swimming without clothes on in an area the elders had declared *horok* changed their dislike into outrage. They warned her but she kept doing it. Then the eels died. Their clan totem had been destroyed. None of them knew about the dumping of the pesticides. They all blamed the woman."

He searched his pockets for a cigarette but without luck. He rested his hands on the desk.

"Rodrigo Duarte and Fidalgo de Queiroz confronted her," he said. "Maybe they were trying one last time to warn her off, maybe she argued with them and they resented it, maybe seeing her naked provoked some other kind of reaction. Who knows? There was a struggle, she fell into the river and drowned. That's their story anyway. They were able to retrieve the body downstream. Helio was brought in to clean up the mess because he was the senior elder. He told them to bury her near where they'd found her and spread a rumour that she'd run off with someone from West Timor."

"Did Helio tell you where she was buried?"

Mateus nodded.

"I sent a team out there this morning," he said.

"So, what will happen to Fidalgo, Rodrigo and Helio?" asked Carter.

"Rodrigo and Fidalgo will be charged with manslaughter," Mateus said, "Helio with the attempted murder of Josefa at Dario's feast, the wounding of Marquita and Cordero, and also with complicity in the death of Josefa's mother."

"What did Helio say when you told him it was toxic liquor that killed his son and most likely the dumped pesticide that killed the eels?" Carter asked.

"He dropped his head and said nothing. I don't know whether that was out of shame at what he'd done or disbelief at what I told him."

Mateus picked up his coffee.

"We saw Bobu leaving as we came in," said Estefana. "What will happen to him now—and to Josefa?"

Mateus took a sip of his coffee, placed the cup on his desk, and spread his hands.

"I let him go."

Carter went to say something but Mateus cut her off.

"Bobu wasn't behind the plan to smuggle liquor across the border and I believe him when he said he didn't know that people had died from drinking it," he explained. "He was being blackmailed by Edi. With his girlfriend gone—or dead as we now know—and Josefa's grandmother almost blind, he wasn't in a position to risk going back to prison and leaving his daughter to fend for herself. So he was a reluctant co-conspirator. I let him go rather than create more problems for his daughter and the grandmother."

He picked up his coffee cup.

"And Edi Sobado?" Carter asked.

"The police picked him up just outside Batugade late last night. He wasn't hard to find. Only crazy people take the road from here to there at night. He'll be charged with smuggling and there'll be charges relating to the deaths of the smuggler, Kosme Tavares, Osorio Lima and Arturo Cabral."

"That leaves a case of embezzlement and another of dumping of the pesticide," Carter remarked.

"Dario came by this morning," Mateus said. "He was picking Marquita up from the health clinic and taking her home. Do you know what a *biti* is?"

Carter didn't and, out of habit, she looked to Estefana to explain.

"It's a mat, *mana*. Sometimes it is laid out for people who are in dispute. They come and sit on the *biti* and don't get up until they have settled their differences."

"Quite right," said Mateus. "I suggested to Dario that he and Juno sit down on a *biti* and talk things out. Juno has lost his son; Dario nearly lost his daughter. The reasons are different but the outcomes are similar. They have something in common in their grief and perhaps that should take priority over their differences. Dario agreed and I have a feeling Juno will as well."

"That's very Jesuitical of you," Carter commented.

Mateus laughed at that.

"Actually it's very Salesian. That's the main Catholic order in East Timor and it's the order I was with when I was in the seminary. The promotion of simple acts of kindness is a big part of what Salesians stand for."

"Kindness is all well and good but what about the embezzlement and the dumping?"

"Oh, Juno will have to answer for that as will his brother-in-law," said Mateus. "But that's something that awaits a Ministry of Agriculture investigation."

Estefana coughed lightly to draw Mateus' attention.

"There's one other thing, commander," she said.

"Yes, what's that?"

"The headstone *Senyora* Tavares wants for her husband's grave," Estefana said.

Mateus nodded.

"I'll order it through Feng," Mateus said. "I've no doubt Juno can be persuaded to pay for that from the money he got from the pesticide affair. He'll also get the bill for the repatriation of the body of our smuggler, Faisal Jollo, to Atambua."

They had all finished their coffee now and Carter checked her watch.

"Do you have somewhere you have to be?" Mateus asked.

Carter smiled awkwardly.

"I thought I'd check on Tino," she said.

"I notice it's Tino now and not Cordero you call him," Mateus said, grinning.

"He rang earlier to say the doctor had come and cleared him to go," said Carter ignoring the comment.

"Already?" asked Mateus.

"Just to Dili," Carter said. "He'll be checked again there. I think the doctor is happy to be rid of the responsibility."

Mateus pursed his lips in a way that suggested her assessment of the doctor was not too far from the truth.

"Estefana got a call this morning to say our vehicle has been repaired as well," Carter added. "We can pick it up in Liquica on the way through. I'll check on Tino quickly before we go to the guesthouse to pack up our stuff and his. We'll pick him up on the way through and be off."

"Do you have enough to write your report for INTERPOL on border management?" Mateus asked.

Carter stood, as did Estefana.

"I have first-hand experience of policing here. That's the best kind of research and I can make a lot out of that. Besides, as you said when we first met, organizations like to bury simple messages in a lot of words. My main recommendation will be that training packages are ineffective without well-schooled recruits and useless so long as officers are denied their salaries. I'll package that in about two thousand words of official sounding bullshit."

"I'll drop by to see Cordero myself in a little while. He's a good man who risked his life to save others."

"Crazy brave," Estefana said, glancing at Carter.

"Crazy brave indeed," agreed Mateus.

• • •

"I didn't go after the bad guy again," Carter said.

"What? When?" he asked.

"Out there on the river."

They were in the health clinic. Cordero was sitting on the side of his bed slowly buttoning up his shirt over the thick wad of bandages around his waist. Carter was seated at the head of the bed. Estefana had taken Cordero's SUV to be refueled.

"Well she jumped in, right? That's what I heard. And she couldn't swim. She was just a kid," he said.

"There was that," Carter said. "But there was more too."

"More?"

She wrung her hands.

"I'd agreed to teach her how to swim," Carter said. "Well, sort of. She asked if I'd teach her when she comes to Dili with her father. I said I would. So I could hardly let her drown."

She tried to laugh that off but the effort was unconvincing.

"There's still more isn't there?" Cordero said.

Carter hesitated. She took in a deep, uneven breath, and lowered her eyes.

"She reminded me of…I don't know, her smile, something in her eyes, her cheekiness. Whatever." She ran a knuckle across her upper lip. "She reminded me of my sister."

He waited.

"When I pulled her out of the water, I thought she was dead. She'd taken in a lot of water and wasn't breathing, you know? I gave her CPR." She lifted her eyes to check. "Do you know what that is?"

"Cardiopulmonary resuscitation," he answered. "Yeah, I know what it is. I grew up in Australia, don't forget. Most Australians live near the coast. Every second person knows how to administer CPR. It's almost a requirement of living in Australia."

She nodded.

"It was like I breathed life into her, you know?" she said. "I've rescued kids before and stopped them from getting hurt or worse. Like you did last night taking that bullet. But I've never done anything like that before."

She rubbed at her eyes hard with the back of her hand. He said nothing.

"It was like I was giving life back to someone."

She looked at him. Her face contorted and she struggled to hold back tears.

"Does that sound crazy to you? Does it make any sense at all?"

"Well I can see how—"

She stood, cutting him off, sniffed, and moved away from the bed.

"Maybe I've been here too long. Maybe I'm just getting rusty and distracted and I need to go home and do some real police work," she said, facing away from him.

He scratched his ear. Raising his arm hurt his stomach and he winced in pain which passed as quickly as it had come.

"You saved a girl's life," he said. "*You gave a girl back her life,*" he added with emphasis. "Isn't that real police work. And you got the bad guy, eventually."

"I didn't get him, the horse did," she said.

"It wasn't a horse. It was a pony," he corrected her.

"You know what I mean," she said.

He noticed her shoulders lift in a quavering fashion.

"Funny thing is I didn't sleep when I got back last night," she said. "Or this morning. Whichever it was. Lost track of time. My watch fogged up from going in the water. So I just lay there thinking."

"Thinking about what?" Cordero asked. It was the question he'd put to her the day before when he asked what prompted her to stay with him after the shooting and not go after Helio. She hadn't answered then and he wasn't sure she'd answer now.

She clasped her hands and walked to the window.

"Everyone I've ever loved I've lost," she said. She took a deep breath. "My mum who walked out on us, my dad who was shot and killed, my sister who was abducted. I've made a life on my own because I couldn't afford to let anyone in and risk losing them too." She turned suddenly and slapped her thighs. "Dragging Josefa from the river, feeling as though it was me who breathed the life back into her?" She sniffled and wiped her nose. "It was like I had the power to determine the fate of someone I cared for. Not my badge, not my gun. Not any of the things I've put between me and other people to avoid further loss. I was virtually naked on the river bank. It was just me! I've been trying to convince myself that I could do it for a long time. Finally I did."

She swiped her nose, lips, cheek. He reached a hand out to her and she took it.

"Does that sound stupid?" she asked, her face red with embarrassment.

"Not at all," he said. "Maybe that's why you stayed with me when I was shot. Sort of like a rehearsal."

"Don't press your luck, Tino," she said.

Their eyes met and they both started chuckling.

"Remember you telling me about the shaman and the sweat lodge?" he asked.

She nodded but didn't speak.

"You said that made you realise how wrong it is to see things from our own perspective all the time. Maybe you've been on your own too long. Too absorbed in your loss and grief. Time to let others in."

She moved away and wiped both cheeks.

"Others, huh?" she said and smiled. "I suppose that includes you? You're a hero after all."

He started to pocket his items from the bedside table.

"I'm sorry that I taunted you about Jesus," she said.

"Jesus?" he repeated, his back to her.

"You know. The picture. At the guesthouse. When we were drinking gin."

"You remember that?" he asked turning.

"I remember everything."

He tilted his head.

"Do you remember what you asked me?"

"Yes," she said. A swift landed on the branch of a tree outside the room and trilled loudly drawing Carter's attention.

"You asked me what I think of you?"

"That's right," she said. "So?"

He paused a moment. She kept her eyes on the tree even though the swift had flown away.

"Well, the answer is I think I like you. A lot."

Estefana came through the door.

"We'd best be going, *mana*. We need to collect all our things from the guesthouse."

Nobody spoke. Carter turned to Estefana and brushed a hand roughly across her face. Estefana's eyes darted from her to Cordero.

"Okay," said Carter. "Let's go. We'll come back for our hero," she said without looking at Cordero.

She walked out of the room and Cordero watched her go.

"Are you okay, *mana*?" Estefana asked when she caught up to Carter.

"Yeah, I'm fine," Carter said and sniffled.

"You know, *mana*, he's cousin's wife, Cipriana, thinks you're his girlfriend."

Carter took a kerchief from her pocket and blew her nose.

"Yeah, so?"

"He hasn't been back to his cousin's for three nights," Estefana said in a whisper. "What is she going to think when we drive up with him this time?"

• • •

As Mateus drove up the health clinic, he noticed Carter and Estefana driving off to the guesthouse. Cordero was at the front door, leaning on a crutch while he thanked the nurses for taking good care of him. The commander pulled to a stop, cut the engine, and stepped out of his vehicle. He gave Cordero a moment to conclude his thanks to the nurses and ambled over to say goodbye. Cordero was surprised to see him.

"Mateus!" he said. "What are you doing here?"

"I've come to say goodbye, what else?"

Cordero's smile seemed feigned, which was not like him, and was quickly gone. Mateus sensed immediately that he was upset about something.

"You in pain?" he asked.

"No," said Cordero. "No, I'm okay."

"Well then, I know you've been shot, *maun*, but you could try to look a little happier about things now," joked Mateus. "You're about to go home a hero and have another several weeks of leave on full pay."

Cordero didn't react. Mateus studied him.

"Want to talk?" he asked. "There's a shady spot over here. Why don't we sit?"

He helped Cordero make his way gingerly on the crutch to the fence of the clinic under a bougainvillea bush. Cordero got as comfortable as he could with the wound to his stomach. Mateus sat and waited. He retrieved a cigarette butt he'd fished out of the ashtray in the SUV and lit it. He held the smoke in his lungs before blowing it out of the side of his mouth away from Cordero.

It was close to 11 o'clock and bells were calling the faithful to the main Mass of the day. In the long procession of families passing by the health clinic on their way to the church, most of the adults waved to Cordero and the children offered him exaggerated smiles.

Cordero raised a hand in response at first before lowering his eyes to the ground.

Mateus took it on himself to acknowledge the passing well-wishes while he waited for Cordero to unburden himself—if that's what he chose to do. After a short while, it was.

"I think I'm a bit of a fraud," Cordero said.

"Oh, how so?" said Mateus.

"When I went to see Father Francedez to talk to him about Bobu, he had a picture of Pope John Paul on the wall of his office. He told me the story of how the Pope kissed a crucifix placed on a pillow on the steps to the altar at his Mass outside Dili. Francedez said all those gathered for the Mass would have figured he was kissing the ground—you know, signifiying that East Timor was a country in its own right."

Mateus nodded.

"I remember it well," he said. "I was there."

"Well Francedez also said that sometimes what we appear to do is more important than what we actually do," said Cordero placing a hand lightly over his wound. "I've been thinking about that all morning."

Mateus played with the butt in his fingers and made no comment.

"The nurses, you, Estefana, people going by, all think I'm a hero. You all think I threw myself in front of Helio to save someone's life and was shot for my troubles." He scoffed at that. "Truth is I'd bumped into Father Francedez, bent down to get his glasses, came up quickly with my hand out to give the glasses to him when Helio pulled the trigger. I didn't intend to get in the way of anything. I guess because no one noticed the glasses drop from my hand in the dark when I was hit it appeared I'd lunged in the way of the bullet."

He eyed the police commander who sucked the last drag from the remains of his cigarette.

"I'm no hero, Mateus. I'm just someone who got in the way."

Mateus extinguished the butt on the fence and went to speak but Cordero hadn't finished.

"She thinks I'm a hero," he said. "And I like that she does."

"I'm guessing you're talking about the American," Mateus said.

"Uh-huh."

Mateus shifted his weight to sit more comfortably on the stone.

"So I'm deceiving her by letting her think how courageous I am because I want her to like me as much as I like her," Cordero said. "Is that wrong?"

"I stopped thinking in terms of right and wrong when I left the seminary," Mateus said and chuckled to himself. "I'm smoking cigarette butts because I deceived Graziela," he said. "I told you, I took money from her to bet on a damn cockfight. So now I have to be punished, not for the money I lost: for going behind her back. For deceiving her. I get it. I don't blame her and she'll get over it. Because we're honest with each other on the important things. Our relationship is strong because it's built on trust."

He brushed cigarette ash off his trousers.

"I doubt the American is fond of you because she thinks you're a hero. I don't think she is the type to be impressed that easily. If she's fond of you, it's because of more than that. She sees things in you that she likes: an inclination to do good, a concern for others. The hero thing just confirms it. To continue to encourage her to believe something that isn't true could undermine all of that." He turned squarely to face Cordero. "All of it," he emphasized.

"Yeah it could," Cordero agreed. "Or it could bring us together, you know. She's due to go back to the States soon. I don't have the luxury of time to allow things to develop slowly."

"You don't have the luxury of deception either," said Mateus.

"What do you mean?" asked Cordero.

"This isn't a silly cockfight you're gambling on," said Mateus. "Are you confident you're not risking the most important thing of all?"

Cordero's expression said he didn't understand.

"What's that?" he asked.

"The thing the American probably likes most about you," said Mateus. "Integrity."

He slid off the fence and brushed the dust off the bottom of his pants.

"You're a decent man, Tino," said Mateus. "And smart. I saw both qualities when you engaged with that boy with the pony who put us on to Bobu and when you spoke to João Lima about the joss paper that led him to explain where he got it. I'm sure with the good sense you have you'll apply it to your predicament now and do the right thing."

He started to walk away.

"You sure you made the right career choice when you decided against the priesthood?" Cordero called after him.

"That'll depend on the decision you make," said Mateus over his shoulder. "Good luck, *maun*."

With that the police commander got into his vehicle and drove off. Cordero sat on the fence and watched the shadow of the bougainvillea dance across the stone.

Estefana drove up five minutes later. Carter got out of the passenger seat and held the door open as Cordero hobbled across.

"We've packed your stuff," she said. "You ride up front. You'll be more comfortable there."

"We need to talk," he said, stopping and balancing on his crutch.

"Something wrong?"

"No," he said. "But I have to put something right."

She gave him a quizzical look. He straightened himself as best he could.

"I knocked the priest's glasses off," he began.

"What are you talking about?" she said.

"I bent down to pick them up. It was dark and he doesn't see good without them. Getting up, the bullet hit me. I had no idea what was happening. I wasn't trying to save anyone. I'm no hero."

Carter tapped her fingers on the roof of the SUV.

"In that case you ride in back," she said and pointed to the driver's side rear door where the seat was clear of the luggage she and Estefana had thrown in in their haste to get on the road.

She climbed in the front. Estefana, who'd been listening to Cordero's confession, reached for the door handle.

"I'll help him, *mana*," she said.

"No," said Carter. "A man has to be taught his place."

Estefana looked across and noticed a grin on Carter's face.

"You appear happy," she said.

"Now we know he's not a hero, he'll be a lot easier to manage," Carter said.

"Manage, *mana*? You mean while he recovers?"

Carter looked at Cordero over her shoulder as he clambered into the SUV. She turned back, settled into her seat, and slid on sunglasses.

"Yeah," she said. "That'll do for a start."

About the Author

Chris McGillion is a regular visitor to East Timor where he has been involved in media development initiatives and conducted research into the communication of agricultural science in remote mountain communities. He is a former journalist whose work has been published in Australia, the US and the United Kingdom and has taught politics, philosophy and communication skills at four universities in Australia. He has authored or co-authored a number of non-fiction books on subjects as diverse as US-Cuban relations, clerical sexual abuse, and religious sociology. He lives in the Blue Mountains west of Sydney, Australia.

www.ingramcontent.com/pod-product-compliance
Lightning Source LLC
LaVergne TN
LVHW031537060526
838200LV00056B/4538